Mr. Brightside

Copyright © 2022 by Abby Millsaps

All rights reserved.

ebook ISBN: 9781737094791
Paperback ISBN: 9798988800361

No portion of this book may be reproduced, distributed, or transmitted in any form without written permission from the author, except by a reviewer who may quote brief passages in a book review.

This book is a work of fiction. Any resemblance to any person, living or dead, or any events or occurrences, is purely coincidental. The characters and story lines are created by the author's imagination and are used fictitiously.

Developmental Editing by Melanie Yu, Made Me Blush Books
Line Editing, Copyediting, and Proofreading by VB Edits
Cover Design © Silver @ Bitter Sage Designs

To all the beautiful humans who staked their claim on Jake from the beginning.

Thank you for really seeing him. This one's for you.

Content Warning

Mr. Brightside is a full-length standalone MM romance novel within the Hampton Hearts universe. It contains content some may find triggering, including explicit language, discussion of attempted sexual assault, and discussion of abuse from a parent, both of which occurred in the past for one of the main characters. It is a dual POV story featuring characters in their twenties. It ends with a happily ever after.

Prologue

"You're the first person I've told."

I glance wearily at the only man sitting at my bar. He looks tired. Defeated. Like a shell of the boisterous, good-natured retired Navy SEAL I'm proud to call my mentor and friend.

I finish pouring his beer and approach with caution. I have never, in the ten years I've worked for Mike Hobbs, seen him this shaken up. Blowing out a long breath, I try to make sense of everything he just confessed.

His mom is sick. He didn't know how bad it was. She somehow managed to sign away her entire life savings to an "investor" who has fallen off the grid. Now, not only is she broke, but she's in debt. Severe debt. And since he just found out she was diagnosed with Alzheimer's more than six months ago, he has no choice but to move to Florida as soon as possible and care for her.

I choose my words carefully, not wanting to come off insensitive but also desperate to know what this means for me.

"What are you going to do?"

There. That should be open-ended enough to err on the side of concerned friend instead of anxious employee. As sympathetic as I feel about his predicament, my mind instantly went to two things: Clinton's Family Restaurant and The Oak Barrel Tavern.

I'm the manager here at The Oak, and I still fill in at Clinton's when someone needs a night off. I also invested $100,000 to get the place up and running last year, making me a silent partner. Between the two establishments, I work at least sixty hours a week, and I love every second of it thanks to the people I work with and the patrons I view as friends. If that's all about to change...

"I have to go."

I nod like I understand. I don't. But I also don't have any living family who would ever need me like that. Assuming my casual bartender stance—leaned back against the bar, arms clasped over my chest, ankles crossed nonchalantly—I try to play it cool, but inside I'm spiraling.

"I'm gonna have to sell, Jake."

I nod again, intentionally slowing my movements so I don't come off as too enthusiastic about him giving up his life's work to help his mom. He said I'm the first person he's told. That means if I express interest...

"Do you want to buy me out?"

Hell yeah. This is exactly where I was hoping this conversation would lead. I suck in a breath and tell myself to stay cool. Given his dire circumstances, I don't want to seem too eager.

"I do. I want them both," I confirm, pushing off the ice maker and coming to stand across from him on my side of the bar.

He nods solemnly. "I figured. And I want it to be you. But it has to be fast. Honestly, I have half a mind to book the next damn flight to Florida..." I swear his eyes cloud with tears before he lifts his glass and gulps down half his beer.

I wait. Watching. Desperate to know what happens next. When he finally sets down his glass, he's all business.

"I'm not trying to make bank. But I need a fair buyout. You've seen the books. You know what both places are worth. And the fact that I own the buildings..."

Tongue stuck into the hollow of my cheek, I weigh my options. I'm well off, thanks to the inheritance my mom left me that my grandma helped me invest. I also own the entire building I live in. A chunk of my savings went into The Oak, but Mike already paid me back with interest, so that's not a concern. I have money. Just not as much as he's going to need.

"Would you consider a payment plan? Monthly payments for the businesses for a set amount of time, then rent-to-own for the buildings?"

His grimace tells me all I need to know. "I'm sorry, kid. That won't work. In addition to moving down there for however long, I need to get my mom set up in a memory care facility. I'm gonna need a lump sum, and I'm gonna need it fast."

I run a hand through my hair and try not to show my disappointment. We haven't even talked real numbers yet, but I know I don't have what he's asking. Even if I sold off some of the condo units, that probably wouldn't be fast enough.

I hold back a shudder as I think about the nuclear option.

Very few people know I stand to inherit more than ten million dollars from my late father's estate. Joe's been dead for years, but my cut remains untouched. His will states that I have to get married if I want my money. Leave it to Joe Whitely to try to dictate my life from the grave.

I've been uninterested in that money my whole life. I don't need it. I don't want it. I'd rather become a monk and take a vow of celibacy than fulfill his dying wish.

And yet...

"I hear you. And I respect that you need this handled as quickly as possible. Can you give me two days to figure out what I can do?"

Mike nods and looks past me to the marquee lights hanging above the mirrored back wall. We poured our literal blood, sweat, and tears into this place. As much as I know he doesn't want to leave it, I have to believe he wants it to go to me.

I want it. I want it bad. But first, I need to figure out *exactly* what Joe's marriage contingency entails. Then I need to decide whether I love this bar more than I hate my dad.

Chapter 1

Jake

"Catch me if you can, bro."

My quads are on fire as I increase my pace. My speed is well beyond the recommended parameters, but if this is what it takes to smoke his ass, there's no way I'm backing down now. I let out a whoop as I pass him on the leaderboard, but instantly regret expelling that bit of extra energy. Less than twenty seconds later, he overtakes me. Again.

I grind my teeth and push the pedals harder. His cardio game has always been stronger, but I got up way too early for this ride to let him win. I'm laser focused as the instructor counts us down.

My chest burns as sweat drips down my front like little rivers running along my abs. My lungs scream at me to slow down, back off, ease up. I'll do no such thing.

I'm blackout-level exhausted by the time it's over, so much so that I barely hear the cool-down instructions over my panting.

It's not until I catch my breath and glance at the screen that I see my efforts were for nothing. My username may be listed above his, but we scored the same number of points. Our rankings are identical. We tied.

Fuckin' A.

I'm getting way too old to push it this hard. Or to be up this early.

I do a quick cool-down ride, then unclip, wiping down the sweat-covered machine. Most days I'd lift or hit the heavy bag, too, but I'm physically spent from going so hard at the end of that ride. I also can't overdo it, because I've got big orders to receive at the restaurant and the bar today.

Instead, I lie down on the mats in front of the mirrored wall in my home gym and do gentle stretches to loosen up my back and thighs. I've only been in a straddle stretch for a few seconds before my mind drifts back to work and, more specifically, to the issue that's been looming over my head for the last forty-eight hours.

The moment Mike told me he had to sell, I knew I wanted to buy him out. It *has* to be me. No one else is better suited or more genuinely interested in owning Clinton's and The Oak.

But he needs to move quickly, and we both know it wouldn't take much effort to get an offer. There's an abundance of rich pricks in this town; Hampton bleeds old money and disposable income. I've been low-key panicked over the last two days thinking about him listing either or both establishments for sale because I know they'll be scooped up in an instant.

Not only do I loathe the idea of working for someone else, but I genuinely care about the staff I've personally hired and trained at both places. Clinton's was my first home. The Oak is my pride and joy. I can't remember the last time I wanted something this much.

I don't fault Mike for needing to sell, and I know this is all happening out of necessity. But I'll be damned if I let the two places I love most in this world be invaded by an outsider.

Not in my house. Not on my watch. It has to be me.

I sit up and reach for my phone, blowing out a long breath as I wait for the inevitable gloating text from my best friend.

Rhett: You almost had me that time. Almost.

I groan and shake my head. Rhett and I are both ridiculously competitive. The moment I bought this damn workout bike, he had to have one, too. Now we do a set schedule of live classes each week—something his wife, Tori, calls "bro bike dates." There's literally no one else I'd wake up at five a.m. for, but I've come to look forward to these rides together. It's one way we can stay connected now that he's not coming back and forth to Hampton like he used to.

I pound out my reply as I lie back and do a gentle spinal twist.

Jake: I DID have you that time, bro. Go check your screen again. My name's on top of yours on the leaderboard.

Rhett: That's because they're listed alphabetically and you know it.

Jake: Tori always says you're a sore loser.

I snicker as I send off the jab. I know the list is presented alphabetically with the same final output numbers, but he sealed his fate when he picked his boring-ass boardroom-inspired username. It's not my fault that JakeNBake69 comes before NSTCEO.

I switch sides for a final stretch, then hop to my feet. One of the smartest things I ever did was convert the second bedroom of my condo into a gym. It saves me a ton of time in the mornings. I whistle to myself as I pass through the kitchen and flip on the coffeemaker to warm up. I'm gonna need a boatload of caffeine to get through this day.

Not only do I have to get to work early to receive the orders, but I have big plans this afternoon that will require a significant amount of energy.

But focusing on my plans and usual to-dos has been virtually impossible. If I'm honest, I haven't stopped thinking about Clinton's and The Oak since Mike broke the news to me on Saturday night.

I asked him to give me two days to figure my shit out. My deadline is today, and I still don't know what I'm going to do.

In the end, this all boils down to two things. First, I need to get the final word from my personal lawyer confirming precisely what counts in relation to the language in my dad's will. Second, I need to decide whether I'm really willing to do what needs to be done to unlock the ten million dollars and change I stand to inherit.

It shouldn't be *that* big a deal. But it is. It really fucking is.

Joe's will says I have to get married to receive my inheritance. Just knowing he put that in a legal document makes me want to lash out and do the exact opposite. I hate any and all reminders of him. Of what he did. Of the hold he once had on me.

But I can't think like that right now. This isn't about him. I've worked too hard to overcome those impulses and pave my own way. This is about me. My staff. The hopes and dreams I didn't even know existed until a few nights ago, when I realized they could all be taken away. This is an opportunity I can't pass up. As much as it pains me, I've come up with a potential solution that just might work.

I've challenged my own ego over and over again about this solution. As much as I hate playing his game, I know I can live with this plan if I do it my way. People get married for practical reasons all the damn time. And it's not like I'm in a relationship or even interested in getting married for traditional reasons. If marriage is what it takes, I can do it. I *will* do it. I just need to confirm my options before I let myself figure out the who, when, where, and how.

I just wish I had someone to talk this out with. Mike asked me not to tell anyone until he'd had a chance to make an announcement. Fair. But isolating for me.

I've almost called Rhett a dozen times over the last two days. He and Tori are the closest thing to family I've got. But there was a nagging in the back of my mind that told me to hold off. I don't really need to seek out his advice. I already know what he'd say.

My best friend is just too moral and good—and a hopeless romantic—to encourage an arranged marriage situation. That, and he'd probably offer to loan me the money, which I do *not* want him to do.

This is something I have to figure out on my own.

And I have to figure it out fast. As in now, *today*, or I might lose my shot entirely.

I huff out a breath as I turn on the shower, shuck off my athletic shorts, and step under the waterfall spray. Usually, a hard workout and a hot shower are enough to clear my mind, but I already know they're no match for the monumental decision I have to make today.

Chapter 2

Jake

I'm dumping ice behind the bar when my phone vibrates in my pocket. Again. I shake my head, but I immediately stop what I'm doing and pull it out to respond.

She's one of very few people I'll drop everything for, and I know better than to ignore her on days like today.

Ashleigh: Fiona can't find her water shoes, and Amelia refuses to put on her bathing suit.

I grin. I can't help it. As much as I despise the Whitely name, I love that my nieces are ornery as hell. I like to think they get that from me.

Jake: Tell Fifi to wear her Crocs instead. And just pack me extra clothes for Mimi. We both know you're not going to win.

I don't bother putting my phone away after I hit send because, if I know my nieces, this conversation's not done. I lean my elbows on the raw-edge bar top and yawn as I wait for my sister-in-law's reply.

Ten seconds later, a picture comes through. It's a selfie taken by Fifi, based on the angle. Her gummy smile with those two missing front teeth takes up most of the screen. Mimi is trying to push into the shot in the bottom corner. She's wearing one of her favorite pop-punk T-shirts—yes, my five-year-old niece is into pop-punk—and now her resistance to ditch Travis Barker for a bathing suit makes sense.

I chuckle when a slew of emojis that makes absolutely no sense comes through next. There's an elephant and a caterpillar and five frowny faces and a beer stein and three rows of hearts...

Cole passes behind me with another bucket of ice. "Ohh, someone's got Jake smiling."

I roll my eyes and resist tripping him since it would create a bigger mess for me to clean up. "Shove off, nosy Nancy," I mutter playfully.

"Ah, come on. Who is she?"

I roll my eyes again and pocket my phone, then lean back on the bar and glare. One downside of having a raw-edge bar with a rustic flare is that it's not as comfortable as my perch at Clinton's. The number of splinters I've had to remove from my ass over the last two years is astounding.

"Or he?" Cole pushes.

I smirk and link my arms over my chest. My sexuality hasn't been a secret for a long time. I've hooked up with more of my coworkers over the years than I care to admit.

My attention shifts at the sound of chimes, and a lanky kid who can't be more than twenty pushes through the front door of the bar.

I pivot to tell him we're not open yet. I also silently curse Cole for leaving the door unlocked after the last order was delivered.

The trucks typically unload in the back, but sometimes new drivers get confused about where to park.

"Hey, buddy. We're not—"

"I'm looking for Mr. Jacob Whitely."

Oof. A "Mr." before noon. I hold in a shudder as I wonder what the hell this guy's playing at.

"That would be me," I hedge. Call it instinct, call it a gut reaction: but after years of emotional abuse at the hands of my family, I'm wary of shit like this.

"I've got a delivery for you from the offices of Hensley and Horr."

It's then that I spot the thick manilla envelope tucked under his arm. I straighten my spine and grind my molars, knowing he's carrying the documents that either confirm or deny what I'm desperate to know.

"Courier service. That's some fancy shit," Cole mutters as I pass him to circle the bar and sign for the package.

I'm just about over his *fancy shit* today.

The courier kid's got at least three inches on me, but he cowers when I come close enough to accept the envelope. He hands me a carbon-backed receipt first, which I sign and tear apart myself. I keep the client copy and give him the signed receipt.

Accepting the packet of papers feels like strapping on eighty pounds of hiking equipment. I'm taken aback by the weight of it and already convinced it's too much for me to bear.

The kid lingers for a moment, looking around the bar like he's never been here before. That makes sense, considering my lawyer's office is in downtown Cleveland. We don't get many people through the doors who aren't already familiar with The Oak Barrel Tavern.

After several seconds, I wonder if he's waiting for a tip. Am I expected to shell out cash on top of my lawyer's astronomical hourly rate? I clear my throat to get his attention, desperate for him to take the hint and go.

"Oh, yeah. Sorry, I got distracted," he mutters when he meets my unamused glare. He turns on his heel and heads for the front door, but not before glancing back to offer, "This place is pretty cool," before taking his leave.

Yeah, kid. Believe me. I know.

"Hey!" I holler, rising off the bench and jabbing my finger at the little shithead who just swiped Mimi's cup out of her hands. "You give that back—you can't just take things from other kids." I level him with a glare, and he immediately drops the cup.

The irony here is not lost on me. I used to buy Solo cups for parties at Rhett's house, but I now buy them in bulk for afternoons at the splash pad.

"Danks, Uncle Jakey!" Mimi yells as she scoops up her cup and goes back to the game she's made up in her head. I watch, amused, as she flits over to one of the smaller water fountains and plops down in a puddle, fully clothed.

Amelia's more independent than her older sister, and she probably could have taken that little punk on her own. But I'm inclined to jump in and defend my nieces more often than not. They deserve to have an adult step in and handle shit for them;

I want them to feel loved and safe and supported when they're with me.

I settle back onto the bench I've claimed, flipping down my Ray-Bans and surveying the scene in front of me. There are at least twenty kids here today, and the place is total chaos. Screaming, crying. It's like last call at The Oak on a reunion weekend when we also have multiple bachelorette parties in the house. The humans are just smaller here.

It's not hard to keep track of my girls: Fifi had a major growth spurt last year. At eight, she towers over most of the middle school boys causing trouble at the far end of the splash pad. Mimi's easy to track, too, considering she's the only kid here rocking a Blink-182 long sleeved T-shirt. At least I didn't have to fight with her about sunscreen.

I stretch my arms out on the bench and look around at the other adults. The girls and I come here a few times a month, and I'll admit to having made the acquaintance of a new fuck buddy on occasion. It's my target market, really, as long as I can discern the housewives from the nannies.

I've lived in this town my entire life, and I have a strict rule about not hooking up with regular customers or my employees now that I'm the manager at The Oak. The nannies of Hampton are the perfect pool for me to pick from, pun intended.

Letting out a huffy sigh, I check on the girls again. I usually love watching them run around and play, but today I'm restless. I can't think about anything, really, except the Post-It note stuck to the first page of the documents inside the envelope that goofy courier kid dropped off a few hours ago.

Legally recognized marriage. No restrictions.

Seeing it spelled out in my lawyer's loopy scrawl brought on a flurry of mixed emotions.

Relief. Excitement. Anxiousness. Spite.

It's the spite that nags at me. Because there's no way my bigot of a father would leave his will so open-ended.

The only explanation I've come up with is that he was too naïve—and too full of hate—to even consider the possibility of marriage being defined as anything besides the union between a man and a woman. He loathed that I'm bisexual and went as far as to try to force me into a relationship in high school with a girl he blackmailed into pursuing me.

That he didn't stipulate that I had to marry a woman in his will tells me he was even more narrow-minded and bigoted than I believed. It also makes me inclined to marry a dude.

I put eyes on my girls again, double-check that all the little shitheads here are staying in line, then drag my gaze past the other benches.

I owe Mike an answer. Today.

That means I have to find someone to marry. Today.

This is impossibly poor timing. Two years ago, I would have had a healthy list of prospects, both male and female.

But life's been coming at me pretty fast lately. That, or I'm just slowing down with age. I've spent the last few years occupied with everyone else's business, coasting through my own life.

Tori and Rhett had their issues, and some days I felt like they shared custody of me as their emotional support human. Then, once Mike came to me with the idea of buying and renovating the old bar next to Clinton's, The Oak became my baby. Throw in all the ways I've stepped up to help Ashleigh with the girls over the last few years, and I guess it makes sense that my prospect list is feeling a little thin.

And by thin, I mean nonexistent.

My phone vibrates in my pocket, so I pull it out to read the message. Ashleigh's leaving the gym and heading our way. I push to my feet, then blast out a wolf whistle that has both girls' heads snapping to attention.

I've been practicing that particular move for months, and can't help but smirk at the way the nannies and housewives gawk at the girls' instant obedience. Never mind that my nieces know they're about to get cake pops from the coffee shop where we're meeting their mom.

I hand them both their towels, then scoop up Amelia and tickle her.

She squeals and thrashes, but when I ease up, she screams, "More butterflies, Uncle Jakey!"

Fiona gathers up all the Solo cups and reaches for my hand so we can cross the parking lot together. I get them situated in their booster seats and shake my head over my own version of the walk of shame as I slide into the driver's seat of Ashleigh's minivan. It's just easier if we switch cars when I have the girls... but still.

Looking like a manny behind the wheel of a Honda Odyssey is the least of my concerns today. I've got cake pops to dole out, a restaurant to check on, a spouse to find, and a deal to close. It's go time.

Chapter 3

Jake

I push through the side door of Clinton's like I own the place. If everything works out, I *will* own the place. And *soon*—Mike's leaving for Florida sometime this week. I could be a small business owner in the next few days.

While I was with the girls, Lia texted to let me know the order arrived, and thankfully she's got most of it put away by the time I circle around the bar to take stock.

"Hey, boss," she quips as she slides a carton of lemons to the prep station. I fight the smirk that's threatening to spill out at her attempted jab. She's going to lose her shit when she finds out I really *am* her new boss.

Lia's all piss and vinegar: this untamed spirit who thrives off defiance. She and I had a thing a few years back. She's just as sassy and wild in bed as she is in real life. But just because she's a spitfire didn't mean she was okay with the casual thing we had going on. I got the nagging suspicion she was hoping things between us would turn serious—which is my go-to indicator to pull away and cool off.

I don't know what she expected. I've always been proud of my relationship virgin status.

Or, I was proud. Until today. Today it would be awfully convenient if I could ask my boyfriend or girlfriend to marry me.

I lean against the empty side of the bar and watch as Lia expertly slices a lemon. She's got her hair tied up in a bandanna, her dark brown curls piled up on top of her head. I'm not sure I've ever met anyone who works as hard—or as often—as she does. Except maybe Rhett. I know for a fact that she wakes up at dawn and puts several hours of work into her family's farm every damn day before showing up for her shifts here.

"Something I can do for you?" she snaps in my direction.

I guess I was staring. When I don't reply right away, she stabs the tip of the knife into the cutting board, puts both hands on her hips, and turns to glare.

She's gorgeous. And savage.

I'm pretty sure I want to marry a guy, just to give the middle finger to my dad's stupid will. But even if I was open to the prospect of a woman, it would *not* be this one. I couldn't handle Aurelia Perry.

"Not at all," I reply, coming around the bar to help. "What needs to be done?"

Lia grabs the knife and wields it like a laser pointer, swishing it back and forth through the air as she speaks. "Ice is filled, and this is the last of the garnishes. Silverware and kids' menus need to be refreshed before dinner, but Cory's supposedly handling those." She gives me a pointed look. I follow the direction of her knife, my eyes landing on a slumped figure sitting on a stool at the very end of the bar.

I hadn't even noticed him—he's hunched low, with his arms crossed on the bar and his forehead resting on them. He's sitting against the wall, blending in with his surroundings. I would have looked right past him if Lia hadn't pointed him out.

"Cory," I call out in greeting. "What's up, man?"

Lia shoots me another warning glance. She's acting like I just opened a can of worms. Maybe I have. But that's my right as their manager. If he's sick or unfit to work, I need to send him home.

Cory lifts his head to meet my gaze, his deep brown eyes more despondent than I've ever seen. He peers down at the bar top, then huffs out an extended exhale.

"Just got some bad news about school," he offers vaguely. "I'm not on the clock until four. I'll have my shit together by then."

I nod, appreciative of his work ethic, for sure. But I'm not as concerned about the schedule for the night as I am about my friend.

Well, maybe the word friend is pushing it. Cory and I aren't exactly friends. We're more than acquaintances, though, considering we're intimately acquainted with each other's bodies.

We had a thing a few years back—a really fucking hot thing, if I'm honest—but it fizzled after a few epic hookups. I don't even know what happened back then. But I do remember Cory going cold on me out of nowhere. He's best friends with Lia, so I have to assume they got together and realized I wasn't kidding when I said I wasn't interested in anything exclusive.

The way I used to cycle through partners meant I had multiple options most nights. A few years ago, I could have taken applications for the position of last-minute spouse. Now I'm struggling just to come up with a candidate.

I watch him run a hand through his jet-black hair, messing up the perfectly coifed style. He doesn't even bother trying to fix it. Now *that* has me concerned. Cory's usually so put together. Right now, he's a wreck.

I sidle up to the bar and lean back, ready to use my best bartender listening skills if that'll help him shake out of this funk.

"You want to talk about it?" I ask.

Lia obviously knows what's going on with him, or at the very least, that something *is* going on with him. But sometimes it helps to talk things out with someone who isn't as close to a situation.

"There's nothing to talk about," he deadpans, sitting up to full height to meet my gaze. His irises are darker than normal—ebony and cold. He's locking it down. I know, because I do that shit, too.

"Got it. No worries, man. I'll be around most of the night, so if there's anything I can do for you, let me know."

I move to push off the bar and head to the kitchen when his words make me falter.

He lets out a sardonic chuckle. "Thanks. But unless you know of any open graduate assistantships or have an extra twenty grand laying around, I think I'm all set."

I freeze where I stand.

I feel like I was just hit with an airbag.

My senses are numb from the impact, but I know with every fiber of my being that what he just said is a big deal. My limbs tingle in anticipation of what this means. Of what he might need. Of what could be.

I turn slowly as not to startle him and to give myself a few extra seconds to think. Is this my opening? Is the universe actually conspiring to help me?

I have no idea how to play this. All I know is that I've got to line it up perfectly to stand a chance.

"Why do you need twenty grand?"

I aim to sound emotionless, unassuming. I try my hardest not to let curiosity, judgment, or hope cloud my tone. Especially not hope.

He sighs again. His exhale fuels my anxiety. It's as if he's blowing out his stress and handing it all to me. If he gets defensive, or if he really doesn't want to answer me... I'm back to square one. I can barely breathe as I wait for his reply.

The tension between us grows more volatile as the seconds tick by. If he shoots down the conversation before I know the full story, there's nothing I can do.

Finally, he speaks.

"I just found out my graduate assistantship was revoked because of funding issues in the department."

Shit. I don't know what any of that means. I forgot that Cory's a bit of a brainiac. He's been in school for years, and I think he's studying to be a counselor or a psychologist or something.

"Uh, you're gonna have to break that down for me. I don't speak academia."

He cocks one eyebrow and assesses me up and down. Almost as if he's asking if I really want to hear this. I nod enthusiastically and take a few tentative steps closer.

"For the last two years, Holt has paid for all my graduate classes and given me a stipend through an on-campus job. It's called a graduate assistantship. I help the head of the program with her classes."

He wipes away an invisible piece of dust on the bar.

"It's not that hard... just paperwork, advising appointments, and grading papers, mostly, and I love working with my boss. But I got a call today saying the department had to get rid of all their GA positions this year because of budget cuts at the state level."

His shoulders slump. "I was literally a year away from graduating. And now I'm screwed."

Fuck. I still don't totally understand what all that means. The typical college experience is foreign to me. I have a business degree from Akron, but I just wrote a check each semester, went to my classes between shifts at Clinton's, and got decent enough grades to graduate.

What I *think* he's saying is that his school funding got pulled, and he unexpectedly needs money. A lot of money. Fast.

I'll. Be. Damned.

What's that line? Of all the bars in all the towns in all the world... the husband I'm desperately seeking might just be sitting in mine.

Even better—he might need me just as much as I need him.

I force myself to nod—to acknowledge that I heard him, even though I have no idea how to respond. How the hell do I play this? I can't just explain the situation or proposition him here... no one even knows Mike's plans yet. Also, Cory's super close with Lia. And Tori.

Fuck.

Mike asked me to keep this whole situation quiet, and I refuse to defy his wishes. Keeping this on the down low benefits me, too. If Cory isn't into this... If I can't convince him to do this with me...

This is a Hail Mary of a shot. This is putting every egg in one flimsy basket. This is risky as hell, with a slim chance of working at best.

But it's the only option I've found that makes sense.

Cory is my age, maybe a year or two younger. He's gorgeous, with this dark and handsome effortlessness that I'm drawn to. He's kind. Dependable. A hard worker. A good friend. He's more serious than the type I usually go for—if I actually did relationships and had a type—but I'm best friends with Everhett Wheeler. I can handle stoicism and seriousness because I've been practicing with Rhett for years.

Plus, we've hooked up before. And those hookups *still* live rent free in my mind. Never mind that he ended things abruptly and without explanation. We were never anything but casual. Even if it was some of the hottest sex of my life.

I don't know if it was a defense mechanism or if I'm just a coward, but I never asked Cory why he stopped taking my calls. Back then, I assumed he'd moved on and found better. Or maybe he compared notes with Lia and realized there was some overlap to my time with her and what he and I shared.

I didn't want to make things awkward, so I brushed it off and acted like nothing had ever happened.

The timing worked itself out. The spring he and I started and stopped our fling was when things really went sideways for Rhett and Tori. I spent the next year and a half being there for my best friend and his girl. When I wasn't with them, I was working my ass off to make The Oak the best watering hole in Hampton.

Even though Cory went cold on me without explanation, I owe it to myself to see if this could lead somewhere. He's most likely going to shoot me down. I know that. But now that this idea is percolating in my mind, it feels like the only reasonable way forward.

I have no choice. I'm out of time. Out of options. But I refuse to give up.

I'm going to ask Cory to marry me.

I'm going to do it tonight.

And I'm going to do everything in my power to convince him to say yes. As soon as he gets off work and I can talk to him privately, of course.

Never mind the fact that Mike is expecting my answer before that.

I return to the bar and spread my arms wide on the polished wood. Gripping the edges for balance, and because I know it makes the veins pop in my forearms, I lean forward until I have his full attention. I intentionally get in his space and breathe in the heady citrus smell of his aftershave. I look him right in the eye and lower my voice an octave.

"So, listen... I don't totally understand what you're going through. But I've been dealing with some things lately, too. What do you say we meet up after work and talk? I think I have an idea about how we could help each other out."

His pupils dilate with my words.

Bullseye.

Okay, so maybe it's not entirely fair to use my sex appeal to convince him to come over. Especially because I really *do* just want to talk. At least at first.

But I have to use everything in my toolbox to see this through. Not playing full out isn't an option right now. Either this will work or it won't. But if it doesn't, it won't be because I didn't try hard enough.

Cory clears his throat, then blinks and shakes his head slightly before finally responding. "Um, yeah. Sure. Where are you thinking?"

He fidgets on the stool, and I can't help but wonder if he's recalling one of the times we hooked up after work. We would sneak off to the walk-in cooler. Or climb into the back seat of my Jeep. We really were hot and heavy for a bit.

I shake my head to clear my wandering thoughts. Business before pleasure. At least for tonight.

"My place, whenever you're done here. Just text me when you're on your way."

I don't give him time to respond. To question this. To reject the idea. I rap my knuckles on the bar, smile, and head for the kitchen.

This is going to work. This *has* to work.

Chapter 4

Cory

My hand is shaking—literally, visibly shaking—as I punch in my table's order at the POS computer in the back. Lia creeps up on me and immediately knows something is wrong.

"Cory—what the hell?"

She bumps her hip into mine, and because I'm so unsteady, she displaces me in front of the screen.

"Give me that," she grumbles, snatching my pad out of my hand and entering the order for me.

I close my eyes and blow out a breath. I thought my nerves would ease up as my shift went on, but if anything, I'm getting myself more and more worked up as it gets closer to the end of the night. I've felt like this for the last three hours. Ever since he invited me over.

Thankfully, Lia thinks I'm still freaking out about school.

And I am. At least in my logical, sensible, reasonable mind.

But the real reason I'm a shaking, anxious mess is because the man I've been crushing on for years just invited me over after work.

Jake Whitely wants me to come over to his place tonight. How did he put it? To help each other out? If I hadn't been sitting down when he said it, I swear my knees would have given out.

I'm not usually such a simp for rich white boys who pride themselves on noncommittal behavior and a total lack of emotional intelligence.

But fuck.

It's Jake.

This isn't even my first rodeo with him. We hooked up a few years ago, right before Tori and Rhett got back together. But then I found out he'd been fooling around with Lia, too, and that she was hoping for a whole lot more than Jake was willing to give.

That was it for me. My friendship with Lia was more important than satisfying my lust for Hampton's most notorious bisexual bachelor. She didn't even ask me to cool down with him—I dropped him on my own. Then I spent several months licking my wounds when I realized he didn't care.

But a lot has changed over the last two years. I'm different. He's different, too. Jake isn't as rowdy or wild as he used to be now that he's the manager of The Oak.

Lia's in a totally different place nowadays, too. She's kinda sorta doing this long-distance thing with her fuck buddy in Pennsylvania. She doesn't talk about it unless she's drunk, and I never push her to share. But I'm sure hooking up with Jake is the furthest thing from her mind.

That works for me. Because right now, Jake is literally the only thing on my mind.

I should be worrying about school, freaking out about how I'm going to pay the tuition that's technically already past due. I should be livid that the department revoked my assistantship, especially after all the work I've done for them over the last few years. Or calculating tuition costs to see how many classes I can afford this semester and how that affects my practicum assignment and plans for graduation.

But I'm not.

Me. Cory Vargo. Worrier extraordinaire. For the first time in a long time, my mind isn't fretting with indecision.

I can't explain it. It's like he's taken over every thought inside my head. I can't even remember my orders without writing them down, as proven by the three drink orders I've messed up so far this shift.

Embarrassingly, the only thought in my head is *him*.

The way his eyes bored into my soul when he leaned across that bar. The way his teeth rolled over his bottom lip when he suggested I come over tonight, almost like he was nervous to ask. The way his scent consumed me with its equally sweet and spicy notes. Vanilla and musk and perfectly Jake. His mere presence dominated every neuron in my brain.

Maybe a casual hookup is just what I need to take my mind off things for a few days. There's nothing I can do about school anyway. Every other GA position is long gone, and there's no way I can pay for the course load I intended to take. I need to regroup. I need a backup plan. But first I need to blow off some steam.

"Earth to Cory," Lia says as she snaps her fingers in front of my face.

Right.

I've still got three hours left of this shift. We're not slammed, but I'm not going to slack off and make Lia work herself to death because I'm distracted by our funny, charismatic, sexy-as-sin manager. The guy who got so close earlier I could feel his minty breath on my face.

Shit. I'm doing it again. He really is the perfect distraction.

Jake Whitely may be a fuckboy who's only interested in a good time. But for once, that's exactly what I'm looking for, too.

I give Lia a sheepish smile and head to the dining room to check on my tables.

I just have to get through these next few hours until we meet up. Then I can really let myself get lost in his specific brand of hot, sweaty, no-strings-attached fun.

Chapter 5

Jake

I called Mike on my way home tonight and told him it was done. That I had a plan. That I would have the money.

We'd already negotiated a price, and there's not time for any sort of formal transition or training. He's literally getting on a plane tomorrow. He'll be back and forth for a while since he still has to sell his house and move all his things.

He knows the deal. Well, not the details of the deal. But he knows I have untapped funds from my dad's will and that I'm sticking my tail between my legs to unlock that money and buy him out.

Thankfully he trusted me enough to agree to an initial down payment with a promise to pay in full as soon as I have the money. According to my lawyer, it shouldn't be more than a few weeks from the time we send the marriage certificate to my father's estate attorney.

It's comically easy. There are no other conditions to satisfy. All I have to do is get married, and the money is mine. For all intents and purposes, I just became the new owner of Clinton's and The Oak.

Well, aside from the part where I still have to actually ask Cory to marry me.

I've spent the last hour psyching myself up. Tidying the condo. Convincing myself that this will work.

I'm prepared to offer him half of everything. No prenup. No conditions. Just half of everything I get. There can't be a paper trail to this arrangement. But if he's willing to help me—to trust me—I'm happy to give him five million dollars.

To think: the man was worried about coming up with twenty grand.

I've pumped myself up so much I feel sick. Little blasts of nausea keep catching me by surprise as I wipe down my kitchen island for the third time. Cory's never been here, and I want to make a good impression.

I snicker at the idea of worrying about sparkly counters when I'm about to propose marriage. I doubt he'll be able to focus on anything once I drop that bomb. Speaking of sparkly...

I don't have a ring.

Doesn't matter. If he goes for it, we can go shopping together. That is, if he wants to wear a ring. I don't care either way.

My lawyer was clear; there are no extra conditions or a time frame included in my dad's will, so we don't have to stay married forever. But I don't want to call any unnecessary attention to the situation by getting divorced too quickly, either. Especially because I know my brothers will catch wind of what's going down. And they'll be watching for me to mess this up.

I don't know if either Julian or Joey would care enough to take me to court, but I'm not willing to fuck around and find out. I don't think we'll cause much of a ruckus if we stay married for two years.

I finally make myself sit. Cory's going to walk in and know something's wrong if I don't cool it. I pick up my phone and open up a social media app, intent on doing a little research on my potential future husband.

Husband.

Fuck.

That's going to take some getting used to.

I find him immediately. Even though we're not connected, we have a bunch of mutual friends. His profile picture is an upper body shot of him laughing and looking past the person taking the picture. He looks really handsome.

I keep scrolling and poking around, but force myself to go slow so I don't accidentally click on anything to let him know I'm creeping. There aren't many recent pictures, but I think that's typical for people our age. I was desperate for everyone on social media to know everything I was doing five years ago. Now I mostly just use it to remember to text my friends on their birthdays.

There are a few pictures of him with Tori and Lia, and one of him with a woman in her late fifties or early sixties. There are also a few pictures of him and a blond man who looks to be five or ten years older than me. In one of the pictures, they've even got their arms around each other, posing in front of a highway sign.

My heart leaps into my throat as I realize I didn't think through a major piece of this puzzle. I have no idea if Cory is seeing anyone right now.

I'm such an idiot. I've been getting my hopes up and cleaning like a maniac for the last hour, nervous as hell to pitch him this idea and ask him to marry me. There are at least a dozen reasons he might say no, and I've come up with rebuttals for all of them. But I hadn't even considered that he could be in a serious relationship.

I don't have time to spiral because my phone vibrates in my hand.

Cory: I'm leaving Clinton's now. I think I know the building, but can you text me your address?

I shoot off my building number and tell him to come to the front door. Inviting him in through the garage seems too intimate.

I don't want to do this—I really don't. It'll tip her off that something's up, and there's no way she won't mention it to Rhett. But now I'm in my head, and I'm starting to panic that this whole thing is dead on arrival because of my narrow-mindedness.

Jake: Hey, baby. Random question for you that I don't want you to read into...

To my relief, she responds immediately.

Tori: Hello to you too.

My best friend's wife has been good friends with Cory since he started working at Clinton's. I know for a fact they're still close and that Tori makes a point to spend time with him when she's in town.

Jake: Is Cory seeing anyone right now?

Tori: Jake...

I cringe at the tone I can hear her using in my head.

Jake: It's not what you're thinking, I swear. It's more of a roundabout question that has to do with a work situation.

That's sort of the truth. It fits the scenario, and it'll lower her suspicions. Although if everything goes according to plan, she's going to know exactly why I'm asking soon enough.

Tori: You have no idea how tempted I am to text Cory right now and ask what this is really about...

Fuck. I open my contacts to call her and talk her down just as another text comes through.

Tori: But I trust you. Or, I trust that the truth will come out eventually. ;) He's not dating anyone right now, unless it's super new and I don't know about it yet. He was with a guy named Andre for about six months last year, but they ended things around the holidays.

Relief washes over me. My plans aren't completely thwarted.

Jake: Thanks, baby. I'll call you later this week to catch up.

Tori: Behave

Jake: Always

I set my phone on the immaculately clean counter, do another pass through of the living room and kitchen, then close the doors to my workout room and bedroom. I stand in front of the open fridge and just stare for a few minutes, trying to decide what, if anything, I should set out before he arrives. Is there a traditional beverage or snack for proposing marriage to a casual acquaintance?

I'm so in over my head. But the only way out of it now is through.

When my unit buzzer rings, I inhale one last breath.

This will work.

This *has* to work.

Fuck. I hope this works.

Chapter 6

Cory

I'm a wound-up bundle of energy walking from the main lobby to his unit. I'm not nervous in the traditional sense, but I'm anxious-borderline-excited about what's happening tonight.

This isn't me. I don't do things like this.

I'm a relationship man through and through. I love being in love: Going on dates. Lying in bed on a lazy weekend morning. Having someone to share things with. Being taken care of. So why the hell does meeting up with the king of casual excite me so much?

Because it's Jake.

The boy has this magnetism. He's a living, breathing paradox that always takes me by surprise. Equal parts cocky and kind, he goes to extreme lengths for the people he loves. I overheard plenty of things he said to Tori when she and Rhett were struggling: how he supported her, lifted her up.

I also remember some of the things he said to me on the few occasions we hooked up. Word for word, in fact. Just thinking about his dirty mouth has me sucking in a shaky breath. How can someone so decent also be so charming and sly?

I have to chill out. The guy's human, after all. He's not perfect. He can't be. There's probably some unidentified childhood trauma bubbling under the surface where Jake Whitely is concerned. But I'm not his counselor. Or his boyfriend. I'm just the guy he invited over to get off with tonight.

Heat rises up my neck and hits the tips of my ears as I think about all the things I want to do with him. I didn't know how badly I needed this until he put it out there as an option. Absolutely perfect timing. I don't let myself hesitate when I reach the door of his unit.

I lift my fist to knock, but the door flies open before I can make contact.

"Hey," he greets me, a grin taking over his whole face, one adorable dimple popping as he lifts an arm and scratches at the back of his neck. "I'm so glad you could make it."

This is the shit I'm talking about. Stupid hot. Genuinely nice.

He opens the door wider and ushers me inside. His hand brushes against my low back as he moves to pass me in the entry, and I stop myself from showing how that subtle graze affected me by clenching my abs and holding my breath.

"Come on in," he encourages as he strolls into a pristine, modern kitchen. I've never been to his place before. I was so excited about tonight, I hadn't given it much thought. It's clean and contemporary without coming off as pretentious. Everything looks expensive, but it also looks lived in. Of course his house is an effortless balance. Just like him.

Anticipation slams into me as I look around his personal space. I'm at Jake's house. I'm standing in Jake's kitchen. And at some point tonight, I'll be in Jake's bed.

He saunters to the fridge before turning back to me. "Can I get you something to drink?"

"No, I'm fine. I brought my water."

I hold up my emotional support bottle and inwardly cringe. I must have grabbed it when I got out of the car out of habit. Phone, wallet, jacket, water. My subconscious knew I'd need to stay hydrated, but I probably didn't need to draw attention to it like that.

Mierda.

"Do you mind if I have a drink?" he asks as he pulls a bottle of Great Lakes Lemon Hefeweizen out of the fridge. "It's been a hell of a week."

I smile at his courteousness, but can't resist teasing him. "You know it's only Monday, right?"

He pops the cap on a fancy wall-mounted mechanism, then takes a long swig. I watch, enraptured, as his Adam's apple moves in rhythm with each swallow. Pulling the bottle away from his lips, he gives up this little noise of satisfaction—a mix between a sigh and a grunt—that makes my dick twitch in interest.

He sets the bottle down and catches me staring, but I don't care. We're both grown men. There's no reason to play coy. I know exactly why I'm here.

"Believe me, I know. That's what I was hoping to talk to you about tonight." He circles the island and hops onto one of the stools, then pats the empty seat beside him.

I slide onto the stool, but have to pivot to face him because it isn't pulled out far enough for my legs to fit. We're close enough that I could reach out and touch him if I wanted—and God do I want to—but if he wants to chat me up first, that's fine, too. I can do small talk. Especially when I know what comes next.

"I found something out over the weekend," he starts. "Something that changes everything."

He's not looking at me as he speaks, which is odd; he's always so direct and confident. His gaze is fixed on the bottle in his hands, and he's picking at the corner of the label mindlessly. Is he nervous?

"I can't really tell you all the details. But it's a big deal to me and to a lot of other people, too. There's something I want to do. Have to do, really. But the only way it all works out is if I can come up with a lot of cash, fast. My dad left me a sizable inheritance, but I have to get married to get it. That's where you come in. Or at least, where I hope you come in."

What? Why is he being all vague and evasive? I'm barely following his monologue, and now he's talking about marriage and an inheritance?

"I'm sorry I can't tell you all the details or explain why this is all happening... I promise I will if you agree to go along with it. I'll tell you everything, and I'll give you half. It's a ton of money, Cory. Like, a stupid amount of money."

Is he already drunk? I'm beyond confused, but he doesn't give me time to interject.

"I've been thinking about it nonstop since I left Clinton's. I think it's fate, honestly. I had to figure this out today, and I didn't know what to do. But then you started talking about your school thing and needing money... it's like it was meant to be."

He blows out an exasperated breath, but before I can ask for clarification, he continues.

"I know it's a lot to process, and we can talk it out and negotiate terms or whatever to make sure we're on the same page. It won't be forever, and I won't give you any trouble when it's time to go our separate ways. I'll make it good for you, I swear. I'll make it worth it. I just need you to say yes."

I'm—stunned. And unnerved. I'm not sure I've ever heard Jake talk this much in one sitting. His words were jumbled and left me with two vague takeaways: he wants me to do something for him, and he's really nervous that I'm going to say no.

I stare at him for a moment, shuffling through the questions in my head. He looks like he's going to be physically ill.

"Jake, I don't..."

"Please, Cory. Please don't say no. If it's not yes right now, tell me what I can do to change your mind. I'll give you anything. I'll do anything you ask. Just please don't shoot me down."

Is he—begging? He really does look unseasonably pale. I can't stand to see him like this. I reach out across the cool countertop and rest my hand on his arm for comfort. He tilts his chin to face me, his hazel puppy dog eyes pleading. The problem is, I still don't understand the actual question.

"What I was going to say is that I don't know what you're asking."

His eyes grow wider as he works to swallow. He moves to place his free hand on top of mine, and it's like his touch alone has the power to start a riot in my body. The gesture feels intimate, albeit desperate. At this point, I'm pretty sure he's not just hoping for a blow job.

"I'm asking you to marry me."

Chapter 7

Jake

He yanks his hand off my arm and physically recoils.

Fuckin' A.

This is so much harder than I expected, and I feel like I'm messing it up further every time I open my mouth. I just droned on for a solid five minutes with vague descriptions of what I actually wanted to say, then blurted out a piss-poor excuse for a proposal.

I'd probably flinch away from me, too.

"This is a joke."

It's not a question. It's an accusation. The very evident hurt in his eyes makes that clear.

"Cory, no. I swear it's not."

"Do you think this is funny? Do you think I'm into humiliation? Is this some form of foreplay for you?"

Foreplay? The tension crackles between us. He's getting more agitated with every word.

"You invite me over tonight, insist I come right after work, and tell me we can help each other out since you've been having a hard time, too."

I nod. Everything he's saying is accurate. So why is he...

"You invited me over to hook up, and now you're playing a prank on me instead?"

Oh.

Fuck.

In all my concern about how this night would play out, I sort of forgot that our original conversation at Clinton's did involve a good amount of innuendo and eye fucking.

"You thought we were hooking up tonight?" I do my best to use a gentle tone. I can tell he's already pissed and maybe even a little embarrassed.

"Yes, Jake. You leaned across the bar, got close enough to kiss me, and talked in that low, growly voice. Of course I thought you were inviting me over for sex."

Oh God. I didn't just screw up. I might have ruined everything.

I figured he'd be curious about what I had to say. I never imagined he'd have specific expectations when he walked through my door.

But he's not wrong. I did lay it on thick to ensure he showed up. This is on me.

"Listen, Cory..."

He's got his head turned away with his gaze set on the door. My heart pounds double time as I recognize the threat. He could very well walk out that door and not give me another thought.

Desperate to get his attention, I stand and gently try to turn his face toward me. He lets me touch him, but he won't meet my gaze.

"Hey," I whisper, running my hand from his jaw down his neck until I'm clasping his shoulder. "You're right. I screwed this up. I implied I wanted something sexual from you. And while that's certainly not a lie..." I give him a playful once-over, gliding my hand from his shoulder back up the side of his neck. He's still wearing his heathered blue work shirt, but I move past the neckline in a caress. His skin is soft and warm under my palm, tempting in a way I can't let myself feel right now. "It's not the primary concern for me right now."

I wait with bated breath to see how he'll react. I'm good at reading people—I have to be, given my occupation. The best bartenders have steady hands, endless patience, and perfectly tuned intuition.

Right now, my gut says that Cory feels rejected, and there's a serious chance he'll shut down because of it. I can't let the rejection fester or it'll only make it harder to claw out of this hole I've dug for myself.

"Co-ry," I try, extending his name for emphasis. I risk moving my hand to his cheek, cupping his face and tilting his head until he's looking at me. "Talk to me. What are you thinking?"

He shudders under my touch—just slightly. Only enough that I notice because I'm scrutinizing him with such intensity. I wait with bated breath, desperate for him to give me something to work with.

"I'm thinking I made a mistake coming here tonight."

Oof. He's looking right at me now, his eyes boring into my soul, letting me see, without a shadow of a doubt, the truth behind his words.

I believe him.

But I'm not done trying.

"Not a mistake," I correct with false confidence. "An opportunity. An answer. A chance for you to finish your degree, pay off student loans, set yourself up for whatever comes after school, and be financially set for life. What are your dreams, Cory? What do you want most?"

Chapter 8

Cory

What do I want most? Until two minutes ago, the answer was him. I wanted to be dripping in sweat while his hips drove me into a mattress until I reached blackout-level bliss.

What I wanted most was to get off. Now what I want most is to get out of here.

I showed up tonight ready to get laid. To forget about everything going on in my life. To let myself get lost in him.

Now my mind is working overtime to keep up.

Jake Whitely just asked me to marry him.

The tip of his thumb grazes just below my bottom lip as he traces it with his nail. His light hazel eyes are warm and sincere. Between his touch and his gaze, I relax a little. It's like he's got me in a trance, and I find myself processing—and maybe even considering—what he's asking.

But herein lies the heart of the issue: I could have a one-night-stand with Jake Whitely. Even though it's out of character for me, I was able to play it cool when we hooked up in the past. Hell, I could probably even manage a friends-with-benefits relationship if I kept my emotions in check. But I'm a sucker for commitment and powerless when it comes to this guy's magnetic pull. The prospect of a committed relationship with a man I've been crushing on for the last several years is likely more than my heart can handle.

I know my own heart. And the emotional baggage I carry from all the times things didn't work out with guys I really liked. I can't do this. Which is why I shock the shit out of myself when I open my mouth and say, "Be honest with me, Jake. Tell me exactly what you're asking of me and why."

He must sense he's been given an opening because he drops his hand from my face and straightens his spine. I miss his touch the moment he cuts off contact.

"Okay. I can do that. I'll tell you everything. But you have to swear to keep this to yourself. I need you to promise, Cory. Promise me you won't repeat what I'm about to say."

I nod my head, curious and a little scared.

"Mike has to sell Clinton's and The Oak."

I can't help but widen my eyes at that, but otherwise, I try not to react.

"He needs a quick cash buyout. I want them. I just don't have the money for it, and he doesn't have time for me to figure it out. I've come up with one single solution: I have to get married. My dad died six years ago. He was a real asshat who got off on making my life hell. I know a lot of people have daddy issues or whatever, but Joe Whitely bore a special breed of hate. He left me ten million dollars in his will, but with the condition that I only got it if I got married. I know exactly why he set it up like that…"

Jake trails off and goes quiet for a moment. It doesn't take a therapist in training to recognize the hurt behind his eyes.

"So that's what this is about. I need to get married as soon as possible. I didn't know what the hell I was going to do, but when you mentioned you needed twenty grand, it was like the universe was saying, 'here he is! This gorgeous man who you genuinely like would make a great husband, and he needs money, too!'"

My whole face heats at the compliment, even though I know he's laying it on thick.

"I'm sorry if I led you here under false pretenses. I was so in my own head about this situation, I wasn't using my other head for once." He winks at me then, because of course he does.

"Do you... have any questions for me?"

Yes. Yes, I do. What's in it for me? What would I have to do? How long would it last? Would I have to lie to my family and friends? Are there rules? Is there sex? And most importantly, at least where my heart is concerned, why not someone he's actually been in a relationship with before?

That's where I start. The question is rooted in self-doubt. But I have to know.

"Why me, Jake? Out of all the people you could have asked..."

He shrugs in defeat. "I don't have anyone else to ask. You and I have always gotten along, and you could use the money, so why not you?"

His explanation is mediocre at best. But I have to hand it to him: he didn't sugarcoat his answer. I respect that.

"And if I say no?"

He gives me a pointed look, like he doesn't want to answer the question. I stay quiet and wait him out.

"If you say no, I'm back to square one, and I'll start over."

Start over?

Oh. Realization dawns on me then. This isn't a special offer for me. I deflate as the reality of the situation sinks in. "You're going through with this plan whether I'm in or not..."

Jake spreads his arms out on the island and hangs his head.

"It's the only way I can think to get the money fast enough..."

"Why don't you just ask someone you've dated?" I challenge.

He and I have hooked up. We've flirted. We've eye-fucked each other from across the room. But that's as far as it's ever gone. And none of that has happened recently. I've been in two relationships since the last time I was with Jake. He and I have been nothing but cordial, platonic coworkers since the spring of my first year of graduate school.

He smirks, making his dimple peek out before he replies. "Asking someone I've dated would be impossible, considering I've never been in a relationship."

"*What?*"

I heard him. But I need him to repeat it.

"I've never been in a relationship. I swore them off in high school. I've never had a boyfriend. Or a girlfriend. I've had plenty of partners, but never an actual *partner*, ya know?"

I rack my brain, trying to come up with an example to refute his claim. But I draw a blank. For the five years I've worked at Clinton's, I can't think of one person Jake has ever referred to as his boyfriend or girlfriend. Huh.

"You said it didn't have to be forever; how long would we have to stay married?"

Jake grimaces. I know from the look on his face this isn't going to be a short-term arrangement.

"Two years, ideally, to be safe. There's not a contingency about the length of the marriage in the will, probably because my dad didn't think I'd ever go for it. But I have two brothers, and they'll be on my ass as soon as they catch wind of this from our family's estate lawyer. I don't think they'll interfere out of spite, but they'll be the first to call me out if they don't think it's real."

"What does *real* mean, Jake?"

He raises his eyebrows in challenge and sticks his tongue in his cheek. "What do you want it to mean, Cory?"

"I—"

I honestly don't know. This isn't some fake dating scenario he's suggesting. He's asking me to marry him. To be his husband. To be... in a committed relationship? Emotionally involved? Physically intimate? I feel way too raw to play games and dance around the details.

"I'm serious. Lay it all out for me right now, or I'm gone. It's not fair for you to talk around things and make me jump through hoops to get the answers I deserve. I'm entitled to all the information before I make a decision. You need to be crystal clear with me if I'm really going to consider this."

He startles and takes a step back, leaving me to wonder if I was too harsh. But he can't really think this is a lighthearted matter, can he?

"Okay, I hear you," he asserts. "This is what I've come up with so far, which is all negotiable—just a starting point. Stop me if you have questions, okay?"

I nod, grateful he's finally taking me seriously.

"We would get married as soon as possible. As in, this week. Do you want a wedding?"

Hell yes, I want a wedding. But I want a real wedding, with the person I love, to celebrate what should be the happiest day of my life. I don't need a wedding for this charade.

"Not for this."

"Okay. So we can do it at the courthouse. How much longer are you in school?"

"I've got two more semesters, then an internship next summer."

"So that takes us to the one-year mark. If you can give me two years, that'll be perfect."

I nod methodically. Not because I'm agreeing to his plan. But because it sounds reasonable. It may take time to find a job after graduation anyway. It would be nice to have a buffer while I'm getting things sorted post-graduation.

"You would have to move in here."

That gets my attention. I gawk but don't have time to object before he starts making his case.

"It... it has to be real. Or at least look real. My older brother has eyes and ears all over this town. If he catches wind that I'm married but not living with my husband, he'll know something's up."

"Why do I have to move in with you?" I challenge.

"I own the building. I can't move out; I'm the landlord."

My eyes go wide at that fun fact. And his nonchalance about the whole thing. I've never even lived in a home that wasn't a rental. To think he owns this entire complex...

"Plus, if you move in here, you'll be closer to school and work."

He has a point.

"Do you have a roommate or something? We could buy them out and pay off your lease if that's what you're worried about."

I gulp as I remember just how little this man knows about me. "I live with my grandmother."

"Oh. Shit. I didn't know that. Do you take care of her?"

"No, no, she's only in her fifties. She doesn't need taking care of."

His face screws up slightly as he tries to work out the math. I'm twenty-five. My mom is forty-one. Abuela is fifty-eight.

We did, in fact, throw a party when I reached the ripe age of eighteen and had not yet fathered a child. Never mind the fact that my family knows I'm gay and that not knocking someone up in high school shouldn't be *that* remarkable. It was a running joke for years that I broke the family curse. We all have dark senses of humor, obviously. That's just how I was raised—laugh through the joy, lean on each other through the rest.

That's all way too much information for this particular conversation, so I keep it to myself. He does need to understand where my family falls in terms of my priorities, though. I know for a fact that Abuela will see right through this ruse.

"She works nights as a custodian for the Cascade Falls public school district. She doesn't need me at home, but she knows me better than anyone, and I know she'll question everything about this. She practically raised me, Jake. I won't lie to her."

He nods slowly, processing. "You won't have to. I'm not suggesting we do this on the down low. Hell, it needs to look convincing and be legit. We'll have to tell all our family and friends."

"So are you proposing a marriage of convenience *and* a real relationship, Jake Whitely?"

My words hit as intended.

"Whoa, whoa, whoa, don't get crazy on me. Relationship virgin over here, remember? What if we start things casual... maybe call it a marriage with benefits?"

I set out here tonight looking for casual. But casual and marriage don't exactly go hand-and-hand in my mind. I love love. I respect the shit out of marriage. I'm so damn grateful to be alive in a day and age where I can marry whoever I want.

Even if what we're doing isn't real, I'm not okay pretending marriage isn't a big deal to me.

Jake continues his crusade while I'm still gathering my thoughts. He does that a lot: doubles down to drive a point home before I've even come up with a rebuttal. He's a fast thinker and a smooth talker. Just two more reasons I always feel off kilter around him.

"If you're my husband, and we're living together..." He pauses and regards me suggestively.

My cheeks flush with desire, even as I'm still trying to gather my thoughts. My body obviously hasn't caught up to the revelations of the last several minutes.

He bites down on his lip, cocks his head slightly, and does this little half smile that puts that damn dimple on full display.

I'm grateful to still be seated. The guy smirks and I'm half hard. Since I'm feeling vulnerable to his onslaught of flirtation, I steel my spine and rely on sass as a defense mechanism.

"So you expect me to marry you, move in here, sleep with you, and still call it casual?"

Instead of replying, he's on the prowl. I watch intently as he closes the space between us. He moves slowly, giving me time to track his motions and pull back if I'm uncomfortable.

But I'm not going anywhere. I want this. I want him.

He hits me with the most delicious smirk before gripping the back of my head, bowing low, and whispering in my ear. "You already know we're good together, Cor. No, not just good. Mind-blowing, if memory serves me right."

Goosebumps erupt on the nape of my neck and travel all the way down my thighs.

"But it's your choice. If you don't want to have sex with me..."

His breath is hot on my skin: his words kerosene that catch immediately and send me up in flames.

"Marry me, Cory. Please. I would be so good to you."

I almost say yes right then and there. His hand cupping the back of my head reminds me just how electric it is when we come together. His breath warm against my skin is equal parts soothing and stimulating.

I'm so close to saying yes. But I owe it to myself to put words to my greatest fear.

"If we do this... you have to be faithful to me."

He stills, then pulls back. His movements are slow and calculated. When he looks into my eyes, it's like he's searching for something. There's a tinge of hostility in the air that wasn't there a moment ago. He almost looks... insulted? I take a move out of his playbook and double down before he can respond.

"I know it's not forever, but if you expect me to tell people I'm married to one of Hampton's most notorious playboys, then I expect you to be faithful."

He crosses his arms over his chest. "Understood."

That's it? Now that I've spoken the fear out loud, I desperately need him to understand how important this is to me. "I'm serious, Jake."

He shakes his head and lets out a huff of agitation. "So am I, Cory. I wouldn't try to convince you to do this with me, then turn around and embarrass you like that. What kind of person do you think I am? If you're my husband, then it's only you."

He looks legitimately angry now. But there's still something about his promise of commitment that doesn't feel right. I believe him. But I also question whether someone can just turn things around and change their behavior that quickly. Rather than push back and challenge him on it, I decide to move forward.

"Okay. So you want to get married. I have to move in here, and we have to stay married for two years. You'll pay for my tuition—"

"And whatever else you want," he interrupts.

I side-eye him at that.

"What? I know how much you make at Clinton's. If you're having trouble paying for school, I just assumed…"

"I'm not some charity case," I spit.

Jake doesn't know it, but I used to be. Shame still flares up when I think about the free lunches and weekend food bags. My abuela worked tirelessly to raise me and give me everything, but sometimes we still needed help to fill in the gaps. There's nothing wrong with receiving help. I know that now. But it doesn't change the visceral reaction I feel when I think about it.

"I'm not implying that you're a charity case. But I don't think you understand how much money we're talking about here. Or how badly I don't want or need it. I never counted on this inheritance. It feels like I've spent my whole damn life trying to make smart decisions to avoid having to rely on this option."

He takes a deep breath and shakes his head before pinning me with those hazel eyes.

"But it's ten million dollars, Cor. That's a lot of fucking money. In my mind, we use it to buy out Mike, invest in the businesses so those are secure, then pay for your school and pay off any student loans. Even after I've paid for the restaurants and we've lived off it for a few years, it's safe to assume you've got four million to your name. We can't have a prenup or a paper trail, so that means when we separate, you automatically get half. I just ask for your word that you won't touch the businesses. Otherwise, what's mine is yours, for better or for worse, and only richer, because it's so much fucking money you'll never be poor."

"Jake..." I can barely wrap my mind around the enormity of what he's offering. "That's so much money."

"I know. And you have no idea how badly I don't want any of it." He sighs, then peers past my shoulder, seemingly lost in thought.

"Accepting it feels like defeat," he admits, shaking his head in shame. "My dad left me that money to mock me. He wanted to remind me of how he tried to force me into a relationship before. I can't be certain, but I'm pretty sure he never imagined gay marriage would be legal in Ohio, hence why he didn't stipulate that I had to marry a woman."

Realization hits me as he candidly shares the real motivation behind his plan.

"I despise having to use this money. It's steeped in hate. But if you do this with me, I'll feel less shitty about the whole thing. Marrying a man and making my dreams come true seems like a pretty good way to give the middle finger to my father's wishes."

I'm sure I'm not thinking this through, but I feel myself nodding again. It's like my body has a mind of its own around this man.

"We can pay off your car or buy you a new one. I might get a new car while we're at it. We can pick a few charities and make big donations. Anything you want to do with it, we'll do. Hell, you can pay off your grandma's house if you want. We'll share everything while we're together. Then we'll split up what's left when we go our separate ways."

My car is on its last wheeze. Tori's dad told me I was months away from needing a new one the last time he looked at it for me. Most of my undergrad student loans are in forbearance, but interest keeps accruing. My abuela rents our 2-bedroom ranch house in Cascade Falls, and she refuses to let me contribute while I'm in school. She's never owned a home. She's going to lose it when she finds out about this.

Then there's my dream. The improbability I hold close to my heart, even though I know it's years away from becoming a reality. Or it was. Maybe it's not so farfetched now.

I want to open a private counseling practice that's run like a non-profit. I want to forgo private insurance and offer high-quality services on a sliding scale fee. Like Planned Parenthood, but for mental health. I don't have any idea how to pull it off, or if it's even possible. And I'm still more than a year out from earning my master's degree and even thinking about opening an office.

But with that kind of money? With that kind of freedom?

I think I'm going to do it.

I rise to my feet to match his stance. "You're asking a lot, Jake."

"I know." He turns his head away, almost like he's preparing to be rejected.

"But you're offering a lot, too. Before I commit, I need to make sure you understand something. Marriage is a big deal to me. So are relationships. This isn't something I take lightly. Especially because when I was younger, I thought I'd have to leave Ohio to even have the opportunity to get married. I don't love that part of this plan. But I can set my personal feelings on the matter aside for now. If you promise to be faithful... and if it means my dreams don't get derailed because of funding... I'll do it."

His head snaps up so fast I'm afraid he pulled a muscle.

"You'll do it?"

I shake my head and laugh—I'm almost as surprised as he is. What the hell am I doing?

"Yeah," I confirm with a grin. "I'll marry you."

His joy is infectious as he comes at me in violent delight. The next thing I know, his arms are around me: hugging, squeezing, lifting. He lets out a whoop, and I laugh again.

This is not how I thought this night would go. This is not how I thought my *life* would go. This is the most reckless, wild thing I've ever done.

But it'll be okay. Because it's Jake. And he really is offering a hell of a lot.

Chapter 9

Jake

He said yes. He freaking said yes.

I squeeze him as hard as I can, pouring every ounce of my gratitude into this hug. He smells like citrus and honey, and it takes everything in me not to burrow into his neck and give him another whiff.

I'm just so grateful.

And relieved.

Now that I'm not stressed and anxious, I realize I'm bone-achingly tired.

Exhaustion slams into me while we're still hugging, my body threatening to collapse now that I can breathe after what might have been the most nerve-racking forty-eight hours of my life.

I finally loosen my grip, then pull back to make sure he hasn't changed his mind in the last ten seconds.

He gives me a sheepish smile, looking up at the exposed beams of the vaulted ceiling and running his hands over his face and through his hair.

"This is crazy," he mutters quietly. I know his words aren't for me. For as long as I've known Cory, he's been a rule follower, the type to play it safe. That aligns with what I know about him. He's one of my most dependable employees. I can always count on him to be early, stay late, and pick up a shift when needed. He's a really good guy. Now I get to find out what kind of husband he'll be.

He's still gazing at the ceiling, shaking his head in disbelief.

Now that things have calmed down, awkwardness creeps in. Since I lured him over here by implying we were going to hook up, I'm a little unsure of what my next move should be. It would be weird to fool around now, considering I just asked him to commit the next two years of his life to being with me. But it's also weird to pretend like this isn't a life-changing moment.

Do I offer him a tour of the place? Do the get-to-know-you thing? Circle back and offer him another drink?

Maybe it's the bartender in me, but the drink seems like the safest bet.

"I'm gonna have one more," I declare, holding up my almost-empty beer bottle. "Want one?"

He meets my gaze and nods so adamantly that I have to hold in a smirk. My instincts were spot on. We both need something normal to cling to in light of what we just agreed to do.

I grab the beers, pop the caps, and hand him one before clinking the necks of the bottles together.

"To us," I pronounce. "To helping each other out and making the most of the next two years."

He puffs out his cheeks, blows out a long breath, and looks at me like I'm crazy. Maybe I am. But we're both about to have our lives changed in big ways. This moment is too important to gloss over.

"To us," he finally relents before taking a long sip.

I watch the way his lips encircle the opening of the bottle, mesmerized when he lowers the glass in slow motion. He's got this perfect mouth—a mouth I remember so clearly in my mind, a mouth I'm craving to taste again soon. But not tonight.

I really am tired, and although I didn't give it much thought before, I think it's best to take things slow. Physically, at least. Emotionally, for sure. Just because we're having a shotgun wedding doesn't mean I expect him to open up to me or want to hop into bed right away. That'll come with time. It almost happened tonight, so it's safe to say it's a foregone conclusion. But for now, I need to make sure he's okay with what's happening and how this is all about to go down.

"Come on," I urge, slipping my hand in his and pulling him farther into the condo. "Let's at least sit down while we drink these."

I guide him into the living room but don't bother turning when I hear his gasp. The view is breathtaking. I live on the third floor of the building, and I have these massive floor-to-ceiling windows lining one wall. The windows look out onto a grassy picnic area and the train bridge that cuts through town. Beyond that are the tops of the buildings of downtown Hampton, plus the clock tower on the green. At nighttime, it almost feels like I live on an island that overlooks the ocean, with nothing but stars and sky and twinkle lights interposing on the darkness.

"It's really pretty during the daytime, too," I tell him as I plop onto one side of the leather sofa. The thing is almost as wide as it is long: like a daybed masquerading as a couch. I sprawl out like usual, then adjust my posture to sit up a little straighter when Cory perches on the edge.

He's turned to face me with one leg crossed over his knee, the beer bottle cradled in both hands. He looks adorable, but I'm acutely aware of how uncomfortable he is.

"What can I do?" I question, jutting my chin in his direction. I've never been in a relationship, but I've been around Tori and Rhett long enough to know how to play the part. At least in some regards. If he's uneasy, it's my job to figure out why and to comfort him however I can. I think.

"How long have you lived here?"

I sit up straighter still. He's mentally freaking out right now; I can see it in his eyes. I've had some time to wrap my head around things, to plan how this will go. But he hasn't had the same processing time. If he has questions, I want to give him answers. I'll do whatever it takes to ease his mind and make him feel better about this situation.

"I moved out of my dad's house right before my senior year of high school."

His brows furrow slightly, his expression contemplative.

"My mom left me an inheritance—she died when I was three—but I couldn't access it until I graduated. Things got... really bad... with my dad."

I grind my molars as memories of Joe flash through my mind. If Cory pushes—if he asks for more details—I'll tell him. But I really hope he lets me leave it at that.

"My grandma helped me out my senior year. I lived in one of the duplexes down by the bakery for a year thanks to her generosity. Then, once I graduated from high school and got my inheritance from my mom, my grandma helped me buy this building as an investment property."

"You bought an entire condo complex when you were eighteen years old?" Those furrowed brows are accompanied by a frown now, his face screwed up in confusion.

"I was nineteen. But yes. Both my parents come from money. My Grandma Patty helped me get it all set up so I wouldn't ever have to rely on my dad again."

"Until now," he retorts.

"Until now."

The moment feels too heavy. I need to figure out how to lighten the mood—fast.

I reach out slowly, tentatively, and he doesn't resist when I hook my pinkie finger with his, tugging on his arm gently so he turns to face me completely. Even once he's staring at me head-on, I don't let go. I run my fingertips over his knuckles, then smooth them up and down his hand.

"The view isn't the only perk of this place. We have an underground garage all to ourselves, too." I continue stroking his hand in what I hope is a soothing gesture. I want him to know it's okay to freak out right now, but that I'm here. I'll hold us together.

"The whole thing is just for us?"

I bite my bottom lip and nod. "Yep. The location of this building is so great—and the landlord is so hot—" I give him a pointed look to make sure the joke lands.

When he rolls his eyes, I smile wider and continue.

"That I can offer street parking for residents. I have a few cars down there, and a whole bunch of my dad's classics, too. It's nearly full, but I guess I can clear a spot out for my husband." I give him a wink for good measure.

"What else?"

The curious glint in his eye spurs me on, and I scramble to think of what to say next.

"There's a pool. I'll only keep it open for another month or so, but it's usually pretty quiet down there, and you can access it twenty-four seven."

He gives me a little half smile that encourages me to keep going. Our hands are still touching, and now I'm leaning in closer, eager to feed into his excitement about moving here.

"We've got two full bathrooms—the master has a dual showerhead with a waterfall feature, and the tile floor is heated. I upgraded the kitchen a few years ago; can you cook?" I ask, genuinely curious about whether he even cares about the kitchen. I'm no slouch, but I'm no master chef, either. Maybe I'll cook for him this weekend.

"I can cook." He nods tentatively. "I like to bake, too. I just don't like to do dishes." He raises one eyebrow as he throws the proverbial ball in my court.

Could I banter with him and push back? Yeah, probably. But I'm on cloud nine right now. And I was serious about what I said when he first arrived: I'll give him anything and do anything to keep him on board with this plan.

"Lucky for you, you're marrying the best dishwasher to ever pass through the hallowed kitchen of Clinton's Family Restaurant."

He barks out a laugh that lights up my insides. I think it's the first time he's genuinely smiled all night. He has this epic smile—straight white teeth surrounded by plush lips with this super chiseled jawline. God, it's going to be fun making this man laugh on the regular.

"You know I already agreed to marry you, right?"

"I know." I encircle his hand in mine. No more teasing, caressing, flirting. I hold it firmly and speak my truth. "I'm just really happy you agreed to do this with me. You could probably get me to commit to any number of household chores or domestic responsibilities right now."

That earns me another genuine, albeit small, smile.

"Speaking of... we have a washer and dryer just down there." I point in the direction of the hallway that leads to the other side of the unit. "Then the bedroom and workout room are down that way, too."

His hand slips out of mine as he pulls back and scowls.

"There's only one bedroom?"

Shit.

Yep. There's only one bedroom.

"There is," I answer honestly, racking my brain to come up with a solution before he changes his mind. I obviously hadn't thought that through when I asked him to move in here. I promised him we could take things slow; guess I forgot to mention the one-bed situation.

He shakes his head, a mix of amusement and disbelief gracing his expression.

"This whole scenario is straight out of a rom-com. You know that, right?"

I see a shot and seize it.

"I call dibs on Jude Law playing me if they ever make our story into a movie."

"In what version of reality would Jude Law play the gay Puerto Rican in the relationship?" he deadpans.

I smirk at his quick wit.

"I didn't know you were Puerto Rican," I throw out. If he wants to share with me, I want to know. I want to know as much as I can about him, everything, really. Now that we're doing this, I'm all in. But I keep my tone casual, just in case it's something he'd rather not talk about.

He nods and holds my gaze. "My mom and grandma are from Puerto Rico. My dad's from Pennsylvania, though, and I was born here in the States."

"That's awesome. God, I feel like there's so much I don't know about you…" I trail off when I catch that look of uncertainty in his expression again. "But we have time. I promise you; we have time."

That brings me back to the whole reason we got off topic in the first place.

"So listen, I'll sleep on the couch for the foreseeable future. I fall asleep out here half the time anyway. And when I close at The Oak, I'm not home until two or three."

"And what about the unforeseeable future?" he asks, that one perfect eyebrow cocked high in challenge. God, he's quick—I love how he challenges me and pushes back. I could shoot the shit with him all day.

"I guess we'll just have to wait and see." I resist winking at him for the third time tonight, but it's tempting. It feels good to flirt after being so strung out and stressed these last few days.

"I guess we will," he relents. He looks around the apartment again, and I give him a minute to take it in.

I track his gaze as he assesses the space, and I mentally make note of some of the things I'll need to do before he moves in—making room on the bookshelves, cleaning out my desk so it's functional for both of us.

It's strange to be making a list of domestic chores. Even stranger that it's intended to make room for my husband.

Husband.

That's going to take some getting used to. But I'm not panicked or filled with dread at the prospect of getting married—not like I thought I'd be. I'm actually excited about this—ecstatic that this is going to work. A lot of that has to do with him.

His yawn pulls me out of my meandering thoughts. A quick glance at the clock confirms it's almost one a.m. It feels too—pushy? To invite him to spend the night now. I don't want him to think this is some sort of test.

"You gonna get going?" I ask, wanting to make sure he knows I don't have expectations about the rest of the night. As if the next two years of his life aren't enough…

He nods through another yawn and gives me a sheepish smile. As he's shifting forward to stand, I reach out and stroke his arm, halting his movements and freezing him in place.

"I have to know something before you leave," I murmur.

I don't know if it's my tone or the words themselves, but that gets his attention. He turns back to face me, his head cocked in question.

"Who *do* you want to play you in the movie?"

He busts out laughing, then bats my arm away before slapping my knee playfully. "You're going to be a handful as a husband, aren't you?"

I stick my tongue in my cheek and eye him up and down before responding as he walks toward the door. "You and I both know that I'm more like two handfuls."

Chapter 10

Cory

"How long have you been up there?"

I don't bother sitting up to answer. If Lia's already starting her morning chores, it's after five a.m. I've been up here since I left his place—scratch that—*our* place, around one.

"I just needed to think," I call down to her. An indignant moo sounds in the distance. The cows are probably pissed that Lia's up and hasn't made her way to them yet.

"I have to get a few chores out of the way, but I'll join you when I'm done."

I groan slightly at the idea of having to evade the reason I've pulled an all-nighter. How can I possibly explain this to Lia when I barely understand it myself?

He implied we were going to have sex.

Instead, he proposed marriage.

And somehow, despite knowing Jake Whitely doesn't "do" relationships and learning last night that he's literally never even been someone's boyfriend, I agreed to marry him.

I'm going to have a husband.

I'm going to *be* a husband.

I agreed to marry him. I can't seem to make myself feel bad about the situation. If I'm honest, doing this to make him happy makes *me* happy. Sure, other things factor into the equation. But he needs me. He needs me in a way no one ever has before. It was the way he looked so desperate, so hopeful. Like I was his salvation. My stupid tender heart got together with my wanton dick and thrust me into this scenario, but I don't regret it.

I've been lying on the roof of this pole barn for hours, trying to make myself feel ashamed of what I just agreed to do.

But I don't.

If anything, I'm excited. Nervous, yes. But also... intrigued and captivated and inexplicably eager about what the whole thing means for the next two years of my life.

I don't make reckless decisions. I've always played it safe. No one would expect something like this from me, which makes it that much more enthralling.

And then there's the money. It's a life-changing amount of money. I thought I'd be riddled with student loan debt for the next ten years. I assumed I'd have to live with my abuela until I was at least thirty just to make ends meet. It's crazy to think that something as simple as getting married will provide a solution to so many obstacles in my life.

Before I left the condo, we agreed to announce our marriage via text to everyone except my abuela and Mike. I balked at the suggestion at first. But Jake made a number of valid points, the biggest one being that everyone in our circle can find out at the same time if we send off a group text. This way, we won't have to decide who to tell first.

It sounded like a good plan last night. Except now I'm faced with the prospect of explaining my emotional breakdown all-nighter to one of my best friends while circumventing the truth about why I'm freaking out.

I still don't know what, exactly, I'm going to say when Lia joins me on the roof half an hour later. She grunts as she heaves herself next to me, then sits there panting for a few seconds to catch her breath.

I swear she works harder than anyone I've ever met. I admire her grit. The way she just handles shit, moves forward, and never complains.

"I'm too tired to stage an inquisition," she huffs as she lowers down to lie beside me. "Spill."

I turn my head to meet her gaze through the early light of dawn. The sun won't be up for another hour, yet a glow is already cast over the entire farm.

I've been sneaking up onto the pole barn forever; Lia and Tori have been doing it even longer. It's where we come to escape. To think. To unwind. To figure shit out.

And now, apparently, it's where I come to share half-truths.

"Something happened last night," I start.

"With Jake," Lia interjects.

Mierda.

Am I really that transparent?

She rolls her eyes and elbows me in the side. "Come on, Cor. I saw how he was looking at you at the bar yesterday. Then I watched you stumble through a shift like you didn't know left from right or up from down. It doesn't take a genius to figure out what he wanted."

Wait... does she think...?

"It's fine," Lia insists, rolling her eyes and shaking her head after a moment. "Seriously. I don't care if you want to hook up with Jake again. I have absolutely no interest in being back on that boy's roster."

A surge of jealousy hits me. Jake promised me he could be faithful. He said that if it was me, it would be *only* me. There's no more roster. Lia just doesn't know that yet.

I promised Jake I wouldn't tell. I may be brand spanking new to this marriage thing, but I want to be a man of my word. After the initial shock of last night wore off, I realized just how thoughtful and gentle he had been: with my feelings, with my heart. Sure, what we're doing is crazy and unconventional. But it doesn't feel overwhelming or chaotic, and that's all because of him.

There's literally no one else I would do this with or do this for. But there's just something about that man—about my future husband—that makes me crave his happiness. When I finally agreed and he hugged me, I was overcome with the most intense warmth. The way he held me, the way I felt so seen and cherished, that's a feeling I want to experience again and again, a high I'll be chasing for a long time.

But maybe I won't have to chase it. Maybe that'll be the norm with Jake. Maybe I didn't just say yes to him last night. Maybe I also said yes to myself.

"Am I really that obvious?" I finally reply, confirming that yes, I'm all twisted up about Jake Whitely like Lia thinks. Even though it's not for the reason she assumes.

"Just be careful, Cor." She sighs, then links our arms together. "I know what Andre did was awful, but Jake is a really big personality to rebound with."

I consider her words and think back to my sleazebag of an ex-boyfriend.

Andre. Just his name elicits a full-body shudder.

Our relationship ended last winter after I caught him getting his dick sucked by a stranger when we were out at the Interbelt. I don't know why I even agreed to go with him that night; clubs are so not my scene. I always felt like I was trying to keep up and prove myself to him.

We had been exclusive—supposedly—for the better part of six months the night I caught him balls-deep down some guy's throat in the bathroom. To this day, I can still see the grimace on his face when I pushed through the door and our eyes locked.

"What are you doing?" he'd demanded.

As if *I* was the one in the wrong.

I respect myself too much to let someone gaslight me. That doesn't mean it didn't hurt like a motherfucker when he broke up with me on the car ride home for being "too sensitive" and closed-minded.

Yikes.

I sure know how to pick them.

I sigh, then give Lia's arm a squeeze. "I know. But Jake's not Andre."

She snorts. "Obviously not. It's not like Jake's going to lock you down, then go gallivanting around town behind your back. Ya know, maybe he *is* a good rebound."

A tickle of dread dances in my gut. I trust Jake—I really do. The way he looked at me earlier and swore his loyalty just felt right. It's the first part of her declaration that I'm stuck on.

Jake already *did* lock it down. She just doesn't know that yet.

I sit up slowly, gather my bearings, and blow out a long exhale filled with all the things I wish I could say. I hate keeping secrets from one of my closest friends, but at least she knows Jake's back in my life in some capacity. That'll have to be enough for now.

"Thanks for the chat," I say, tapping her foot with the toe of my shoe before I shift over to the ladder and make my descent. "I'll text you later, okay?"

She smiles and nods but doesn't lift her head off the corrugated metal of the pole barn. I hope she stays up here for sunrise. She deserves a minute of peace before she has to get back to her chores.

I head to my car feeling lighter—better—now that Lia knows something's brewing with Jake. I yawn and check the time on my phone: 5:28 a.m. Abuela gets off at six. I'll get home before her, make breakfast, and break the news to the one person I *am* allowed to talk to about all this.

"What did you do, nieto?"

I knew she'd call me out the moment she walked in the door.

My abuela works nights, cleaning the public elementary school while the rest of the world sleeps. She's had the same job since I was in middle school—something that allowed her to be home when I got up each morning and be around to help with homework and make me dinner each night.

She's sacrificed so much for me over the years. Even though it's not just about the money, I get a little thrill thinking about Jake's offer. He mentioned we could pay off her house. I want to do more than that: I want to buy her dream home.

"Good morning to you, too," I tease, bending to kiss her on the cheek as she peers around my shoulder. I'm just finishing up the eggs, and everything else is done and laid out on the table.

"You are awake too early. Or maybe you have not even slept? You better start talking, nieto," she chides as she washes her hands.

She's ruthless. And she doesn't tolerate anyone's crap. This is precisely why I just have to come out and say it. I turn the burner off and grab a bowl to give myself a few extra seconds. "Let's at least sit down," I offer, ushering her over to the table.

We both take our seats, but she tents her hands and eyes me skeptically. I know for a fact she won't touch her food until I say what I need to say.

"I need to tell you something."

She nods, an iron fortress of indifference, as I suck in a shaky breath and force out the words.

"I'm getting married."

Her face screws up in confusion, the wrinkles in her forehead deepening as she frowns. There's a charged silence between us that drags on for a beat and then another.

"I know this question does not make sense, but I have to ask it. Did you get someone pregnant?"

I roll my eyes and hold back a chuckle. Our family really does have fertile genes—both my abuela and my mom got pregnant in their teens. But my grandma knows I'm gay, and that it would be extremely unlikely for me to impregnate someone unplanned.

"No, Abuela. It's a friend. Someone I've known and liked for a long time." I bite my lower lip at that admission; saying I've liked Jake Whitely for a long time is a major understatement. But I want her to know that I'm not just jumping into this with anyone. "He needs a favor," I add weakly, reaching for the bowl of arroz con dulce to bide my time.

"And *you* are the favor?" she presses.

I hold back a smirk but mentally catalog the remark so I can tell Jake about it later.

"I know him from work. He used to be my manager; now he runs the bar next door. The man who owns both places is selling them, and Jake—that's his name—wants to buy them. He needs money fast, which he can get from his inheritance if he gets married."

"He is gay?"

Could she at least throw me some softballs? I crack my knuckles under the table and sit up straighter in my seat.

Jake is bi. But trying to explain the sexual spectrum to my grandmother just might throw her over the edge, so I choose the path of least resistance. Besides, gay, straight, bi, pan, or anything in between doesn't matter—he asked me to marry him, and I asked him to be faithful. He's nothing but *mine* for the next two years.

"Si, he's gay, and he wants to marry me. I've already said yes," I declare with more confidence than I feel. I give her a pointed look before she can interrupt. "We have to stay married for two years. Then he's going to share the money he gets from his inheritance."

Her eyes sparkle at that revelation.

"So he is like your sugar daddy?"

She watches too many telenovelas.

"He's not paying me to marry him," I clarify. Because there's a difference. I've stayed up all night convincing myself there's a difference. "I'm marrying him, and we'll share the money like any married couple would while we're together. Then, when it's over, we'll split whatever's left."

I reach across the table and take her hand. Her skin is impossibly soft aside from the callouses on the pads of her palms. She always wears gloves when she works.

"Abuela, it's a *lot* of money," I murmur.

"Cuánto cuesta?"

I look from the untouched coffee in front of her to her arched eyebrow. It's a stupid amount. Embarrassing, really. More than I ever dreamed of possessing. More than he needed to share.

"It's four million dollars."

She slams her fist on the table with enough force to make the silverware rattle and the orange juice sway in her glass.

"Why didn't you lead with that?" she exclaims excitedly. "When is the wedding?"

I laugh out loud at her enthusiasm and exhale a sigh of relief. But I quickly school my expression and prepare for impact. I was less worried about telling her about my marriage of convenience with a big cash windfall than I am for what I'm about to say next.

"Abuela... don't be mad..."

Fire erupts behind her eyes at my warning.

"We're just going to the courthouse and signing papers. There isn't going to be a wedding."

This time when she smacks the table, her juice actually sloshes out of the glass.

She's on her feet a moment later, mixing English and Spanish in a tirade made for the stage. I know better than to interrupt her or try to talk her out of this reaction. She just needs to get it out of her system.

She starts grabbing dishes from the table and clearing them, even though neither of us has taken a single bite of food. I stand cautiously and try to stay out of her way. She's still muttering as I follow her over to the sink. She sets down a plate of toast, and I see my opening.

I grab her in a one-armed hug and feel her tense immediately. Before she can start in on me, I kiss the top of her head. "When it's real, you'll be there," I promise. She hits me with a surly scowl. "I am not getting any younger, nieto."

Oh boy. Now she's just trying to pick a fight. She's not even sixty years old.

"Te amo hasta la luna y de vuelta," I murmur as I ignore my rumbling stomach and retreat from the kitchen to my bedroom. I need to let her have her moment. She'll cool down. I know it. And when I tell her more about my plans for the money...

I yawn deeply as I tread to the other side of our small ranch-style home, desperate to finally get some rest.

Chapter 11

Cory

For as frustrated as I am about the assistantship debacle, I can't help but smile as I stride up the familiar incline from the parking lot to Gray Hall. There's just something about Holt State University's campus that makes me feel a boundless sense of optimism.

Maybe it's the cheesy marketing banners all over campus. Maybe it's the eclectic mix of students meandering on the path in front of me. Or, as corny as it sounds, maybe it's because my dreams are on the precipice of becoming reality thanks to Holt.

I'm a first-generation college graduate. Earning my bachelor's degree was the most significant accomplishment of my life thus far. My parents and Abuela were proud, of course, but I didn't do it for them. There was something intrinsically satisfying about accomplishing that goal and pursuing my dreams. Soon, I'll have my master's degree in a field that I'm passionate about so that I can actually help people.

I didn't set out to become a therapist when I started at Holt. I was undeclared my freshman year, and I took a lot of general education classes to begin with. I had never even considered working in mental health until I was invited back to my high school alma mater to give a presentation about the college experience.

It was my former high school guidance counselor, Mr. Stamos, who suggested I chat with Dr. Deshong, head of the School of Psychology and Human Services at Holt. They had gone to school together and stayed in touch over the years. It was his off-handed comment and their connection that led me down this career path I genuinely love.

I had considered going into education for the first few years of my program, but the restrictions on school guidance counselors, even at the high school level, just feel too ingenuine to me. I want to help the kid who's trying to come out to their parents or experiencing their first heartbreak. I don't want to write college recommendation letters and dole out personality tests for the rest of my life.

I pull open the heavy door to Gray Hall and inhale the musty scent of linoleum and paper. This is one of the older buildings on campus, a preserved snapshot of eighties architecture and décor among a sprawling landscape of new builds.

I forgo the questionable elevator and take the stairs to the fourth floor. I'm not even sure if she'll be here today, but I figure it's worth a shot since I'm on campus anyway.

The light in her office is on, and her door's propped open. I can't help but smile when I spot the feminist bumper stickers and equal rights decrees covering every inch of her office door. I tentatively knock to announce my presence.

She lifts her eyes to meet mine, and a compassionate smile blossoms on her face.

"Cory." She sighs, a mix of sympathy and sadness clouding her tone. "Please, come in."

I take a seat across from where she sits behind her desk, but she doesn't even give me a chance to settle in before she launches into a hurried explanation.

"I am so sorry about your assistantship, Cory. The absolute audacity of this institution to toy with people's futures like this." She huffs out an agitated breath. "I spent hours yesterday demanding the dean do something—*anything*—to save our GA positions." She looks at me with a mix of frustration and defeat. "Obviously, that was all in vain."

I nod in understanding. I figured she had absolutely no control over the situation. I could tell as much by how forlorn she sounded yesterday when she called to break the news.

"I've put feelers out to every other department on campus. Sometimes life happens—there could be a number of reasons someone passes on an assistantship at the last minute. I know working for another department wouldn't be ideal, but at least your tuition and stipend would be secure."

I can't help but smile at her concern. It means the world to me that she's hustling to try to help me figure this out.

"I appreciate that, but I actually think I've got it under control." I hold her gaze and watch her expression morph from concern to confusion.

"Did you find another assistantship on your own?"

I shake my head. "No, but I figured out a way to pay my tuition. It's an option I... hadn't fully explored until now," I offer vaguely. I inwardly cringe at my aloofness. But there's no way I can explain to my mentor and professional idol that I agreed to marry a man who is going to pay my tuition and my student loan debt.

Dr. Deshong peers at me over her glasses, no doubt trying to work out how I could possibly come up with a way to finance my education in the twenty-four hours since she broke the news.

"I've seen the financial aid office work its magic over the years," she offers reservedly. "It may be worth your time to make an appointment—"

Fueled by the familiar prickle of shame whenever the topic of money comes up, I raise both hands to cut her off. "I appreciate your concern. But I've got it under control."

She nods in slow motion, accepting my answer even when it's clear she doesn't understand the solution.

"Okay," she declares, spinning in her chair to grab a file from the bookshelf behind her desk. "Onto the next order of business then." She grins before opening the manilla folder in front of me.

"Each year, the Office of Diversity, Equity, and Inclusion hires a student ambassador to represent Holt State at a number of community functions and admissions events. I nominated you, and yesterday I got the call that you're their top choice."

What? This is the first I'm hearing about any of this.

"You'd be required to have an elevator pitch to share at most events. Just a few remarks about your experience at Holt. It's not so much about regaling the university," she rolls her eyes to show her disdain before continuing, "as it is about showing a candid look at a successful student. It's an excellent way to network, both across the university and in the community. It's a prestigious position, and you'll receive a stipend for the semester. It's not nearly as much as you're worth, but I think you'd get a lot out of the experience."

Again with the money talk. The emphasis she keeps placing on it puts my financial situation into context.

"I didn't want to say anything yesterday on the phone, what with the assistantship news and the uncertainty about your enrollment status."

My jaw ticks as I remember just how close I was to losing this opportunity.

"But I think you'd be perfect for the job, and it's something I could see you really enjoying, too."

I give myself a moment to gather my thoughts and regain my composure. My education and my career path mean everything to me. And they almost slipped out of my grasp.

"I appreciate your vote of confidence. I want to think about it and make sure I understand the commitment, but it sounds like something I'd love to do."

"I understand. I'll forward you the email with all the details. They don't need an answer until the first week of classes anyway. No need to rush to any decisions with a commitment like this."

I bite down on the inside of my cheek to keep from smirking. If she only knew the rash decisions I've rushed into over the last twenty-four hours...

"Oh shoot," she mutters as an alarm dings on her computer. "I have to be on a call in five. I hate to rush you out—"

"No worries," I insist, rising to my feet and gathering my bag. "We'll catch up once the semester begins."

"Yes! Lunch the first Friday of classes?"

That's our regularly scheduled catch up time. I'm grateful that some things won't change, even if I'm not her GA anymore.

"Wouldn't miss it."

I pull the door closed behind me as I leave her office, then slide my phone out of my pocket to check the time. I've got a text message from Jake waiting for me, which has me grinning like a fool in the stairwell as I pause on the landing to read it.

Jake-Work: Do you have plans tonight?
Cory: I don't. Did you have something in mind?
Jake-Work: I do. I'd like to take you out on a date.

My stomach somersaults as I read the sentence again.

A date.

I guess that makes sense. We're going to be married soon, so we probably should go through the motions of getting to know each other.

Cory: Okay. What should I wear?

Mierda.

What the hell kind of question is that? I slump against the painted cinderblock wall of the stairwell. I sound pathetic. And I just set him up to reply with a cringe-worthy joke at my expense.

Jake-Work: Something casual. Bring a jacket or hoodie. Let's meet in the parking lot behind Clinton's at 9 pm. I'll drive.

I blow out a long breath, grateful he didn't take the low-hanging fruit and tease me. I like that we're meeting on neutral ground and that he offered to drive. I'm exceptionally curious about what sort of date starts at nine p.m., though.

I heart his text so he knows I saw it, then second-guess that response, too. He won't read too much into that, will he?

I repocket my phone and jog down the four flights of stairs. It's already late afternoon, and I still have to stop by the registrar's office before I can head home and get ready. I've got an extra spring in my step as I walk out of Gray Hall.

I have a date with Jake.

The practical part of my brain reminds me that I also have a pending marriage ceremony and two years of commitment ahead of me, but I don't let those thoughts linger. I'll have plenty of time to stress about this whole marriage of convenience arrangement in the coming days. For now, all I want to worry about is finding the perfect "casual" outfit for tonight.

Chapter 12

Jake

I turn into the gravel driveway, easing up on the gas as my Jeep joins the line of cars waiting to get in. I've been sneaking peeks at Cory the whole way here, but now I really can't resist drinking him in.

He's wearing this sharp cream-colored pullover with dark jeans, and his hair's meticulously styled. He's got this comb over fade and a hard part that's hot as hell. I itch to outline the edge of his clean-shaven jawline and graze my fingers over the blunt sides of his head.

He must feel my eyes on him because he smirks in my direction, then sits up straighter in his seat. "You brought me to the drive-in for our first date?"

I spent most of the morning Googling "best first date ever" and "unique date ideas." It wasn't until I saw the suggestion online that I remembered the drive-in past Holt had been running old movies on weeknights. And by "old," I mean classics from the eighties and nineties. Tonight's lineup is a Jim Carrey double feature.

"I did." I grin proudly. I'm pretty pleased that I came up with this idea on my own. All damn day, I was tempted to text Rhett, but I knew he'd have too many questions about *who* I was taking on a date and why. Cory and I agreed not to tell anyone except for Mike and his grandma about our marriage until things were official, and I didn't want my best friend asking questions I couldn't answer.

Cory makes a sound of contempt that gets my attention.

"And here I thought you said we were going to take things slow."

My eyes go wide at the callout.

"We are!" I insist, frantically looking from Cory to the car in front of me, then back as we inch forward toward the ticket booth.

"People usually come to the drive-in for a specific kind of date, Jake," he teases.

Shit. Yeah, okay. He's not wrong. But we're not in high school, and it's not like we've never hooked up before. I thought the drive-in stereotype didn't apply after a certain age. But I'll feel like a douche if he thinks I have an ulterior motive for tonight.

Do I want in his pants? Hell yes, I do. But only when we're settled into this new relationship, and we're both ready for that step.

I grip the steering wheel and grind my molars together as I scramble to come up with an alternative plan. There are two cars ahead of us still, so it's not too late to turn around and take him somewhere else.

"Jake."

His hand is warm on my arm, the contact sending a tingle of electricity through my body when his fingers run a soothing path back and forth over my skin.

Mischief dances in his eyes when I meet his gaze. "I'm just teasing you. Seriously. We're both grown men. If you want to make out with me, just ask. We don't have to sneak away to the drive-in for a bump and grind."

I bite down on my lip and huff out a sigh. He really had me going.

"Sexual expectations aside"—I give him a pointed look—"I thought it was a decent idea. I brought snacks and we get to enjoy some quality entertainment."

"It's more than a decent idea," he assures me, reaching across the console to grip my thigh.

I watch, transfixed, as his hand stretches out right above my knee. My abs clench with desire when he squeezes my leg once. Why is that so damn hot?

A car horn blasts behind me and jolts me back to reality. He chuckles under his breath as I pull up to the ticket booth. I roll down my window to pay for our admission, then accept the handout with the radio station information on it. I scope out a perfect spot a few rows from the front but off to the side. Once the Jeep's in park, I unbuckle, reach behind me, and unpack the snacks.

"What are we watching?" he asks.

"It's Jim Carrey night," I explain, handing him a water bottle, a can of Cheerwine, and a beer. I may have overdone it with the beverage choices, but I wanted him to have options. "First up is *Liar Liar*, followed by *The Truman Show*."

He wrinkles his nose and looks at the various drink options now taking over every cup holder in the vehicle. "*Liar Liar*? Really?"

I scoff at his dismissal. "It's a classic! Please don't tell me you don't like it, or I'm going to have to rethink this whole arrangement."

He shoves me playfully and mutters something about "already too late" under his breath as I dump my bag of tricks on the dash. I admittedly went overboard with the snacks, too, but I don't know what he likes, and I didn't want to text him and give away the surprise. I brought chips, Skittles, Junior Mints, Sno-Caps, Sour Patch Kids, Airheads, and Buncha Crunch.

"That's probably something you should know about me. I love movies from the nineties. Like, seriously love them. My dad had this theater room in the basement of the house where I grew up, and I would spend entire weekends camped out down there, watching movies. That and my bedroom were the only places I liked in that damn house."

"How many people were you planning to feed tonight?" he muses, looking over his choices before reaching for the box of Sno-Caps. So he's a chocolate guy. Noted.

"I just wanted my future husband to have options." I eye him playfully, then snag a bag of Skittles for myself. "I'll admit, though, I'm grateful you didn't try to claim these." I shake the bag for emphasis before tearing it open with my teeth.

His pupils dilate as he watches me, and I can't hold back the *hmph* of satisfaction at knowing I affect him just as much as he affects me.

"Would you have let me have them?" he asks huskily, leaning close enough that I can smell the chocolate on his breath.

"Yes," I answer honestly. "What's mine is yours, right? Marriage is about compromise."

He bites down on his bottom lip, and a carnal urge to replace his teeth with mine hits me. He's got these full, plush lips that I'm aching to get reacquainted with. His eyes track mine, and he cocks one eyebrow, his smile deepening.

"Good answer," he whispers, leaning in another inch and getting close enough I can feel the heat of his breath on my neck. But just as quickly as he kicked things up, he pulls back.

"So you love movies from the nineties, and your favorite candy is Skittles. What else do I need to know about you, Jake Whitely?"

"Ask me anything," I offer, waving my hand with a flourish.

"And you'll answer honestly?" he challenges.

I don't miss the hint of skepticism behind his question.

"Tell ya what," I say, glancing at the screen as the opening credits start. "From now until the end of this movie, I'll be Fletcher Reede. Ask me anything, and I'll tell you nothing but the truth."

"No exceptions?"

"Nope. Nothing's off limits. But I do have a condition."

He scowls slightly, creating this little wrinkle above his nose where his eyebrows pull together.

"What's that?" he questions.

"I get to ask you questions, too."

Chapter 13

Cory

I'm sitting in the privacy of Jake's Jeep, totally ignoring the movie he brought me to see, completely transfixed by him. He's given me an opening: I can ask him anything, and he'll answer honestly.

I don't even know where to begin. I'm going to be a therapist, for crying out loud. This should be second nature. I settle on simple to start, knowing I want to grill him and really dig deep before the night is over.

I clear my throat before speaking. "Okay. What did you want to be when you grew up?"

"Alive," he answers without hesitation.

Mierda. Is he serious right now? He holds eye contact as I try to read him.

"I told you my dad was an ass. He beat me when I was little. Then he found other ways to make my life hell once I was old enough to fight back. I spent most of my teen years just trying to survive, one day to the next."

"I'm sorry you had to deal with that," I murmur. "But I appreciate your honesty. So why did your dad want you to get married so badly? That's the only requirement for your inheritance, right? Just to get married?"

He lifts the package of Skittles to his mouth, pours some in, and chews slowly.

"My dad hated me," he offers nonchalantly before pinning me with his gaze. "I don't really want to psychoanalyze it. It's something I've accepted. He was a bigot, but it wasn't just about my bisexuality. He hated me long before I tried to come out to him. I've always been the black sheep of my family. He probably didn't think I'd go through with it—getting married, that is—if he put it in his will. Joke's on him." He smirks before glancing back up at the screen.

Jesus Christ. When he promised to be honest, I had no idea he was going to open up like this. His candidness surprises me, but I don't want to miss this opportunity. There's so much about him I want to know. We're going to be married in a few days, after all. This may be my one chance to really get to see past the mask he wears for the rest of the world.

Besides, there's no way I can revert to questions about his favorite beer or pizza toppings now that we've taken it to this level.

"What did you mean when you said you tried to come out to your dad?"

He snaps his head in my direction, then gives me this crooked smile. "You don't miss a thing, do you?"

I blush at his praise but stay quiet, intent on waiting him out.

He sighs, then mutters something along the lines of "you asked" before taking a sip of Cheerwine.

"When I was sixteen, something bad happened—with someone older. It stopped before I was physically harmed, but it still scared the shit out of me. Rhett helped me out that night, and then I tried to tell my dad about it. His reaction... was horrible. He called me names. He told me I was probably asking for it. To be drugged and almost assaulted. He spit on me in disgust."

My eyes widen in horror—both for what his dad did, and for Jake's ability to just sit here and recall the incident with such a calm demeanor.

"Jake..." I feel compelled to reach across and console him, but I let my hand drop. I don't know how he likes to be comforted. And I don't know what sort of lasting trauma he deals with because of what happened.

"Being shoved back into the closet when I came out to my dad was honestly more traumatizing than almost getting sexually assaulted. It ate at me for a long time, but I eventually found ways to push past the memories and move on."

How did this get so heavy so fast? Jake has literally only ever been jokes and good times around me. The fact that he's opening up like this—taking his promise seriously and answering every question I ask as honestly as possible... I swallow past the lump in my throat, the weighted significance of this moment holding my emotions hostage.

I feel for him on such a deep level. I'm also low-key panicking that he took this honesty thing so seriously. If he's being this candid with me, he's going to expect the same level of intimacy in return when he's the one asking questions.

"Is that why you went to both Archway and Hampton?" I ask, desperate for a subject change. This is supposed to be a date. I have to lighten the mood—fast.

He smiles before he answers this time. "It is. What happened... the guy worked at Archway Prep. It was just too hard to go back and face what I had done. What had happened that night, I mean."

I don't miss the self-deprecation in his original word choice, but I don't call him out on it, either.

"Tori's the one who convinced me to switch schools, actually. She and Rhett know what happened that night. Back in high school, the three of us were the very best of friends. They're the closest thing I've ever had to family. They helped me more than I think either of them knows."

His eyes light up when he talks about his best friend, Rhett, and one of my best friends, Tori. It's wild to think that they're married, and soon we will be, too. We could go on a double date next time they're in town.

Jake stretches one arm out and rests it on the back of my seat before he hits me with another playful smirk. "What else ya got for me?"

I like that he's undeterred by this conversation. It's refreshing to be on a date without worrying about the subtext of every word or action. I guess that's another benefit to this marriage with benefits thing.

"How did you, Tori, and Rhett become the three musketeers?"

That one has him grinning from ear to ear. "Obviously Tori and Rhett were inevitable. Rhett and I met at Safety Town before kindergarten—our last names are Wheeler and Whitely, so of course they lined us up. The first picture taken of us together is the two of us hanging out the windows of the Safety Town fire house. We were wild back then."

It's my turn to hit him with a pointed look. "Opposed to now?"

Chuckling, he brushes his hand down my arm. "Rhett settled down," he relents. "But I guess I still haven't been tamed." He leans in then, circling my wrist with his hand in an iron-tight grip that has me craving more. "Is that what you want from me, baby? You want to tame me?"

I bite hard on my lower lip, silently willing him to kiss me. But then I come to my senses. Did he just call me baby?

"I don't think you should call me that," I reason, pulling my arm out of his hold and creating more space between us. My brain instantly protests over the lack of contact.

"Oh. You don't like it?" he asks earnestly.

God. This man. How does he go from over-the-top flirtatious to totally genuine in the space of a breath?

"I don't *not* like it. But I've heard you use it with Tori for years."

He sits back and brings his hand to his chin, looking thoughtful as he peers out the windshield at the movie screen. When he focuses back on me, his expression is alight with authenticity. "I think I want to call you baby. Would it be okay if I stopped calling her that and only used it for you?"

I crack my knuckles quietly as I consider his offer. Why does this feel like we're negotiating so much more than a nickname?

"You would do that?" I question. Not because I don't believe him. But because I can't imagine him making such a big change for something that's supposed to be a temporary arrangement.

"You're marrying me, Cory. Of course I'd do that for you."

I'm grateful for the darkness that surrounds us so I can downplay the grin threatening to take over my whole face. I pretend to pay attention to the movie for a few seconds before murmuring a soft "okay."

"Okay," he repeats salaciously. "Pretty sure it's my turn to get in some questions, *baby*." I don't miss the way he emphasizes my new nickname. And I don't hate it one bit, either.

Chapter 14

Cory

"Why did your abuela raise you instead of your parents?"

That's a softball question compared to the hard-hitters I just lobbed his way.

"Abuela raised me, but my parents did, too. We all lived together when I was little. My parents had me when they were teenagers. My mom and my dad got married, and they stayed together until I was in first grade. There was nothing dramatic or messy about their divorce. They just decided they were better off as friends and co-parents."

I shrug as I try to explain my family dynamic. My parents have always made me a priority, and I've always known they love me. They just weren't the ones who raised me.

"After the divorce, Dad moved out first, then he met someone and started a new family. My mom met a guy when I was in fifth grade, and she eventually moved out, too."

"They just left you?" he asks. There's no judgment in his tone. Just genuine curiosity.

"Oh no," I insist. "They both wanted me to come with them, actually. But I refused to go. My parents were only sixteen when they had me. We all grew up together, in a way. My abuela was the parental figure in my life when I was a kid. She still is. I love her just as much as I love my mom and dad. And honestly, I didn't want to have to choose between them."

"That makes sense," he murmurs under his breath as he nods to himself.

I'm not sure if my explanation was what he expected or not. My family is non-traditional in a lot of ways, but I always had my parents' support; I always felt their love. I feel like an asshole talking about them so much, though, after everything he revealed to me just now about his own home life growing up. I'm glad for the subject change when he asks his next question.

"What were you like as a kid?"

Well, here goes nothing. Jake gave me his honesty. I guess it's my turn to give him mine.

"I was a total dork," I admit. "I had glasses by the time I was four, and Abuela had to shop in the husky section until I got to high school and finally hit a major growth spurt." I chance a glance to gauge his reaction and see the hint of a smirk playing on his face.

"Don't laugh!" I defend, smacking his arm as his grin grows wider.

"I'm not laughing *at* you," he insists, adjusting his position so he's facing me completely.

"Well, I'm not laughing, so you're not laughing *with* me," I chide.

He sticks his tongue between his teeth and scrunches up his nose. "I'm just picturing it in my head, is all. You were probably so stinkin' cute. I want to see pictures from when you were little."

My eyes search his in question. "You do?"

"Yeah," he replies automatically. "I really do." He runs one hand up my leg in a move that's more direct than anything he's tried to pull so far tonight.

I watch, fascinated, desperate for him to make this move. My cock is acutely aware of his palm traveling up my pants. I try not to squirm as I feel my dick hardening without my permission. But as soon as he reaches mid-thigh, he redirects and snatches up the box of Sno-Caps I had resting on my lap before dumping some into his mouth.

"What do you want to be when you grow up?" he asks through a mouthful of chocolate.

I blink slowly to regain my composure, avoiding his gaze for a few seconds so he doesn't see how deeply his touch affects me.

He wants to call me baby, and he can get me hard with a graze of my thigh. I'm so screwed.

I clear my throat and crack my knuckles before responding. "You know what Planned Parenthood is, right?"

"Yes...?" he draws out his response in question.

"My dream is to open up a clinic—or lots of clinics, eventually—that's like Planned Parenthood, but for mental health. It would be donation based with suggested fees, but we'd never turn anyone away who needed help. It would be open to everyone, with an emphasis on serving young people, people of color, and the LGBTQ community. Basically, anyone who faces barriers to obtaining mental health services for whatever reason."

"That is..." He trails off as he looks at me, wonderment in his gaze. "That's amazing. And very specific. Have you been thinking about this for a long time?"

"For years," I admit with a nod. "It's always just been a dream, something I hoped to work toward but that I knew would take years to figure out..."

"Wait," he interrupts, sitting up straight in his seat and reaching over to grip my thigh. "Cory. With the money... you could totally make that happen."

Warmth blossoms through me at his genuine enthusiasm.

"I know," I murmur, tracing the veins in his hand with the tips of my fingers. He doesn't pull back, and I boldly find the courage to lift his hand and place it higher on my thigh.

He squeezes me through my jeans, his fingers curling under and wrapping around my inner thigh. His hand's only a few inches higher than before, but his hold on me is everything. I have to physically hold myself back from thrusting against his touch. Or forcing his hand higher.

"You trying to make me be bad for you, baby?"

Fuck. I want him so bad.

"Why do I get the feeling you don't want to take this slow anymore?" His tone is guttural and strained, as if he's working to hold back from what we both know is inevitable.

Slow. He promised me slow. I agreed I wanted slow. Maybe if he just slowly strokes up and down my...

Mierda. I have to get it together. I don't want our first *anything* as an actual couple to happen in the front seat of this Jeep. We've got two whole years together. I blow out a long breath and silently plead with my dick to deflate. Why am I such a manwhore for Jake Whitely?

My brain scrambles for something that'll get us back on track as I shift out of his grasp. I don't even think the question through before I rush out and ask it.

"How many people have you been with?"

He audibly hisses as he grits his teeth and lifts his hand from my thigh.

"You promised you'd be honest," I remind him.

"I did. And I will be. The answer is a lot," he responds with a pensive nod.

"I want to know the number, Jake."

"Well, that's not going to happen because I don't know the number, Cory."

His tone is a mix of defensiveness and shame.

I assess his slouched shoulders and sullen expression. I don't think he's lying, but now I'm morbidly curious to get to the bottom of this. "Why don't you know the number?" I pry.

He blows out a long breath before turning to face me head-on. "Look, I'm embarrassed to admit this, but once the number hit a certain milestone, I stopped counting."

"Dios mío," I mutter, a flurry of concern and jealousy swirling inside me.

"I *always* used protection, and I used to get tested regularly."

"Used to?" I challenge.

His cheeks color for just a few seconds at the callout. "Yeah, used to. I haven't actually hooked up with anyone in a long time. It's been well over a year, maybe two."

What? This is Jake Whitely we're talking about. He's been the town's most notorious playboy for as long as I've worked at Clinton's. I could line up everyone within a certain age bracket, man or woman, and it'd probably be easier to pick out the people he *hasn't* had sex with. Sex is who he is. It's what he's known for.

And yet.

He's sitting beside me, under a vow of honesty thanks to this stupid movie, and I don't think he's lied to me yet.

I'm inclined to believe him.

"Can I ask why?" I cautiously inquire.

He shrugs. "You can. But I don't have some revolutionary answer. Casual hookups stopped feeling like something I enjoyed and started feeling more like a chore. I can't even pinpoint when it happened because I didn't know it was happening at the time, ya know? Tori and Rhett were both going through a lot, individually and together. I started hanging out with different people. My entire schedule changed because of The Oak. I guess I changed, too."

He pulls out his phone then, determined. "I've been tested since my last hookup, of that, I'm sure. I'll forward you the results right now." He fiddles with his phone for a minute. Then, as soon as he locks the screen, I feel mine vibrating in my pocket.

"I don't mean anything by sending that," he rushes to explain. "I just want you to believe me. We don't have to rush into anything, and we'll obviously use protection. I just want you to feel like you can trust me and to know I'd never put your health at risk."

I don't know what to say. I pull out my phone to buy myself a few seconds, desperate to come up with an adequate response to match his openness and honesty.

I click on the PDF he just emailed me, squinting to see all the negative results on the STI panel. I'm about to close out of the screen when I notice the date and time stamp at the bottom of the page.

The results are from eighteen months ago.

Jake and I hooked up for the last time just before Tori's birthday during my first year of grad school. February of last year. *Eighteen months ago.*

"You haven't been with anyone since this panel?" I confirm.

"I have not."

Realization slams into me and knocks the air out of my lungs. If what Jake says is true—and I really do believe him—then his last sexual partner was actually *me*.

I try to temper the shit-eating grin threatening to give away my delight. Knowing I was his last and that I'm about to be his only for the next two years turns me all warm and gooey on the inside. It also strokes my ego in a way, this possessiveness I didn't know I had in me rearing its head once again.

I don't tell him any of that, though. I wouldn't dare. Instead, I rely on my tried-and-true future therapist response.

"Thank you for sharing that with me."

He nods solemnly before turning the tables. "Okay—same question. How many people have you been with?"

"Six," I reply without having to think about it.

"That is... admirably low." He chuckles to himself.

"I told you before: I'm a relationship guy. I had a sort-of secret boyfriend in high school. He wasn't out, but I was, and you know how that always ends up." I sigh as I recall the heartache of that first love feeling.

"Then I was serious with a guy my freshman year of college, and I dated a soccer player during my senior year. I was with a guy in my grad school cohort but just for a few months. Then my most recent relationship was with a guy named Andre. Even though that ended at the beginning of the year, it was a really hard break up. I haven't dated anyone since."

"That's five," Jake counters as soon as I'm done speaking.

My cheeks flush as I realize he's right: I skipped over one.

"Who's six?" he presses, taking a sip of his drink without taking his eyes off me.

I pray for courage and steel my spine before answering. "I didn't think I had to mention you in the lineup since you're obviously aware of our history."

"Wait. *I'm* six?" he boasts. Leave it to Jake to be proud of his place on my very small roster.

I roll my eyes to tame his ego. "Technically, you're number four. I've had two relationships since you and I hooked up."

"But everyone else you mentioned was a boyfriend?" he challenges.

I meet his gaze and let him see right through me: to the heart of what I'm about to confess, to the truth behind the power he has—has always had—over me. "I told you. I don't do casual, Jake. I only ever did it with you."

He mutters something I don't make out under his breath, then we both busy ourselves by crumbling up our candy cartons and reaching for more snacks. I'm grateful he doesn't push me or call me out on what I just confessed.

He's always been the exception for me. And now, tonight, he finally knows it.

I don't want to drown in my own self-doubt. I don't want to let him see me at my most vulnerable. This has been the most bizarre, revealing, and weirdly intimate date I've ever been on. Part of me can't wait for it to be over, while another part yearns for it to never end.

I think we're both running out of steam, the heaviness of our Q&A session weighing us down. But I feel compelled to wrap it up with one final question. "You've honestly never been in a relationship?"

He shakes his head but offers me a little smirk.

"I've got this, though. I'm a quick study. I promised I'd make this good for you. I'm going to Google the shit out of how to be the perfect husband and rock these next two years.

Just you wait. I've got plans for you, baby. Two years' worth of plans."

Out of everything he's shared tonight, that's the one truth I want to hold on to.

Chapter 15

Cory

I wake up slowly, reveling in that quiet moment of bliss between sleep and awake, past and present, dreams and reality.

Tingles of anticipation course through me as I blink my eyes open and remember the events of the last few days—and think about what lies ahead.

Even when the reality of my decision comes back to me each morning, it doesn't fill me with dread. The only issue I'm struggling with is why I'm not bothered by this situation. Why did I agree to marry a man—who, admittedly, is hot and rich and just a little bit rowdy in that way that makes me feel untamed when I'm around him—I really don't know?

I reach for my phone to check the time, and am surprised to see that it's eleven thirty. I slept most of the morning away, which I guess makes sense considering my sleep schedule has been messed up all week. I better get it under control before the new semester starts. I check my notifications and almost drop the device on my face when I see three texts, all from Jake.

He's been doing that every day this week. Sending me cute texts. Just checking in to say hello. The other day he even requested my shirt and suit size but refused to tell me why he needed the information.

If I didn't find it so endearing, I'd probably tease him about it. Although I guess neither of us needs to play it cool or try to impress the other—we're already engaged.

There's no way he knows the hold he has on me. I have no intentions of playing hard to get (obviously), but it feels like too much too soon to admit how okay I am with this whole scenario.

Jake-Work: Hey, handsome. What do you have going on today?

Jake-Work: I hope you slept well. Shoot me a text when you get up.

Jake-Work: I've got a lunch thing at Clinton's, so I won't be on my phone much. Stop by if you have time.

I smirk at the label next to his name in my phone. I don't even know another Jake, but I friend-zoned him—hard—once Lia and I compared notes. That little "Work" moniker may or may not have been my way of reminding myself not to be tempted to reach out.

Obviously, I need to change it. Should he just be Jake? Would it be weird to label him "husband" in my contact list? Maybe the label would have the same effect: remind me of who he is, given our new arrangement.

Cory: Good morning. I'm just now getting up.
Jake: You okay?

Oof. Why do those two words pluck at my heartstrings? He didn't even type out a complete sentence. And yet...

Cory: I'm good. Someone just kept me up late on Monday, and my sleep's been wacky ever since. I've got to do some packing today. What do you have going on?

Jake: Guilty. But no regrets. ;) I'll be at The Oak or Clinton's most of the day. If you want to stop by for lunch, we can hang out...

I smile at my phone before typing out my reply. Of course I want to hang out. After last night's date, I'm itching to spend more time with him. The idea of marrying Jake has taken root inside me over the last few days. Aside from questioning my own lack of contemplation, there's no question of what comes next. I'm all in.

Cory: I was planning to go up to campus today and try to sort through my tuition payments. I'll stop by Clinton's on my way.

Jake: I'll be here or next door. See you soon, baby.

I should roll my eyes. I should scoff. I should be offended that he's recycling a nickname I've heard him use on Tori for as long as I've known them, even though I told him yesterday it was okay.

But I don't.

Instead, I swoon.

A million questions try to swarm my conscience, but for once in my life, my mind isn't in overdrive. Instead, I just feel happy.

I stroll in through the side door of Clinton's, even though I'm not scheduled to work. It doesn't even occur to me to use the front door. The restaurant is bustling—this is one of the few sit-down places in town open for lunch. I'm surprised when Jake isn't behind the bar like usual. Maybe he already went over to The Oak...

A wolf whistle has me snapping my head to the main dining room, my gaze locking in on him like he sent out a damn sonar signal. When our eyes meet, my abs clench. It's stupid how good-looking he is. Perfect head of wavy, light brown hair. Hazel eyes with that ever-present glint of flirtation behind them. Soft, symmetrical, kissable lips that I'm aching to feel against mine.

We flirted last night. On the drive home, we held hands. When he dropped me at my car, he hugged me. But that was it. There was literally none of the physical contact I expected or craved from a date night with Jake Whitely. That's something I hope to rectify soon.

I grin and walk toward the table as he watches me. It isn't until I'm around the half-wall partition that I see he's not alone.

I almost trip over my own feet when two blond-haired little girls sprawled out in the booth across from him come into view. They're both focused on the kids' menu coloring sheets in front of them. The little one even has her tongue stuck out of the corner of her mouth in concentration.

I stand there, perplexed. What did he tell me earlier? To meet him for lunch? I glance around the restaurant, looking for a parent or another human who might be responsible for the small children at our table. It's not until I look back at Jake that he cracks a grin and waves me over.

"It's okay; they don't bite."

"Yes, she does! Mimi bit me last week, Uncle Jakey," the older girl maintains without even looking up from her paper.

She called him Uncle. Are these kids related to him?

I slide into the booth beside them.

"Hey." He knocks his shoulder into mine, then squeezes my thigh under the table. That touch grounds me, reminds me to focus on the present and just ask him what's going on rather than let my mind spiral.

"Hi," I falter. "I didn't realize this is what you meant by 'hang out.'" I cock one eyebrow in question, urging him to explain.

His hand lingers on my thigh, his fingers stroking back and forth right above my knee.

"Girls," he commands, finally looking away from me to address the small humans across from us. "I want you to meet someone special."

The older child looks up and squints at me quizzically. The little one can't seem to be bothered.

"Earth to Mimi," Jake teases, reaching across the table to boop her on the forehead. She cracks a grin, but doesn't put down the crayon or lift her gaze. Even if they didn't look like him, it would be unquestionable that these children are related to Jake Whitely based on their demeanor alone.

"Okay, fine. I bet Cory doesn't want to talk to you anyway."

That gets her attention.

"Hey!" Mimi declares, mock outrage—or maybe real outrage? I don't know much about kids—painting her expression. "I want to meet da special someone!"

Jake smirks, then turns to me. "Girls, this is Cory. Cory, these are my nieces, Fiona and Amelia."

"Nice to meet you, Cory," the older one says as the little one talks over her.

"My name is Mimi!"

"Hi," I greet, awkwardly lifting my hand even though they're sitting right across the table. Kids don't shake hands, do they? "It's nice to meet you girls."

The older one is unfazed and resumes her coloring. It's the little one, Mimi, who's staring at me with beady eyes and pursed lips. I swallow—hard. Now what do I do? She can't be more than four or five years old. And yet, she makes me inexplicably nervous. "Is he your bestest friend, Uncle Jakey?"

Jake grips my thigh as he smiles in amusement. I glance down and am instantly distracted by the sight of his large, tan hand gripping my quad.

"I don't know yet, Mimi. He might be." He squeezes me one more time before he resumes the comforting, hypnotizing strokes. "I'm hoping he wants to be."

This. Man. The last part comes out low, just for me. I'm so out of my league here. I'm half afraid to turn and let him see my truth. His eyes are boring into my profile, but I still don't look over at him. I know if I do, all bets are off. One look at how I'm affected by his touch and he'll know the power he has over me.

I'm saved when the older one—Fiona, who has resumed coloring but seems fully capable of multi-tasking—speaks up.

"What do you call him, Uncle Jakey?"

"You can just call me Cory," I insist. I don't want to confuse them about who I am. And I definitely don't want Jake to feel pressure to reveal what we're doing. He said we'd do this out in the open, that it would be real, but I hadn't considered that there would be kids involved.

Apparently, my answer isn't acceptable.

"I know your name," Fiona declares. "But what does he *call* you?"

The words are the same, but I don't understand what she thinks she's asking. I turn to Jake for clarification just as the little one pipes up.

"Uncle Jakey gives everyone nicknames. I'm Mimi. Fiona is Fifi. Your name is Cory, so you can be Coco or Riri."

Jake is already laughing—busting up, really—as I finally understand the question. He catches his breath long enough to ask, "What'll it be, baby? Coco or Riri?"

I scowl. "You better not call me either of those," I hiss under my breath.

Jake's still laughing when the younger one speaks again. "I like Coco. So Coco you'll be."

I'm sort of scared of the small one. She seems extra feisty. Rather than argue, I grab a crayon and an extra kids' menu from the center of the table, busying myself with the word search on the back of the page.

I watch through the corner of my eye as Jake snatches up an orange crayon, and I pause my motions as he reaches over and puts an *X* on the tic-tac-toe board on my paper. I smirk but join right in.

"So what do you think about Friday?" he whispers. His hand isn't on my thigh anymore, but we're sitting close enough I can feel his warm, strong leg resting against mine.

"For?" I ask as I watch him place another *X* on the board.

He lets out a little scoff before responding. "Getting married."

Now he has my full attention. My head shoots up, first to look at him, then across the table to see whether the girls are paying attention. They're laser focused on their coloring sheets. When I turn back to meet his gaze, Jake is laser focused on me.

Friday. That's just two days from today.

In typical Jake fashion, he continues before I have time to formulate a response.

"There's no waiting period in the state of Ohio. We can go down to Akron, get our marriage license, and do it that afternoon. I've made a few calls and have it all figured out; I just wanted to check in with you first."

I could ask a million follow-up questions. Grill him. Make him squirm. Give a voice to the anxiety that creeps up every time I think about what I agreed to do with him: to embark on this marriage of convenience, where both loyalty and sex are mutually expected and encouraged.

But I don't do any of that. I'm not myself around Jake Whitely. Or, I'm a version of myself I don't recognize. I am surprisingly disarmed around this man.

I add my *O* to our game, then turn to meet his gaze. "Friday," I confirm, inspiring the biggest grin on his face.

He glances at the game, then looks back up at me. His words come out low again, probably because he doesn't want his nieces to hear. When his voice hits that register, all bets are off.

"Can you stay over tomorrow night? We could get ready together on Friday morning."

I clear my throat and try to ignore the unexpected heat creeping up my neck. "Okay," I choke out. Because I guess I'm only good for one-word answers today.

I don't doubt what we're doing, and I'm not hesitating because I've changed my mind. I'm just so out of my element right now. I'm lust-drunk on Jake Whitely, and yet I somehow need to come to terms with the fact that in less than forty-eight hours, he'll be my husband.

Rather than let myself get lost in those thoughts, I change the subject. I point my crayon toward the girls and cock my head in question.

"Will you explain this to me later?" I ask. It's part curiosity. And part challenge. He didn't mention them at the drive-in last night. But I also didn't think to ask.

He answers without hesitation.

"I will. I promise," he vows. "You win," he mumbles as he nods toward the table. It's not until I glance down at the paper that I realize he's right—I just unknowingly won the game.

Chapter 16

Jake

I spent the whole damn day doing everything I could to prepare. I've been to the bank. Half the bedroom closet has been cleared out, and I rearranged the bathroom so he has a drawer and a shelf. I even reprogrammed my coffee machine so it would brew a full pot tomorrow morning.

Because it's not just me anymore. At least not for the next two years.

I spent the last few hours reading over the title and sale paperwork for the businesses. It was a futile exercise, really. Mike and I already agreed to the terms, and my lawyer is combing through the details now. I just needed the distraction—the reminder about why this is happening, and how it will all go down.

I needed to keep myself busy—to resist doing the thing I've wanted to do all week. I don't need approval. In fact, I'm pretty sure he'd be the first to challenge me and push back against this whole idea. But any time I've faced something like this, he's been my first call. Now, he can't be. Cory and I agreed to tell everyone about us at the same time, so that means I haven't talked about any of this with Rhett.

We've exchanged a few texts about normal, random things, but that's it, which is weird for us. Now that he and Tori are both in Virginia, I talk to him on the phone at least three or four times a week. But if I call him now, he'll call me out. I could simply breathe into the phone and he'd know something was up. No one can read me quite like Rhett.

It sucks shutting him out and keeping this from him. Even knowing he wouldn't approve, and that he'd pick apart my plan—I still want him to know. I want someone to know what I'm about to do. And why.

"Uh, pretty sure that section is going to be a different color and texture if you don't cool it."

My head snaps up at Dempsey's words. I look from him to the cloth in my hand, just now realizing I've put some serious elbow grease into wiping down the same spot of the bar for several minutes.

I chuckle, then throw down my bar rag in defeat.

"Thanks, man," I nod appreciatively.

"You know, I've got this covered."

We're fully staffed, so they don't need me here. Dem's scheduled as the manager tonight. I'm sure he'd prefer if I didn't hover. But I have nowhere else to go. Home doesn't feel right anymore—everything's shifted, and it looks empty without Cory's stuff to fill in the newly created space. I'll be okay once he joins me. But right now, I'm standing on the edge of a cliff, just waiting to make the jump.

"Yeah, I know," I finally respond. "I'm just wasting time and trying to get my head straight."

Dem assesses me for a moment, then looks down along the bar. We're busy, even though it's only dinnertime.

"You want to talk about it?"

Do I ever. I pause and think through the consequences of sharing some—or all—of the details about what's about to happen.

Dempsey and I have grown closer this summer. I used to hang out with his twin brother Fielding just about every day, but that changed earlier this year after Fielding became unhinged and made some selfish, shitty choices.

Now Dem is the Haas twin I hang out with most, both here and outside of work. He reminds me of Rhett in a lot of ways: sharp, responsible, always worried about everyone else. We don't talk much about what happened—about his brother and how he's doing now—but I can read him well enough to know it's not good. He deals with a lot because of his mom, too. Even though he's a millionaire—hell, probably a billionaire—he holds down this job at my bar and works like he actually needs the paycheck. Maybe he does need something from this arrangement—but it's definitely not money.

It would be easy to open up to Dempsey. I know I can trust him. And I would probably feel better. But there's a nagging at my subconscious that pumps the brakes on spilling the beans. I could tell him everything, and no one would be the wiser. But I made a promise to Cory, and I don't want to break his trust. For the next few years, my promises to him take priority.

"I'm okay," I reply. Not because I actually am. But because that's what people say when they want to lock it down.

A hint of rejection flashes in his eyes, but he nods in understanding. "Well, I'm always around if you need to talk. Standing offer."

He doesn't give me a chance to respond before he heads to the other end of the bar to check on the patrons.

I trace one finger along the ragged, uneven edge of the natural wood bar top I picked out. In the establishment I helped design. The rustic industrial lighting overhead. The smooth, polished, obsidian-colored bar stools. The old sports photos and memorabilia on the walls featuring decades of teams from both Hampton High and Archway Prep. The blending of old and new, of past and present.

When Mike asked me to help him renovate The Oak Barrel Tavern into the kind of place people would flock to, I wasn't sure how we'd pull it off. But we did it. We really freaking did it. It's hipster without being pretentious. It's equal parts trendy and cozy. It feels like home, because that's what it is for me. More than my condo has ever been, and a far cry from the house I grew up in. The Oak, and by extension, Clinton's, are where I feel most like myself. And now they're mine.

I quietly slink out from behind the bar, intent on heading next door and helping the staff close. Cory's supposed to stop by at the end of the night so we can head to the condo together. There's a nostalgia I feel as I walk out of the front door of the Oak, pass the narrow alley between the buildings, and stroll through the front door of Clinton's.

Chapter 17

Cory

He left the side door unlocked for me. So even though Clinton's closed nearly an hour ago, I let myself in, then lock it behind me.

I was wary when he texted and said to meet him here. I've been avoiding Lia as much as possible, relying on short texts and insisting I'm stressed about school to keep her off my case. She knows something's going on with Jake and me, but nothing more than that. And since we agreed to tell everyone together once it was official, I'd rather avoid putting myself in a situation where I'd have to lie by omission.

The end justifies the means. I want to be a man of my word. I want to keep my promises. I want to be faithful to my husband.

When I walk into the restaurant, I know right where I'll find him. He doesn't hear me approach, which gives me a few seconds to admire the guy I'm going to marry tomorrow.

I still can't believe I'm doing this. But the idea of not going through with it seems even crazier than the reality of what I've committed to.

He's leaning up against the back bar, looking down at his phone. His brows are pulled together in concentration, creating the cutest little indent in the center of his forehead. My hands twitch with the urge to smooth it out and massage away the concern. I could tease him about premature wrinkles, but it's pretty pointless. He's got such a baby face—he'd be hot as hell with a few age lines to go along with that dimple.

"When's your birthday?" I ask, loving the way his head snaps up at the sound of my voice.

He grins, jutting his chin in my direction as I approach. My feet move a little faster, eager to close the space between us.

"May fifth." He pushes off the ice machine to meet me around the bar. Instead of joining him, I lean forward near the opening. It's not lost on me that our positions are similar to how we were standing just a few nights ago when he first invited me over to his place. Except this time, I'm standing too, facing him head-on. We're on equal footing, about to embark on something new and crazy and potentially amazing together.

"When's yours?" He leans forward farther, getting so close our foreheads almost touch.

"December twenty-fourth."

His eyes light up. "I guess the holidays will be extra special this year." He smiles again, blinding me with those dazzling white teeth, before pulling back a fraction and giving me room to breathe.

"How are you?" he asks, sounding like he genuinely wants to know.

I blow out a breath and decide to be honest.

"Not great. Abuela is on my case about moving out, and I've had to avoid Lia all week. Plus, when I went up to Holt the other day, I found out that they unenrolled me from all my classes since my tuition is past due. I'm low-key stressed about not getting back in to the classes I need to stay on track for my degree."o

Jake's eyebrows pinch together again. "Seriously? They're the ones who canceled your GA thing! What sort of asshat decided to pull your classes, too?" He glowers as he waits for my reply.

Oh. He's pissed. My happy-go-lucky, hot as hell soon-to-be husband is pissed on my behalf. Why is this such a turn on?

"It's okay," I assure him, fighting the increasingly persistent urge to touch him. "I think it was an automated thing, honestly. Once they changed my student status, it looked like I hadn't paid for the semester. It's just an administrative issue I'll have to figure out."

He doesn't look convinced. He stands up straighter but keeps his arms spread long on the bar. God, he has the best arms. What is it about his tattooed forearms, muscles, and veins for days that turns my insides to mush? It's August, so he's also super tan. Our skin tones almost match, thanks mostly to the fact that I haven't had time for fun this summer.

"We'll get it taken care of tomorrow." He looks me straight in the eye. "Or tonight, if it's something you can do online. Do you have to write a check? Or can we put it on a card?"

"I—" I don't know how to respond to that.

He waits, not filling the silence for once, which gives me a second to process my thoughts.

"I assumed I'd just take care of it next week once we're officially married."

He rolls his teeth over his bottom lip, assessing me in a way that makes me squirm.

"Would you rather it be handled now?"

Of course I would. This thing has been a nightmare, and I already know I'll have to email my professors individually and beg them to put me back on their class rosters. There's a sequence to the courses I have to take to earn my master's, and knowing I don't have my perfectly planned schedule secured is enough to give me mild hives.

"Well, yeah," I answer honestly.

"Then it's settled."

Something about this doesn't feel right. How can he just trust that this is all going to work out?

"Jake..."

He raises one eyebrow in a move that I swear he must have practiced in front of a mirror. The effect is instant. I shut my mouth and feel my eyes go wide at his opposition.

As if sensing that he's disarmed me—again—his expression softens. "Look, it could take weeks or maybe even a few months, for my inheritance to make its way to us. I went into this assuming we'd take care of your tuition before anything got sorted out with my dad's will. I have the money. I'll pay for it."

Everything he's saying makes sense. But doesn't he see the vulnerability in his plan? "Don't you want to wait until after tomorrow?"

That would be the sensible thing to do. The smart move. The way I'd expect him, or anyone in this situation, to play it. But Jake's not just anyone.

He scoffs, then assesses me like I'm dense. "Cory, you agreed to marry me. You asked me to be faithful. We already decided this was going to be real. I trust you."

I say nothing, turning my head to avoid his gaze.

He's so damn charming. I love and hate the way I feel around this man.

"Don't believe me?" he challenges, forcing me to meet his gaze. He's still got that eyebrow cocked up again, his expression hiding nothing as he shows me his truth. "Here's what I've been up to today." He turns on his heel, grabs a manilla envelope near the POS computer, then comes back to stand in front of me. He keeps his attention fixed on me as he pries open the little metal closure, then dumps out the contents with a flourish.

I don't know where to look first. Which is fine, because Jake takes over right away.

He moves things around, lining them up in order as he points and explains. "Condo key. Mailbox key. Garage door opener. Keys to both my Jeeps."

I do a double take at the identical keys—he has two of the same car?

"Storage unit key. Master key for Clinton's and The Oak. Damn... I should have bought you a key ring for all these." He chuckles as he pushes the small pile of metal toward me.

His tone changes from amused to serious in the next beat.

"In case it wasn't clear, I'm all in with you. And I take care of what's mine. Your new credit and debit cards have been ordered. You're officially on all my accounts. We're getting married tomorrow: what's mine is yours, in every way. So you'll either use my card and get your tuition taken care of tonight, or I'll write a check and we can drop it off tomorrow. But just so we're clear: there is no choice when it comes to me taking care of you."

I don't know what to say. Or how to react. There's this relief and this magic coursing through me, because as crazy as it sounds, I believe every word out of his mouth. It's beguiling to think so highly of someone, then find out that they're even more perfect than you imagined.

Arguing is futile. So I circle the bar, peeling one of his arms off the edge and forcing him to let me into his space.

He lets me in, all right. He lets me slip between him in the bar, then he settles his hand right back where it was, essentially locking me between his arms.

"Thank you," I whisper, resting my hand on his chest, right over his heart. That little bit of contact sends a zing through me that starts in my brain and travels all the way to my balls. I'm so gone for this guy. He has no idea. For someone who supposedly doesn't do relationships, he's nailing it so far.

He gives me a little smirk. Without overthinking it, I rise up on my toes and kiss him. It's just a peck—an admission of what I've wanted to do all week, and for much longer if I'm honest with myself. But I want him to know I'm all in, too. How did he put it? In every way?

He bows his head and gets so close we're sharing breath. There's this virility to him that sparks each and every one of my nerve endings. I'm practically panting as I wait to see if he'll kiss me back.

I startle when his hand works its way between my back and the bar. He spreads his fingers wide, digging in and using his grip to pull me closer. His hold is everything. It's also the only thing. I realize he's only touching me on my back—making a concerted effort to keep his body and that delicious mouth hovering just out of reach.

"I want to kiss you, Cory. Is that okay?" he asks without a hint of his usual playfulness.

If I wasn't pinned between his body and the bar, I'd probably drop to my knees and swoon. The only thing hotter than a secretly rich, genuinely nice fuckboy is one who confirms consent.

"Kiss me," I beg.

And then he does.

His mouth crashes into mine, consuming me as he tilts his head to get a better angle. His lips—God, his lips—they map across my mouth like he's memorizing every inch of me. He licks the seam of my lips and hums quietly, again with his hot-as-hell permission seeking. I eagerly let him in. His free hand grips the back of my head and moves it where he wants it, granting him deeper access. I see constellations form and universes burst into existence as he hypnotizes me with his mouth. I'm instantly addicted to the feeling he inspires in my body. In my mind. In my heart.

I've waited for this for days. I've secretly wanted this for years. Because even when we hooked up before, it was casual. Transactional. Sure, we've kissed, but never like this.

This is the type of kiss people write songs about. The type of kiss that makes you forget your own name. The type of kiss I never want to end.

But it does. Jake breaks it off first, abandoning my mouth to pepper my jawline with little pecks. When he reaches my neck, he doubles down, eliciting a moan that takes both of us by surprise.

He chuckles against my neck, but doesn't stop working me over. His teeth pull on my earlobe as his breath warms my skin.

"I've been waiting to do that all week," he confesses.

I work a hand between our bodies and press against his chest. "Then why didn't you?"

He looks at me with his signature smirk and shrugs. "I remember how good it was when we were casual. I had a feeling this was going to be about a hundred times hotter. And I wanted to give you time. I wanted you to make sure this is what you want without making things murky because of sex."

While reasonable, his answer shocks me. He still thinks about the few hookups we shared? And he purposely wanted to give me space to figure things out on my own?

"I can't believe this is all so easy," I marvel, wrapping my hands around his trim waist and pulling him closer to me.

"Why wouldn't it be?"

"We just... we don't know each other. Not really. And yet I feel so comfortable with you. So hot for you. So sure about what we're doing. It's not supposed to work like this."

He tilts my chin up and holds it in place with his fingers. "How do you think it's supposed to work, baby?"

He pins me to the bar with his hips, pressing hard enough that I can feel his erection through the seam of his jeans. I hold back a groan when I realize that, intentionally or not, he's lined up his length right along my completely hard dick.

I need to stay focused—this is his go-to move. Or at least one of them. The man has more game and swagger than anyone I've ever met. For as open as he can be, Jake Whitely is also a master at shutting down and relying on sex when things start to feel too real.

I reach out and stroke the side of his face, willing him to feel my sincerity and not shy away from this moment. I want to know what he thinks. And now I'm genuinely curious about whether he'll open up and not just brush me off.

"You know what I mean," I try. "We're not doing things the "right" way, and yet it all feels right to me. That's scary to admit out loud. But it's the truth."

He doesn't turn away from my touch, but he doesn't lean into it, either. He's preoccupied with watching me, considering his next move. I know him well enough to know that he's deciding which version of himself he's going to let me see.

I freeze when he speaks.

"I grew up thinking I'd never get married. It wasn't something I wanted or respected. I didn't... I didn't think I'd get to have someone care about me in this way."

He closes his eyes and gives his head an almost imperceptible shake before he returns his attention to me.

"So for you to agree to do this with me... to accept me, see me, push me, just like you're doing now, when everyone else just lets me crack a joke and change the subject? All this feels like a bonus. It doesn't matter that this isn't how people traditionally do it. It's the way *we're* doing it. And I gotta admit—I really like it. Mostly because I like who I'm doing it with."

I'll. Be. Damned.

His words are honest, his gaze intent. It takes an extra surge of effort on my part, but I don't shy away from his praise. I soak it in, revel in it, let it fortify what I've known all along: this feels right. It feels hopeful. Beautiful. *Real*.

"I'm really excited to marry you tomorrow," I confess. Because I am. As stupid, crazy, and lovesick as I might sound, I really, really am.

Instead of replying, he kisses me again. This time there's less urgency to it, his kiss a slow, tantric caress. He explores my mouth with his tongue and squeezes my obliques as I feel his aura blend with mine. When he sucks on the tip of my tongue, I moan again, louder this time, as the snowballing pulse of desire inside me grows more intense with each passing second.

His hips piston into me in rhythm with his mouth, and I can't help but wonder if we're going to hook up right here, right now.

But in the most surprising move of the night, he abruptly pulls back. I've literally been on my knees in the walk-in cooler with him before—so I know it's not modesty or even sanitation he's worried about. Especially not now that he owns the damn place. But his gaze searches mine before he takes my face in both hands, smiles sincerely, and kisses me softly three times.

Once I catch my breath, reality hits me. He's intentionally taking things slow. Just like he promised.

Jake shifts back on his heels and blows out a long breath, like he's trying to find his own composure, then hits me with one of those giddy little-boy grins. He links our fingers and pulls me around the bar before I even know what's happening.

"Come on, baby. Let's go home."

Chapter 18

Cory

My eyes fly open, and I frantically scan the exposed beams above me. It takes me only a second to remember where I am and why I'm here. Once I do? I'm even more panicked.

I'm in Jake's bed.

I slept (or, if I'm honest, barely slept) in his bed last night. I knew this was the arrangement. But I really hadn't thought it through.

The plush charcoal gray sheets and comforter smell so distinctly of him it's like I'm lying in a fluffy cloud of Jakeness. Vanilla. Musk. Something poignantly familiar and addictively delicious. My senses are overwhelmed by him, and he's not even in the damn room.

I curl up slowly, letting a full-body yawn work through me and hoping it's not too early to get up for the day.

Because that's the thing: I spent the night here for the first time, meaning that while I was tossing and turning in the bedroom last night, Jake was camped out on the couch, just like he promised. Even though things already feel different from they did four days ago when he proposed this arrangement.

I was disappointed when we got home last night and he didn't make any moves to pick up where we left off at Clinton's. He showed me where to park. Gave me an overview of all the space he'd cleared out for me. Helped me carry up and organize the carload of belongings and clothes I'd brought with me. Then gave me a lingering-but-chaste kiss, told me to come get him if I needed anything, and left me alone.

I reach across the nightstand for my water bottle but silently curse when I find it empty. I wasn't even thirsty until I realized water wasn't an option. Now I'm so parched I can't accumulate enough spit to swallow.

I'm petrified with indecision. Do I fill my water bottle in the en suite bathroom? Do I risk sneaking into the kitchen and waking him?

Or maybe the real question is: do I risk sneaking into the kitchen and letting him see me like this?

I'm not second-guessing our marriage. I'm all in with this plan.

But that doesn't mean I'm not so nervous I might puke.

I shake my head a few times to rattle myself out of the anxiety spiral looming over me. I'm marrying the man later today, for crying out loud. I should be able to stumble into the kitchen with bedhead for a water refill without overthinking it.

Still.

I slowly guide the bedroom door open but wince when it creaks as I slip out of the room.

"Good morning."

His words startle me so badly I yelp and drop my water bottle. The metal clangs against the polished wood floor. I cringe as I scoop it up and assess the damage. There's a little dent in the floor near where it hit, but I have no idea if that's new or not. Do I ask him? Do I offer to... what? Use his money to pay to have it fixed?

"Cory."

My name is a two-syllable benediction laced with emotion. On command, I lift my head to look at him. I could scurry away. I could lock my feelings down. Instead, I show him everything.

I stand there in my doubt, radiating unease and worry, and I let him see me. Rumpled. Frazzled. Anxious. And now, apparently, dehydrated.

We stand across from each other like that: me positioned at one end of the kitchen, his feet firmly planted at the far end of the living room. Seconds tick by as the tension builds between us. He's staring at me with an intensity that should unnerve me. But this is Jake. I'm galvanized by his gaze, assured that even though this is the craziest shit I've ever done in my life, it'll be okay. He'll make sure of it.

He doesn't break eye contact as he finally approaches. When he leans into my space, I feel his hot, minty breath on my face.

"I'm going to get a workout in before we get ready. You're welcome to join me if you want to blow off some steam."

He pulls back quickly, brushing past me to head down the hall to the second bedroom he's transformed into a gym.

Was that an invitation? I stand there, perplexed, and now thirsty in a completely different way.

I fill up my water bottle and screw the lid on tighter than necessary, not trusting my hands to hold steady now. I pop back into the bedroom to make the bed and change into a cutoff, athletic shorts, and sneakers. What I'll do when I join him in the gym is beyond me. I just want to be in his orbit.

I can hear him as I make my way down the hall. When I reach the doorway and peek inside, my heart catches in my throat.

There he is: shirtless, straddling a bench, dumbbell in hand, dripping in sweat, radiating sex appeal. He's facing away from the door, but on full display thanks to the mirrors lining the front and side walls.

I freeze in the doorframe. Not because I don't want to go in. But because I'm spellbound by the show.

Every time he lifts the weight, he grunts. It's not quiet, either. It's deep. Guttural. Pornographic in the best possible way. Each grunt skates down my spine and tugs at my core.

I'm so transfixed watching his bronzed skin glisten with sweat and the muscles in his arms bulge that it takes my brain a second to register when he's finished his set.

He rolls his shoulders out once, then again. I'm mesmerized by the way the muscles coil and ripple. He's tension and chaos, release and control. This perfect specimen on the inside and out. And most importantly, as of today?

He's mine.

As soon as I think the words, our eyes connect in the mirror. He sticks his tongue in his cheek, then gives me a pointed look that can only be described as lust personified.

I keep my feet planted and cross my arms over my chest, smirking back instead of shrinking under his gaze. We may be in another silent standoff, but this is nothing like what just happened in the kitchen, and we both know it. This is carnal attraction, unfettered longing.

I stand there expectantly, excited for him to begin his next set. I could watch him do just about anything, but watching him lift shirtless just shot to the top of the list of my favorite pastimes.

Except he doesn't start up another set. Instead, he cocks his head slightly, his voice lascivious as he grits out, "Come here."

Those two words and that mischievous glint in his eye are like gravity: I'm pulled into the room, consumed with the need to be near him. He turns around as I approach so he's still straddling the bench, but facing me head-on.

I stop right in front of him, but he doesn't rise to stand. Instead, he reaches out, hooks one finger in the waistband of my shorts, and uses his hold to pull me closer.

Dios mío.

He's so fucking close.

His face is just a few inches away from my erection. A second hand joins the first. His fingers explore *just* under my elastic waistband, grazing the sharp v cut of my hips. He strokes the definition of my stomach, outlining the valleys where my waist tapers in. It's not until his nails scratch against my trimmed pubic hair that I grunt.

He gives my shorts a little tug while nuzzling his face against me. His mouth is *right there*. I can feel heat radiating off him—warmth and sweat and desire that matches my own. I raise a fisted hand to my mouth to stop myself from moaning. When he bites me through the fabric, I almost lose it.

"Cory?"

I look down to find his eyes on me, his hands still hooked in my pants, his expression inquisitive. My dick pulses in anticipation when I see the intent in his gaze.

"Yes?" he asks, nudging my cock with his nose and making it abundantly clear what he's after. What he's *offering*.

"So much yes," I pant.

He's got my dick out and in his hand a moment later.

He strokes me once, and I have to imagine I'm rooted to the floor to keep myself from thrusting forward into his touch. Every muscle in my core clenches in anticipation as I watch him scrutinize every inch of me.

"Goddamn," he whispers in reverence, peering up at me as he licks the tip and runs his tongue back and forth over my slit.

I spread my legs wider in encouragement as he grips me right at the base. His hold is firm, confident. His touch is instantly addictive.

He swirls his tongue around the crown a few times, then takes me deeper. One hand stays firmly wrapped around my dick, stroking me as he sucks. He works the other hand around my body, fingers digging into my ass cheek and anchoring me in place.

When he moans, I almost come from the vibrations.

I run a hand through his hair, more to ground myself than because he needs any sort of guidance. I'm both infatuated with and infuriated by how good he is at this. Because this? Me receiving? We've never done this before. But this is obviously not the first blowjob he's given.

A flare of jealousy creeps up my neck, quickly replaced by my need to possess him. I roll my hips forward in rhythm with his mouth and pull hard enough on his hair to get his attention. His eyes shoot up in question, but like the champ he is, he doesn't break pace.

"Mine," I grind out through clenched teeth, doubling-down on my efforts to fuck his face. "Your mouth is mine. Your body is mine. As of today, you. Are. Mine."

His eyes light up at my declaration, but I don't have time to think about that. Right now, I only have one thing on my mind: a desperation to explode in his mouth.

I feel his hand move from my ass and circle my thigh. It's the only warning I get before he cradles my balls. He kneads them in one hand, then when it starts to feel too good, he gives them a tug. I moan his name, completely consumed by the rhythm he's establishing and the way he's working my body.

Suck, swallow, suck, tug.

Suck, swallow, suck, *fuck*.

I'm so lost in him I can barely choke out a warning before the first spasms of my orgasm tingle up my calves. My abs clench as I cry out his name. He laps me up, sucking and moaning like he can't get enough, milking my cock for everything I'm worth as I shoot into his mouth over and over again.

Even when I'm empty, he doesn't pop off my dick. Instead, he savors me, licks me clean, then peers up as he kisses the tip.

He pulls my shorts back up, rises to stand, then slants his mouth against mine in a deep, heady kiss that forces me to taste myself on his tongue. It's not until I'm breathless that he pulls away, only to lean right back in again and whisper in my ear.

"Yours."

That one word has me silently groaning in want. I watch as he walks out of the room like he didn't just flip the script and make me come harder than I've ever orgasmed in my life.

I'm starstruck and lust filled and so fucking gone for Jake Whitely.

It takes me another minute to get myself sorted. I have to physically sit down on the bench he was just straddling, otherwise I worry my knees will buckle. Once I've caught my breath and my pulse has settled, I realize he didn't let me return the favor.

No. No way.

I stalk out of the workout room and head for the master bedroom, confident that's where I'll find him. If the steam billowing out of the en suite wasn't enough of a giveaway, my king of an almost-husband left the door open for me. For someone who swears he's never been in a relationship, he sure knows how to play his part.

I walk into the bathroom with purpose, kicking off my shoes and stripping out of my clothes so fast I stumble. Ten seconds later, I'm stepping into the glass block shower, my target finally within reach.

The whole shower is massive, lined with tiles and two fancy showerheads I have no idea how to operate. Doesn't matter—I came in here for one thing and one thing only.

His skin is slick when I yank his body into mine, his taut, defined muscles slippery and covered in suds. I drape my arms over his shoulders, the need to be as close to him as possible dominating my every thought.

"Cory?"

Concern. Desire. Perfect, gentle care. How does he make my name sound like a hopeful prayer every time he speaks it out loud?

"I'm fine," I insist. "I'm right here with you."

He may not be looking for reassurance, but I offer it willingly.

His completely erect cock nestles between my dick and my thigh, reminding me of why I came in here in the first place. I work a hand between our bodies, gripping him at the base just like he held me in the gym.

I stroke, relishing the solidness of his girth in my palm. Knowing that I did this to him—that getting me off made him this fucking hard.

I kiss his neck, suckling the skin between his jaw and his ear until he finally gives up a moan.

"Hey," he protests. "Don't you dare give me a hickey before we take pictures today."

Of course he's concerned about appearances. That just makes me want to mark him more. He said he was mine. If that's the truth, he can wear the proof on his neck.

I savor the same spot until I'm satisfied it'll bruise. He doesn't protest again, instead letting me have my way with him as I continue to stroke his dick. I'm fully hard again, so he takes the opportunity to wrap his fist around me, too. It feels incredible—to jack each other in perfect sync, to match our lust stroke for stroke. I could absolutely go for round two already. But I have a point to prove.

I reluctantly pull out of his grasp and release him, kissing his chest as I work my way down his body. I'm stooped low, two seconds away from dropping to my knees, when I feel his big hands catch me under my arms.

His action halts my movement and sends a pang of rejection through me. I've given him head before, and right now, the need to claim him and return the favor has me practically panting to get that dick in my mouth. Why doesn't he want this?

I don't meet his gaze as his arms hold me in place. It's not until he releases one hand and reaches past me that I focus on what he's doing.

He takes a step back, separating us further, then bores right into my goddamn soul as he forces eye contact and works something over in his hands.

He folds a towel on itself twice. Then he bows slightly and places it on the floor, right in front of his feet. When he rises back up to full height, he looks from the towel to me and winks.

My soon-to-be husband just made me a goddamn cushion so I could suck him off in the shower. If I wasn't already lowering to my knees to please him, I'd be dropping down in worship.

I run my hands down the grooves of his chest, letting my fingers trace the pronounced muscles of his abs as I slowly lower down. My kneecaps make contact with the plush, sopping wet towel, and now I'm face to face with his gorgeous, perfect cock.

I still and just admire the damn thing for a moment—long and fat with this prominent vein running the entire length. The crown is perfectly symmetrical, flared and so damn tempting. The few times I sucked him off in the past, I didn't have the time or patience to appreciate the rock-hard power of this man's assets. I lick my lips in anticipation, delighted to have the chance to savor him now.

A firm hand finds the back of my neck just as I grip the base of his cock and stroke him once from root to tip.

Jake's head drops back on a groan, then he tucks his chin and scorches me with his gaze and his liquid hot words.

"Put me in your mouth and put me out of my misery before I shove you against the tiles and do it myself."

I clench my ass cheeks together and try to ignore the way his words have my cock in a proverbial chokehold. Right now, I want to be choking on him. I don't need to be told twice.

My eyes flare in wanting as my heart thrums against my chest cavity in anticipation. I follow his commands and shove his dick in my mouth, taking him as deep as I can go, swallowing around his length in rapid succession until he's gasping for breath.

"Yes, baby," he hisses through clenched teeth. "Make me yours."

His words spur me on. I'll make him mine, all right. I'm about to blow the memory of every partner he's ever had right out of his mind and give Jake Whitely the best fucking head of his life.

Chapter 19

Jake

We're driving north on Route 8 with the top down in my dad's yellow 1969 Pontiac GTO. It feels goddamn poetic to be behind the wheel of one of Joe Whitely's most prized possessions as life comes full circle and I fulfill his dying wish.

I smirk at the thought—my awful excuse for a father got what he deserved for everything he did, and didn't do, over the years. His bisexual son and biggest disappointment is officially married, just like he wanted. I just happen to be married to a man.

A gorgeous, complex, intelligent, possessive man who surprises me at every turn.

I sneak a glance at my husband sitting in the passenger seat beside me. He's grinning from ear to ear, wearing the Ray-Bans I bought him that match mine, his arm resting on the side of the car as he caresses the air tunnel created by going seventy-five miles an hour in a convertible.

He's so freaking adorable. I can't believe how wrapped up in him I am. After all the ups and downs of this week, and despite everything that felt uncertain, Cory just feels right.

I've been so engrossed in the logistics of pulling off this plan that I haven't spent nearly enough time appreciating the perfect specimen of a man who's making my wildest dreams come true. Thankfully that's about to change. If he likes the idea, that is.

I reach across the console and take his hand, clasping it in mine and grinning when he looks back at me. The wind is too loud for words. That's okay: my heart feels too full to come up with anything worth saying anyway. I pour my gratitude into my gaze and squeeze his hand even harder before turning my attention back to the road.

I pull off the highway four exits before Hampton. He looks at me quizzically as I ease the car to a full stop at a red light.

"What are we doing?"

"We're celebrating."

Two minutes later, I'm cruising into a specially marked reserved parking spot at Swenson's. Almost immediately, a young kid jogs out with the order I placed in advance.

Cory beams at me, his grin lighting me up in the best way.

"How did you... wait, did you know?"

He hasn't actually asked a question, but I give him the answer he's seeking.

"I heard it's your favorite. I may have had a little help getting the order right..." I hand him the peanut butter milkshake and a Galley Boy, plus a pile of napkins. I don't give a shit about making a mess. I'm half-tempted to grind some potato teasers into the seats and leave them for my brother Joey to deal with when he gets the car out for the next Hampton Days vintage car show.

But Cory does care about the brand-new dove gray suit he's wearing. The one I rush-ordered from Nordstrom and surprised him with today. I almost gave the surprise away when I texted him earlier this week to ask his shirt and suit size. But damn, was it worth it to see the way he lit up when I unzipped our matching garment bags.

I like spoiling him. I love seeing his delight when I put him first or plan a surprise like this. There's something about taking care of him that feels utterly satisfying in a way I've never felt before.

"I have one more surprise for you," I confess as I turn to face him. I watch as he dips a French fry into a white crinkle carton of ranch dressing—gross—then eyes me skeptically while he chews.

"I know this isn't *the* dream, but I promised I'd make this good for you."

He looks like he wants to interject, so I rush to finish.

"The businesses aren't officially mine until September first, and your classes don't start until next week. I want to spend more time with you before we both get super busy and have crazy schedules to maintain... so I booked us a honeymoon."

He balks and says nothing. I squirm through the silence as I realize maybe I should have run this past him first. Asked his opinion? Confirmed he was free?

Shit.

Did I fuck this up already?

I scramble for something to save the moment, but he speaks first.

"Are you serious?"

When I finally lock in on him, he's assessing me through squinted eyes. I have no damn idea how to respond.

"I mean, if you're too busy, or if you don't think it's a good idea..."

Fuckin' A.

After this morning's epic blowjob exchange, I thought for sure he'd be excited about this. All I want to do is eat seafood, drink fruity drinks, and explore the chemistry brewing between us. That's what a honeymoon is about, right? Who wouldn't want to go on a gluttonous, sexy vacation?

"It's the best idea. So where are we going?"

He has the most earnest expression—like he can't believe I did this. Relief washes over me as I snag my chocolate milkshake from the tray hanging off the window and suck down a few strong pulls.

"I booked a private villa at an all-inclusive resort on the treasure coast in Florida. We'll have a two-story beachfront house all to ourselves. There are a few restaurants and lounges on property, and we'll have access to the pool, too. We only have two nights because I have to get back to the businesses, and I didn't want to ask about a passport and spoil the surprise, but—"

"Jake."

I stop blabbering and meet his gaze.

"It sounds perfect."

Chapter 20

Cory

Navigating through the airport with Jake is like traveling with a celebrity. He unwittingly captivates every person we encounter. He's enigmatic on a typical day. Add in the happy-go-lucky, shit-eating grin he's been sporting since we said 'I do,' and people just flock to him.

My brain short-circuited when he told me he booked a honeymoon. I haven't been on a real vacation in years. Given the shotgun nature of our marriage, I assumed all the wedding traditions were off the table. I assumed wrong.

As if it wasn't enough to surprise me with a gorgeous Tom Ford suit. Or to whisk me away in a vintage convertible. Or to plan a pitstop at Swenson's, complete with "reserved parking" and all my favorites ready when we pulled in.

The only thing that would have made the day more perfect was if he hadn't had to work. He apologized endlessly for having to go in on our wedding night, but in order to take off for the next few days, he felt like it was only fair if he closed. He didn't want to upset his staff, and he didn't want anyone to work all weekend without a day off. That's just who he is.

I was originally thankful when I saw his calendar for the week. Why wouldn't he go to work on our wedding night? Up until two days ago, we'd done nothing more than hold hands and hug. Neither one of us could have anticipated the visceral spark that ignited when we hooked up again.

Something shifted at The Oak on Thursday night. I knew we'd get here eventually, he and I. The chemistry between us is too intense to be ignored. But I never imagined it would happen this fast or feel this right.

Now we're here. At the Cleveland airport on a Saturday morning, surrounded by other couples and families bustling through the terminal.

No one would look at us right now and think this was a shotgun marriage for financial gain or that we aren't emotionally and physically invested.

Jake's waiting patiently as I relace my sneakers near the security checkpoint, one large hand resting just above my knee while he fiddles with his phone.

When I finally push to my feet, he hits me with the most dazzling smile. "Ready?" He slings his carry-on over his shoulder, then picks up my messenger bag, too. He effortlessly slips his hand into mine, ease and care coursing between us like we've been doing this for years, not just days.

"Are you hungry? Do you need more coffee?"

I haven't flown anywhere in years. I forgot you can't take liquids past the security checkpoint and had to abandon my to-go travel mug in the car. Of course he noticed.

"Coffee would be great," I confess as he veers off and guides me toward a kiosk. He drops our bags on a bench, then leans in and kisses me quickly. "Wait here," he murmurs as he heads to the back of the line.

I watch, spellbound, as he strikes up a conversation with the two women in front of him, making them laugh with quips or anecdotes, I'm sure. His dimple pops when he smiles, listening intently to their responses. It's fascinating to watch him move through the world—this hot-as-sin human dripping with sincerity. He's a storm of magnetism, authenticity, and humility. It's disarming in the best possible way.

After Jake makes friends with literally everyone around him, he places our order, sticks a twenty in the tip jar, and moves to the end of the kiosk to wait for our drinks. Once they're ready, he returns, beaming as he hands me a cup and straw.

I eye the beverage skeptically, wondering if it's what I think it is.

"Iced triple shot oat milk latte with vanilla syrup," he declares.

I shift my gaze from the cup to my husband. How the hell did he know that?

His smile falters.

"Wait, did I get it wrong?"

The earnestness—the concern. I bite my lip and resist teasing him.

Just like everything he's done for me over the last week, it's perfect.

We meander through the terminal and stop in some of the shops to kill time before we board. Jake won't let me carry my own bag, which is endearing, albeit foreign to me. I'm learning that that's his MO: He shows he cares by the things he does. His actions say more than his words.

When we turn the corner toward our gate, I stop in my tracks. I've always wondered why airports have jewelry counters. Who wants to buy diamonds and precious metals before they get on a plane?

Apparently, me.

"I want rings," I declare, tossing my empty cup in a recycling bin and striding toward the brightly lit kiosk in the middle of Terminal A.

Jake keeps up with my hustle, but questions my intent.

"What kind of rings?"

I side-eye him as I scan the glass display cases, my heart skipping a beat when I spot the men's wedding bands.

"Those kinds of rings," I confirm, pointing to the small selection of traditional wedding bands. We shift over and peer into the illuminated case. The display is so bright I'm tempted to fish out my sunglasses.

Jake sets our bags at his feet and snakes his arm around my waist, pulling me close.

He bows his head low to whisper in my ear. "You want to wear a wedding band so everyone knows you're mine?"

His question sounds like liquid seduction and sends a shiver down my spine. Goosebumps erupt on just one side of my body as the warmth of his breath dances over my skin.

It's his presence. His essence. That word.

Mine.

Except his claim on me isn't what I'm interested in: he already has me in a vise grip—around my heart and my cock—whether he knows it or not.

I shake my head, then lift my gaze in challenge. I lean in and let myself get as close as I dare before leveling him with the truth.

"I want one, too, but it's not what you think. I want *you* to wear a wedding band so everyone knows *you* belong to *me*."

I can't stop staring at my ring. It's a simple platinum band that matches his, and it fits like it was molded just for me. I saw Jake eyeing the blingier options, but I convinced him to get a matching set. Between the Ray-Bans, our wedding suits, and now the rings, he's a sucker for matching.

I can't stop touching it. Just like I can't stop glancing over and looking at his.

I'm sure he knows what I'm doing. He smirks every time he catches me out of the corner of his eye. He stretches his hand and settles it on my thigh, sending bolts of electricity through my femur when he flexes his fingers, bunching the fabric of my linen shorts with each motion.

I grab for his hand and squeeze, silently pleading with him to stop torturing me. I'll have to stand up and board the plane at any minute, and in these light-colored shorts, my hard-on would be more than obvious.

We're surrounded by kids on all sides. Apparently, the Saturday morning flight is popular for families traveling to Florida, too. Two little girls whiz by, both wearing mini backpacks and oversized bow headbands. I catch him grinning as he watches them, smiling even wider when the little one catches up and pulls her sister's bow off her head.

"What are you thinking?" I ask.

His smile falters. He side-eyes me sheepishly, almost as if he's been caught. "I was just thinking about my girls."

"I have to admit, meeting them shocked the shit out of me. I didn't think you had any family in the area."

He tilts his head toward me, not speaking right away. I'm learning that when Jake's quiet, waiting him out is imperative. He's usually so quick and conversational. Any pause from him is intentional.

"My mom died before I turned three, when my little brother Joey was born. My dad died when I was twenty. My older brother Julian is the girls' dad, and his wife's name is Ashleigh. I honestly only see my brothers once or twice a year, and those are usually chance encounters around town or at events I can't avoid."

"If you only see your brothers a few times a year, how are you so close with your nieces?"

Jake shifts back in his seat and fiddles with his wedding ring. Watching him run his fingers back and forth along the polished metal does something to my insides. The sensual way he fingers the platinum band has me wishing his hand was on me instead.

When he finally answers, his voice is low, almost shaky. I'm surprised by his tone. The man's unflappable. I can't imagine what he's nervous about.

"Julian and Ashleigh got married during my senior year of high school—he's ten years older than me," he explains. "I was at their wedding, but then I didn't see them again until my dad's funeral two years later. After that, we didn't talk for years. One day, I'm in the Acme parking lot because Rhett was home from school for the weekend and had picked up a few shifts at Clinton's."

"So he could be with Tori," I interject with a knowing glance.

Jake smirks and nods. "Mm-hmm. Funny. She was the only one who didn't have his number figured out back then. Anyway, you know how the place gets when the regulars know Rhett's in town."

He twists the ring on his finger a few times before he continues.

"So it's a Sunday morning, and Mike sends me over to Acme to pick up extra celery for Bottomless Bloody Marys. As I'm getting back in my Jeep, I notice this woman a few spots down from me. She's got a screaming baby in one arm, and she's trying to wrangle a feral toddler into a car seat. A whole bunch of produce had rolled out of one of the bags she set on the ground, and it was about to become fruit salad if someone didn't help her."

My heart folds in on itself as I listen to what it's like to live in the World According to Jake. This man walks around with the purest intentions, always looking to be a helper.

"I rushed over to save a cantaloupe and to see if I could help. When the lady turns around, I realize it's Ashleigh. It's my own sister-in-law. With my nieces I didn't know existed."

He shakes his head and plants his elbows on his knees. I can feel the anger radiating off him.

"As soon as she saw me, she burst into tears," he grits out through his teeth. "Julian travels for work a lot, and he'd been out of town for something like three or four weeks that time. She hadn't talked to another grown up in days."

He shakes his head again, still agitated, but more resolved.

"The whole thing rubbed me the wrong way. I couldn't stand to see her like that. It killed me to realize I didn't know my nieces. So I asked Ashleigh if I could come over sometime when Julian was out of town. To this day, I'm surprised she let me. And really, I think the timing was kismet; she was burned out and lonely… just desperate enough to say yes."

Jake leans back in the vinyl chair again, hands on his thighs and a half smile on his face.

"I went back to their house—to the house I grew up in—for the first time in years because of those little girls. They stole my heart immediately. They're the brightest parts of my life."

"Now that they're older, Ashleigh lets me take them on adventures around town. We go to the park and the splash pad. I spoil them rotten with cake pops and ice cream and all the fries and tots they want at Clinton's. I love spending time with them, honestly. And it gives Ashleigh a much-needed break since my brother's too busy to spend time with his family."

I smile serenely as I absorb the weight of his confession. He's always been a jokester with boundless energy. He's always been a helper, too. It's sweet the way their family came back together because of the girls.

"What does Julian think about all this?" I ask.

Jake chuckles. "Julian doesn't know."

"Wait, what? What do you mean he doesn't know?"

He shrugs. "He's literally never home. And when he is, I get the impression that he doesn't talk to the girls or engage with them in any meaningful way. He doesn't read to them. He doesn't play. Mimi calls him 'father,' for crying out loud, like she's one of the kids from Peter Pan."

"So let me get this straight," I push. "You have a relationship with your sister-in-law and you spend time with your nieces on a regular basis, but their father—your *brother*—doesn't know you know they exist?"

"Yep." He pops the *p*, and I read it for what it is: the end of a conversation. We're done talking about this. Instead of letting things get awkward, I grab his hand and lift his knuckles to my mouth.

Before he can respond, the overhead announcement chimes in to explain boarding procedures. We're sitting first class; we'll be first in the lineup, so I double-check my carry-on to make sure I have everything.

"Hey, think we should share the news before we board?"

I whip my head around to look at him. Is he serious? I squint at him in question, urging him to go on.

"If we text them now, we can put our phones on airplane mode and not be subjected to everyone hounding us," he explains.

Oh.

Right.

He has a valid point, actually. We've been planning all along to send a text to establish an equal playing field among our friends and coworkers. There will be talk—so much talk it makes me cringe to think about—but this allows us to control the narrative, avoid the initial reactions, and give everyone the information at the same time.

After taking a moment to consider the scenario and possible fallout, I nod. "Yeah, okay. Let's do it. Is it weird that Tori is one of my closest friends, and Rhett's your best friend, and we just got married without telling them?"

Jake sighs. "Sort of. Rhett will call the second he sees the message."

"And you'll answer?" I challenge. If the whole point of the text is to give everyone time to process, maybe it's better if he really does ignore all follow-up questions.

He cocks one eyebrow. "I *always* answer for him."

Oh.

Jake's loyalty to his best friend stirs up an unexpected pang of envy. The logical part of my brain knows I have nothing to be jealous about where Rhett is concerned. But my baser instinct still gifts me with a surge of bitterness I didn't expect.

I've never been a jealous person, let alone possessive. I honestly have no idea why this greedy, envious side of me springs into action with Jake. I was insecure when I was younger, especially in middle school and then again when I came out. But this outright jealous thing is new.

"I don't really want to have to explain things just yet," I admit on an exhale.

"Then don't. I'll send the text, and you turn your phone off. It's better to give everyone time to process and cool off anyway. Just because I'm going to take Rhett's call doesn't mean you have to answer to anyone." Jake stands up and stretches his arms overhead, exposing a strip of tanned, taut stomach that I want to trace with my tongue. "Anyone but me, that is," he adds when he catches me staring.

Damn. I can't wait to get this honeymoon started.

"Okay. Let's do this."

Jake offers me his hand and pulls me out of my seat, then unlocks the screen on his phone. He flips the camera around, slings his left arm around my shoulders, then tucks his chin against my neck so we're both in the frame. His hand is spread wide across my chest, the brand-new wedding ring unmissable on his finger.

"Hold up your hand, baby. Let's make sure they know you're mine."

We both smile as he takes a few shots. Then he proceeds to squeeze, lick, and bite me until I'm squirming and laughing as he takes a dozen more pictures.

"One more," he whispers before resting his head against mine, genuine affection clear in his eyes on screen.

That one is my favorite.

A few seconds later, he shows me the picture he plans to send, as well as the message to go with it.

Jake: Yo. Life update. I found myself a husband, and we're heading to Florida for a quick getaway. We're literally about to board the plane, then we'll be preoccupied as soon as we land because #honeymoon. We'll explain everything next time we see you. About our marriage, that is. NOT about the honeymoon. ;)

I tentatively nod my approval after I read the message three times. It's not what I would say—but I don't have any other suggestions.

"Here goes nothing," I mutter as I watch him hit send.

He smirks with that saucy glint in his eye. "You mean here goes *everything*."

Chapter 21

Jake

I blow out a long breath as I wash my hands in the huge-ass bathroom attached to the master bedroom. We're staying in one of the resort's private, two-story, beachside villas with uninhibited ocean views and complete privacy.

The place has this modern, beachy vibe with its whitewashed wood and touches of turquoise, teal, and coral. I felt relaxed the moment I stepped into the open-air lobby and spotted the ocean beyond the seagrass barrier wall. Once we checked in, we walked hand in hand down the pier to our villa. I'll never forget the look on Cory's face when we walked through the front door of our home away from home for the next few days.

After the week I've had, I'm ready to kick back with a few drinks at the pool and get even more intimately acquainted with the man I married. Working last night—on our wedding night—sucked, but I owed it to my staff to take a weekend closing shift before heading out of town. They don't know it yet, but I'm going to be their "real" boss very soon. I like to lead by example and earn respect with action.

And the way things have clicked with Cory? Totally unexpected.

I don't believe in soulmates or shit like that—especially not after watching my best friend wring his heart out over Tori for years. Those two are my family—but they almost destroyed each other with years of push and pull, hot and cold, all in the name of love.

A soulmate isn't in the cards for me. But there's no denying my connection with Cory—or the heady chemistry that's coursing between us.

I assess my reflection in the bathroom mirror, marveling at how perfectly everything has come together.

Still.

Rhett's words from earlier keep playing on repeat in my mind.

I hope you know what you're doing.

I knew he'd call me the second he read the group text. I knew others would, too, but his was the only call I was willing to take. He lobbed question after question without giving me time to respond. That went on the entire time Cory and I boarded the plane and got settled into our seats.

Then, just when I thought he was losing steam, Tori added her two cents from the background, which my best friend was more than happy to pass along. Between the two of them, I barely got a word in, even though I was the one being interrogated. Eventually I explained about the restaurants and Cory's school and even got Rhett to admit I had a solid plan. What we're doing isn't conventional, but it's mutually beneficial, given the circumstances. But his parting words gave me pause.

"Bro, I say this from a place of love and genuine concern… don't hurt him."

I get it. I do. Rhett knows that I'm more likely to fuck this up than Cory. I've never even been in a relationship, and I have no idea what I'm doing. But there's something Rhett doesn't know, because it's something I don't even fully understand myself.

This may have started as a transactional marriage of convenience. But it has quickly, magically, inexplicably transformed into so much more.

"I wouldn't dream of it. Truly. We've been super clear with each other about what we want out of this. We're both fully committed to seeing this through, and I don't take that lightly."

The flight attendant was scowling at me by then, giving me the perfect excuse to end the call and settle in for our flight. I had planned to listen to music or maybe catch a nap, but I got wrapped up in talking to Cory about his parents, his abuela, and the courses he's taking this semester. I could listen to him talk for hours. I'm endlessly fascinated by the smallest details he's willing to share.

I grab my Ray-Bans and phone off the counter, connect my device to the sound system wired through the entire villa, and put on a Mac Miller playlist.

When I step into the bedroom, I spot him on the balcony off the master suite, and it's like my feet can't move fast enough. I pull open the sliding glass door and step out into the sticky Florida heat. Ominous storm clouds are swirling off in the distance, miles away out at sea, which is typical for afternoons in the sunshine state. It's impossibly hot, and it's still mostly blue skies above us for now. But that storm—the clouds are the darkest possible shade of blue without being black. It makes the air crackle with a heavy inevitability.

My husband is leaning against the banister smack in the middle of the balcony. He's shirtless and in his swim trunks, the muscles of his back glistening thanks to the sun pounding down on his golden-brown skin.

"What do you think?" I ask as I cross the balcony, wincing as the heated planks scorch the soles of my bare feet.

He turns as I approach and gives me the most thorough perusal I've ever been subjected to. I feel scandalized in the best possible way.

"The view's incredible," he replies as I reach him. I don't bother standing beside him, instead sidling up behind him and notching my dick right into the crease of his ass.

He lets out a sharp inhale when I thrust forward and slink my arms around him to pull him to my chest.

"Agreed," I whisper in his ear. "And it feels even better than it looks."

He melts as I brace him against me, his back melding into my chest. Our combined mass of muscle and definition makes me want to dig in and squeeze him tighter. I glide both hands across his torso in opposite directions, using one hand to grip his throat while the other teases the drawstring of his trunks.

"No one can see us up here, you know. I made sure we'd have complete privacy."

He arches back and rests his head in the crook of my neck, his lips seeking mine. He gives up a whimper when I nip him with my teeth.

"Cory?" For as right as this feels, I can't let myself forget that what we're doing is rushed and uncharted in so many ways.

He pushes his ass back against me. "Stop doing that," he murmurs as he rolls his hips again.

His body is telling me yes, but I need to make sure.

"Doing what?" I demand, using the hand I've got resting on his happy trail to give myself more leverage and grind against him.

"Asking for permission. Doubting whether you're reading me right. Questioning if I want this. I've said yes to you a dozen times in the last five days, Jake. It's yes. It's hell yes. With you, it'll always be yes."

Okay then.

I sink my teeth into the top of his shoulder, inspiring a full-body shudder in him that I feel all the way in my balls.

"Take what you want," he grunts.

I smile against his neck, then run my tongue over the spot that's already reddening in response to my bite. "What I *want* is to drive you crazy."

I push my hand down the front of his shorts, loving the way he hisses when I wrap my fist around his dick. I squeeze his throat in tandem, then nip his earlobe lightly before I move.

Cory braces his arms on the rail, giving me room to work. With a slow, tight stroke, I savor the solidness of his completely hard dick in my hand. He sighs and spreads his feet wider.

When I pull my hand out of his trunks, he whimpers, but he doesn't resist when I tilt his chin so he's looking at me.

"Spit," I command, lifting my hand to his mouth. His pupils blow out as he follows my instructions. They grow even wider when I bring my hand to my own mouth and follow suit, never breaking eye contact.

I cup our combined fluid and work my hand lower once more. This time when I grip him, he thrusts his cock into me.

Fuck. His eagerness spurs me on in surprising ways. I shake my head to focus, then bring my lips to his neck. Licking up the salty sheen of sweat that coats his sun-kissed skin, I jack him in rhythm with my mouth.

I rub his neck—squeezing and thoroughly enjoying the sensation when he swallows. His dick throbs in my hand when I stroke him from base to tip, then back again. I've got him panting already—this pliable, beautiful man getting all worked up with my hands all over him.

The velvet skin of his dick is slick against my palm. I squeeze him with each stroke, but change up the pressure and speed as he tries to match his thrusts to my movement.

"Jake," he whines. Ohhh, this poor thing. If he's already whimpering, he's going to hate what happens next. At least for now.

But I'm a man of my word. And I promised to drive him crazy tonight.

"You like that, baby? You want me to make you jizz all over my hand so I can lick it off my fingers?"

He moans—*he fucking moans*—in response to my words.

"Or maybe I'll use your cum to work into that tight little hole and see how far I can stretch you..."

He lets out a choked cry.

"You want that, too, baby? You gonna let me in? I want to make you feel so fucking good tonight."

I abandon my hold on his throat to tease one finger between his cheeks.

He shudders under my touch, arching back to give me access and gain more friction right where he wants it.

Fuck, he's so responsive. The way he tells me exactly what he wants without speaking a goddamn word... he's a king. I can't wait to worship at his feet over the next few days.

I'm so keen on making him unravel, I almost don't go through with it. But then I think about what he's gonna be like tonight: desperate and love drunk for my dick. Maybe he'll even beg.

I push my hips forward and pin him to the railing, then slowly loosen my hold on his cock.

It physically pains me to do this—but I have bigger plans for my man tonight.

I kiss his neck once, then pepper kisses along his back.

He whips his head around when he realizes what I'm doing. "Jake?"

"Sorry, baby. But I want to make this trip unforgettable. I promise it'll be worth it when you finally get to come."

He spins around in my arms, a fire behind his eyes that I've never seen before. He's not just mad. He's seething.

I doubt my plan to edge him the second I meet his gaze.

"What happened to 'I want to make you feel good'?" he scoffs.

I bite on my bottom lip to keep from smiling. "Did that not feel good?" I ask innocently.

He charges me then—gets right up in my space and smacks both hands against my bare chest with so much force I stumble. "It did. But it doesn't now," he hisses.

His face is inches from mine. I can't resist capturing his mouth in a deep, sultry kiss.

He doesn't resist me, but he doesn't kiss me back, either.

"Baby," I mutter against his lips. "Don't be mad. Think about how good it'll be tonight when I finally let you come."

"*Hmph*. You don't *let* me do anything, Jake Whitely. I'm your husband. Not your plaything."

I still at his words, pulling back to assess if I've read him all wrong. I thought he'd be game for this. But I'll drop to my knees and suck him off right now if he really doesn't want to play.

He glares, huffs out a frustrated breath, then runs a hand through his perfectly styled hair. I know the second he goes soft and accepts his fate. A rush of relief washes over me then. I didn't fuck this up. I keep watching him as he cools off—I've never seen him get worked up about anything like that in all the years I've known him. He's adorable when he's flustered, and I can't wait to really break him down.

"Sorry," he mumbles as he meets my gaze. "I didn't mean that. I'm good. I'm into this. You just caught me off guard. I'm the sexual equivalent of hangry right now."

"Horngry?" I offer.

His smile takes over his whole face, but he doesn't give me the satisfaction of eliciting a real laugh.

"Let's go to the pool," I suggest, wrapping my arms around his waist and pulling him close. I have to stifle my own moan when his dick brushes against mine. "Then the bar. I want to show off my new husband and see what this honeymoon business is all about. Then, I promise," I kiss him for emphasis, "to bring you back here and make you come so hard you see stars. Trust me, Cory. I want to make this good for you in every way possible."

He nods and kisses me back, greedy and eager. I meant what I said—I'm determined to do everything I can to make this night, this trip, the next few years, worthy of this man.

Chapter 22

Cory

We spent the afternoon poolside, cuddled up in a half-dome cabana with bottle service, unlimited snacks, and a privacy curtain. It was literal paradise: the type of vacation I've only ever dreamed of taking. The only thing that would have made it better? If my tease of a husband would have taken advantage of the damn privacy curtain instead of working me up not once, but twice, in public, only to pull back when the first tingles of release had my toes curling in anticipation.

The first time was my own fault. I fell for it when he offered to feed me a strawberry and quickly replaced the fruit with his tongue. He didn't even touch me anywhere below the neck and shoulders... just sucked on my tongue and kissed me senseless until I was rock hard and writhing on my pool lounger. He pulled back, and when I reached out for more, he just shook his head apologetically and took off toward the pool to participate in the afternoon water slide races.

When he came back, he did pull the privacy curtain, and my dick-drunk ass fell for his antics again. The man was straddling me in the chair, under the very unconvincing guise that he wanted to apply oil to my back. Having him on top of me like that... pinned down by his rock-solid thighs and delicious body weight...

He had me crushed down so securely I couldn't have grasped my own dick if I tried. But I'd be lying if I said I didn't love it.

He let the sun oil drip all over my back, then rolled down my swim trunks a few times, dribbled it over my ass, and massaged it into my cheeks until I was dry humping the lounger.

Just when I was about to beg, he popped up, kissed me on the cheek, and called for another round of drinks.

We came back to the villa and noshed on a huge platter of sushi, oysters, and shrimp that room service had left in the fridge. Then, after I took an unsatisfying solo shower, we made our way back to the main building for another round of drinks.

Now we're sipping mojitos and sitting in a kitschy lounge called Cousteau's Cabin. Or at least I'm sitting. My husband can't stay still or get enough of this place. The walls are lined with nautical instruments and artifacts, and he's been making the rounds, checking them all out. Of course he then has to strike up a conversation with every person in the vicinity of each display. I'd be more amused watching him so in his element if I wasn't so horngry.

I finish off the last sip of my drink, and whether it's his bartender prowess or this profound connection we're exploring together, he looks over at that moment and meets my gaze. He winks at me from across the room—which would be an eye roll-worthy cringe move if it came from just about anyone else. But Jake pulls it off. Because he's Jake.

He smiles broadly and says one last thing to the older couple he's chatting with near a large display of old-school scuba gear before excusing himself.

I can't help but watch him as he walks—no, prowls—toward me. He's laser focused on his target. My cheeks heat, but it's not from sun or rum this time. It's him. It's all him.

"Hey, handsome," he greets me as he bows low and gives me a chaste kiss. He snatches the empty glass out of my hand. "I'll be right back."

The second he sidles up to the bar, the bartender, Jerry—who he's already on a first name basis with—pours us another round. I oscillate between watching my husband flirt with everyone at the bar and watching the three-person band set up on the other side of the lounge.

By the time Jake makes it back to me, the band is doing a final sound check and introducing themselves as The Renegade Pesos. My brain sparks with recognition as the guitarist strums the first sultry chords of "Banana Republics."

"Why are you smiling like that?" Jake teases as he plops down beside me and hands me another mojito.

"I love this song," I reply as the singer starts up.

"You *know* this song?"

I scoff and take a swig of my new drink, the mint and lime dancing on my tongue and warming me from the inside out.

"Of course I know this song. It's Jimmy Buffett, Jake. I'm shocked you *don't* know this song. JB's basically you, just fifty years older."

"JB, huh?" He juts his chin in the direction of the band, looping an arm around my shoulders in the process. "Who knew my husband was a secret parrot head?"

"I've been listening to Jimmy Buffett since I was a kid," I explain. "Every year for as far back as I can remember, my dad would take me on a summer road trip. We never had a destination or a plan. We'd just get in the car and drive. We'd stay in cheap motels and explore weird towns. He'd let me chart the course and pick the route. He'd play Jimmy Buffett exclusively on those drives. I know the words to every song by heart."

He's on his feet the moment I finish.

"Dance with me."

He holds out a hand but doesn't wait for me to take it, instead grasping my arm and pulling me to my feet. I laugh as I try not to spill my drink.

"Jake..." I draw out his name in warning. No one else is dancing. We're surrounded by strangers. If he thinks he's going to get me all worked up in a room full of people right now...

As if reading my mind, he leans in and whispers, "I'm not trying to tease you. I just want to hold you."

Mierda.

I'd almost rather he edge me than hit me with these heartfelt moments that leave me feeling like mush in his big, strong hands.

Maybe it's the scratch of the brush against the cymbal. Or the familiarity of the lyrics. Maybe it's the rum warming me from the inside. But in that moment, as my new husband's invitation lingers between us, all other thoughts dissipate. I let him pull me toward the band, then we start to sway together on our makeshift dance floor.

He wraps his arms around me and pulls me close, just like he promised. I lead, moving my hips in time with the music and adding in a few sultry rolls when the tempo changes. The crowd starts to whoop and holler, but I don't pay them any mind. The band is loving everyone's response, so much so that they repeat a verse to prolong our dance.

I hum in Jake's ear, then whisper the next line of the song, rolling my tongue much longer than necessary when I croon about hustling the senoritas.

He groans quietly, just for me.

"You can do that thing with your tongue?" he questions, nipping at my earlobe as he waits for my reply.

"I'm half Puerto Rican, Jake. I can do it on command and without thinking."

One hand snakes down my spine and settles on my low back. His hold is possessive, the feel of him addictive.

"I'm gonna need you to prove that later when my dick's in your mouth."

I smirk into the crook of his neck and continue to guide him in the dance. The way his hips follow mine and respond to every sway has me dick-drunk and wanting. I'll gladly do a lot more than roll an *R* against his cock tonight.

"Today has been amazing," I croon in his ear. "But I'm ready to be alone with my husband now."

He's grabbing for my hand and leading me to the exit a moment later. "Come on, baby. I owe you an orgasm, and you owe me a lesson in linguistics."

Yes. Finally.

Chapter 23

Jake

We're barely through the door before I've got him shoved against the wall, pressing my body into his with surprising intensity. I love everything about this man's body, or at least what I know of it so far. He's responsive and pliable when he wants to be, then hard and forceful in the next breath. He had me panting like an animal on the dance floor tonight as his hips made promises to my body. We affect each other in such surprising, intense ways. I love how I can make him whimper with one touch, but when I smash my mouth into his and grind my pelvis into him, I know he'll push back and give as good as he gets.

"What do you want, baby?" I grit out as I bite his bottom lip.

He digs his fingers into my back, begging me with his touch. "Jake." My name is a scolding, a punishing command. "You've edged me all fucking day. You could look at my dick right now and I would come. I need it."

"You need it?" I whisper as I cup him through his shorts. "Or you need *me*?"

"I need you. I need you to get me off right now, or so help me..."

I suck his neck until his knees buckle, then bend low to catch him under the ass and lift him against the wall.

"Jake!" he protests, squirming where I have him pinned.

"I've got you, baby," I promise, running the tip of my nose along his jaw.

He wraps his legs around me to help hold himself up as I move my hands to cup his face. His deep brown eyes are blown out, his expression soft and wanting thanks to the mix of mojitos and edging.

"You know this is more than sex, right?" I press my forehead to his and will him to understand. "Earlier this week, when I called this a marriage with benefits... that was then."

His eyes shoot open and assess me. I don't have anything else to say—I can't articulate what's changed over the last few days. But this is suddenly so much more than money and sex. And before we do this for the first time as a married couple, he needs to know that. He needs to know that was then, and this is now. *Now.*

The magical, ethereal, alternate universe where I'm married and so damn happy.

"I know. I feel it, too," he replies earnestly. "But I can't even think straight right now, Jake, let alone talk about the state of our relationship. That's on you. Make me come as fast as you can, then I'll make love to you and show you just how deeply I'm feeling it, too."

I gulp at his demand, lowering him and guiding him to the second story of the villa. I don't think anyone's ever offered to make love to me before. A week ago, I would have scoffed at the very idea. Now I can't wait to explore it with him.

"Get on the bed," I command when we're finally upstairs. I shuck off my shirt and push down my Bermuda shorts. Cory pulls his own turquoise T-shirt over his head, revealing his gorgeous, smooth chest with just the faintest hint of a happy trail guiding me to my target.

"Show me how much you want me."

I stand a few feet away, towering over him, watching expectantly as he unbuckles his belt and lifts his hips to remove his pants and boxers. His dick—his hard, glorious, beautiful dick—springs free with an eagerness that makes me giddy.

"Sit on the edge," I instruct, smirking when his eyes shoot to mine in question. My man doesn't challenge me, though. Instead, he positions his body right where I want it.

His hands brace the edge of the mattress, his cock standing erect and ready.

I prowl toward him, then drop to my knees.

His eyes are clouded with lust as I lean in close, tracing a path from root to tip with just one finger. I lock him in my gaze and make him watch me take his cock in my mouth, lapping up the generous bead of precum on the tip. I lick him clean, then hold out my tongue and arch one eyebrow, making him moan. He may be the one who's been edged all day. But I want him so damn much I ache.

"I'm not gonna last long with my dick in your mouth," he warns.

"Good thing I'm not going to put your dick back in my mouth," I tease as I swallow his saltiness and stretch up to kiss him. He tastes like coconut rum and mint—his tongue greedy as he clashes with me for dominance. I grasp his dick in one hand

and squeeze so hard he moans into my mouth, making me want him even more. Kissing the shit out of him, I set the rhythm, giving him that firm, steady pressure he's been craving all day. I fully expect him to come in less than a minute. I can't wait to make him unravel for me.

I force myself to break our kiss, sitting back on my heels as I continue to jack him. There's no teasing now. No more edging or working him up just to cool him off. I'm a man on a mission.

I duck low, cupping his balls in my free hand before I lick the underside of his dick. He jolts on contact, and I chuckle. If he thinks that feels good...

"Fuck..." he hisses when I suck his nuts into my mouth.

I'm still stroking him, determined to make him explode. His hand lands on my head in encouragement as I relax my jaw. He's a literal mouthful, and I love it. Just like I love being under him, pleasuring him with my hands and my mouth. Giving him what I deprived him of all day.

I alternate between swallowing and sucking his sack, teasing his balls as I stroke his dick.

"Fuck. Jake. Yes. Jake..."

He can barely get the words out. I know he's close. It takes everything in me to keep up the rhythm and timing—steady with the pressure, maintain the perfect pace. He pulls my hair so hard I see bursts of light when he finally hits his peak. I keep working him over, wanting him to ride out every delicious wave of this well-earned release. I've got his dick pointed right toward his abs, intentionally making sure to drain him of every drop so I can make good on my promise.

When I finally come up for air, he's resting back on his elbows, his eyes hazy and soft, looking so damn satisfied.

I use his thighs for leverage as I lean up and lock him in my gaze.

"Did that take the edge off fast enough for you, baby?"

He nods lazily. His eyes are unfocused, like he's in a different universe.

"Look at you," I tease, running two fingers through the cum covering his stomach. "You made a mess, Cory. You completely unraveled and made such a delicious mess for me."

I suck two cum-covered fingers into my mouth and eye-fuck my husband as I lick my hand clean. On the next swipe through his release, I trace one finger down his stomach, past his dick, and all the way down to his hole.

I circle him, pressing up without pushing in, letting him stay lost in the headiness of his post-orgasm bliss. I'm not going to edge him again, but fuck if I don't love teasing his tight little hole. Just like with everything else we've done, he's perfectly responsive. His ass clamps down on my hand and tries to trap me when I pull away. Who am I to deny him? I have enough moisture on the tip of my pinky to push in, so I give him just a little, just like he wants.

He moans and flops back onto the bed completely. "Fuck, Jake. I'm already getting hard again."

"Good," I grunt as I work my finger deeper into his ass. "I'm not done with you tonight."

He sits up in protest, dislodging my hand when he pulls himself upright. "No. We're in this together. Your turn," he insists. "I can't stop thinking about your dick."

Now we're talking.

I slowly and deliberately rise to stand. I'm rock hard and right in his face once I reach full height. He licks his perfect lips, and I don't know where to focus. His chiseled face. His pert brown nipples. His trim, tight waist. That glorious, velvety dick which, like he said, is already hard for me again. Those solid, defined thighs. Every inch of him does it for me.

To my surprise, Cory rises to his feet, too, meeting me where I stand. He pulls me into a searing kiss, flips our positions, and pushes me back on the bed. I can feel his release slick between our stomachs as I sink into the sheets. I shift higher, propping my hands behind my head as I rest against a mountain of pillows.

He's on his hands and knees, crawling to meet me a moment later.

When he takes my dick into his mouth, I can't help but thrust up. I may have been the one edging him all day, but this game has been torture for me, too.

He sinks lower, taking me so deep the crown of my cock hits the back of his throat. Then somehow, miraculously, even with a mouthful of dick, my husband rolls an *R* with his tongue that has me hissing through my teeth.

Holy. Shit.

A few more of those, and I'll be coming faster than he did.

"Baby," I croon, lifting his chin with two fingers so he pops off my dick. "Will you turn around for me while you suck it?"

His eyes light up in understanding as I reach for the lube I left on the nightstand.

He flips around and crawls backward until his thighs are straddling my torso with his ass planted firmly on my pecs. He's got the best butt. Two perfect orbs just begging me to knead and massage and smack them until they turn red with want.

"That's perfect," I praise as I run my palms over his ass and around his thighs, teasing along the well-defined V of his hips. "Now get my dick back in your mouth."

I feel the warmth of his tongue two seconds later.

He's on his hands and knees, which is just how I want him. I quickly pop the top off the lube, then squeeze a generous amount in his crack and on my hand.

I let him work me with his mouth as I tease between his cheeks. Every time he deep throats me, I reward him with a grunt and more pressure on his hole. When I peek at him, I can see him bobbing up and down on my length, and fuck does he look good. When he swallows me down his throat, I breach him, pushing in slowly with one well-lubed finger.

He moans, and it's enough to have my abs clenching in anticipation. I hold steady for a second, letting him get used to this angle. When he starts to suck me again, I move, too.

I swirl my finger around a few times, then drag it in and out. I know right when I've found my target because his jaw goes slack and he hisses. Crooking one finger over his prostate, I grin and watch a few drops of precum drip from his dick to my chest.

I pull out slowly, not because I'm done. But because my baby deserves more. I reenter him with two fingers, and the man moans so loud I feel it in my balls. It's that moan that almost throws *me* over the edge. This angle and this view—fuck. There's definitely something to this mutual pleasure thing.

I beckon against his prostate with two fingers this time, massaging him and loving the way his body responds, only stilling when he speaks.

"Fuck, I'm close again Jake…"

Delight courses through me as I realize I'm about to get him off twice in the span of ten minutes. Refractory who? Maybe he'll let me edge him all the time.

"Can you come like this, baby?" I press down and pet his prostate for extra emphasis when I say "this."

He nods vigorously and makes upside-down eye contact with me through his legs. His sweat's on my legs and his cum's still coating his chest. I love every filthy thing about it. I want him to jizz all over me next.

"Fuck, baby. I want to do this together. Ease up on me a second. Let me get you there again."

He backs off just like I asked. I get to work thrusting in and out, massaging him for all its worth. I could reach down and grab his dick too, but now I'm fascinated by the idea of getting him off like this.

"Jake, fuck…"

I know he's close. His quads are tensing around me.

"Gimme that mouth, baby. I want to come with you," I command, smacking his ass with my free hand as I massage his insides.

A moment later, he sheaths my entire length. I'm a fucking mess of pleasure as I finger him and thrust against his lips. He tries to cry out, but his mouth's so full of dick, I feel his vocalization instead of hear it. I triple my efforts and stroke his prostate faster as the vibrations of his moans unlock my release.

I watch, transfixed, as ropes of cum shoot all over my abs. Then my vision goes blackout-level hazy as my own orgasm rips through my core. It's so intense, I feel the pulsing from my toes to my neck.

Cory slumps down when he's done, his head resting on my legs as his hips and ass wrap around my chest. I can't see what he's doing anymore, but I can feel the little licks and kisses he runs up the length of my totally satisfied dick.

I pull out of his ass, and he whimpers, as reactive as always. I can't resist massaging his glutes with my hands, digging into each perfect cheek with my thumbs. I curl up slowly and run one hand up his spine as I sink my teeth into the meaty flesh of his butt.

He shudders as he chuckles against my legs.

"I didn't know you were such an ass man," he quips as he sits up and turns around.

"Come here," I plead, sounding needier than I intended. The sex was incredible, but now I just want to hold him.

He scoots up the bed and tucks himself into my body. He lets me wrap my arms around him and spoon him.

"I'm not just an ass man," I defend as I run one hand up and down the length of his body. "I'm *your* ass man."

His smile is evident when he says, "Yeah, you are. You're mine."

And fuck if that doesn't light me up and satisfy me just as much as anything we've done tonight.

Chapter 24

Cory

My eyelids flutter open after what might have been the most restful night of sleep of my life. I drifted off curled into Jake. One strong, tatted arm wrapped around me as he whispered the perfect mix of sweet nothings and dirty talk in my ear. I think I've found my new version of heaven: completely sated, exhausted from sun and sex, surrounded by crisp white linen sheets, nestled against his chest.

I stretch my arms overhead and yawn. I'm surprised I don't have more of a hangover after all the mojitos I enjoyed yesterday. But Jake made sure I drank plenty of water, munched on fruit, and had a huge plate of seafood for dinner. He also had me pop two vitamin B capsules before we went to the lounge—an old bartender trick he swears by.

I can't help but smile when I think about last night. The way Jake bounced around the room, chatting up everyone and grinning from ear to ear. How he lit up my insides when he asked me to dance, then held me so tenderly as we swayed to the music.

And then there was the sex.

Although sex doesn't seem like a strong enough word to describe what we shared last night. I had a full-blown out-of-body experience when he sucked on my balls and jacked me to finish after edging me all damn day. Seriously. Out of body. I saw the floating head introduction to *Reading Rainbow* against my closed eyelids when I came.

Then there was that second orgasm.

I thought I saw stars the first time because he'd withheld my orgasm multiple times. Nope. Turns out, Jake just knows how to wring my body out until I'm a panting, sloppy, needy mess.

My second orgasm was just as intense—with his dick in my mouth and his fingers in my ass.

I don't know what it is about this man. Being here, knowing we're in a committed relationship, yet figuring each other out and sharing new experiences together... it's everything.

When I finally open my eyes, I realize Jake's not next to me in bed. I glance at the clock and am shocked to find that it's already ten thirty.

After a quick trip to the bathroom to pee and brush my teeth, I pull on a pair of drawstring linen shorts, then set out to find my man.

I open the sliding glass door to the balcony and squint. The sun is shining, and there isn't a cloud in the sky. Jake's wearing his signature Ray-Bans and a pair of bright teal swim trunks, which he's got hoisted up to tan his thighs. I lick my lips involuntarily at the sight.

He's lying on one of two loungers, with a full room service breakfast spread laid out on the other chair. I could grab a rocking chair and drag it over to join him. But that's not where I want to be.

He grins the second he sees me. I wordlessly straddle his calves and lean forward, intent on getting as close to him as physically possible. I slither up his oil-slicked body, then cross my arms along his lower abdomen and rest my chin on my hands.

"Hi," I greet him lazily, nuzzling into his stomach and inhaling the intoxicating scent of coconut, lime, and salt from his sweat. It takes all my restraint not to dart out my tongue and lick him. He's like my own personalized cocktail—tangy, salty, and sweet.

"Hi," he croons back with so much tenderness my heart catches in my throat. He reaches down and runs his hands through my hair, playing with my tresses and scratching my scalp.

"You sleep okay?" he asks as he continues his ministrations. I don't reply right away. I'm too busy drinking him in, memorizing the way he looks and feels and smells right now. We may have only been able to escape for two nights, but I already know these are memories I'll hang on to forever.

"Mm-hmm," I murmur eventually, peppering each one of his defined, glistening abs with a kiss before resting my cheek directly on his stomach.

He tenses under me, but after a few breaths, he relaxes.

"Are you always this cuddly in the morning?" he teases as he goes back to playing with my hair.

"I guess you're just going to have to find out when we get home." I smirk, but my mind also goes to the heart of what I just said. Will things still feel this magical when we're out of this honeymoon bubble and back in Hampton?

My gut tells me yes. This is it. This is life with Jake. The next two years have the potential to be this joyful, playful, and hot if I let them.

I can't be sure it'll always be this magical, but I am sure of one thing: he's crazy if he thinks he'll be sleeping on the couch once we get home.

I run my tongue between the grooves of his abs, tracing the literal eight-pack of his stomach and loving his taste on my tongue. I can feel him growing hard beneath me, so I do what any good husband in my position would do: I double down and lick him faster.

"Mm, Cor... you feel so good, baby. You make me feel so good." He hooks his hands under my biceps and pulls me up, shifting my body until our faces are just a few inches apart.

He kisses me once, then pulls back and murmurs, "Can I fuck you tonight?"

I know exactly what he means.

"Yes," I reply automatically. I want it so much I ache. I want him. I want to feel him everywhere.

"Are you nervous?" he whispers against my mouth before licking my neck and nipping at my jawline.

Those three words dance up and down my spine until I feel a tingle in my core. I swear this man is the sexual equivalent of nicotine, and I'm already on the cusp of being considered a heavy user. It's his words, his tongue, the way his voice sounds huskier than usual, like he's already so hot for me.

"No." My one-word answer comes out harsh and defensive. He doesn't know I'm trying my hardest to hold back a moan. "I want you."

He cups the side of my head and moves his lips to my ear. "I'm going to make love to you so good, baby. You're gonna be addicted to my dick when I'm done."

I chuckle at his crudeness, but don't bother arguing. What's the point in refuting facts?

"If we need to slow down or you want to stop at any point, just tell me. I want this to be so good for you."

I scoff at the idea of stopping anything. I want him. I want him in every way possible. There's no way I'll be asking him to slow down or hold back tonight.

"I don't need a safe word from you, Jake Whitely," I quip as I grind my hips forward. The sharp grunt he gives up when I press my body into his is hard to miss. I smile into his neck, thrilled that he's clearly affected by me, too.

His fingers flex and knead against the nape of my neck. He's massaging my scalp with this tenderness that makes my insides feel like mush.

He pulls back a few inches to lock me in his gaze. "Why not?"

I honestly don't have a response to that. I can't even remember how to form words in either language I speak as he stares at me intently and massages the crown of my head. He digs in harder until my back is arching in pleasure.

Yep. It's official. I'm putty in Jake Whitely's hands.

"Don't we all deserve a safe word in life?" he asks earnestly.

I blink once. Then again. It takes me another second to realize he's being sincere. Am I really being hit with philosophical truth bombs from my emotionally despondent fuckboy husband? How the hell is he so hot *and* funny *and* wise?

More importantly... *how is he mine?*

I shake my head and try to focus. What are we talking about? Safe words. Okay. I can do this.

"Fine. My safe word is lemonade."

He cocks one eyebrow but doesn't challenge me. He just shifts back a bit more, assesses me up and down, and smirks.

My whole body sparks with need from that one look. My cheeks flush under his gaze. I worry I might be spiking an actual fever. I feel like I'm about to internally combust when he finally bows his head to kiss me.

His lips hover just an inch from mine. He's got this mischievous glint in his eye.

"Okay then. Mine will be Shirley Temple." "You're ridiculous," I tease as I lean forward to kiss him.

"I brought two boxes of condoms, just FYI."

My eyes go wide at his confession. I love that he's prepared. But two boxes? Jesus Christ. I've been thinking about this since our date at the drive-in, but I hadn't really made a decision until this moment.

"We don't need condoms unless you want to use them," I offer, putting the ball in his court.

His arms tighten around me as my words sink in.

"I'm clean," I explain. "I got tested after my last relationship ended because my ex-boyfriend wasn't faithful to me." I deliver the information in what I hope is a cool and unaffected manner. Being in the arms of my husband has this heady effect on my confidence, I guess. "I have the results saved in my email if you want to see them."

"I trust you," he replies automatically. "And you've already seen mine."

"I have. And you said you haven't been with anyone since then?" I confirm, tilting my head to make eye contact. I wait with bated breath for him to confirm what he revealed earlier this week.

He shakes his head. "No one."

I bury my face to hide my delight.

"I saw the date on your results," I say into the side of his neck. I didn't feel comfortable enough to say anything when I connected the dots at the drive-in. But now there's part of me that desperately wants him to know what I know. "Jake... was I your last partner?" I keep my face hidden in the soft, warm dip of his shoulder and hold my breath as I wait for his reply.

His abs tense under me as he wraps his arms around my low back, digging into the muscles right above my ass. A super-charged tension thrums between us. I'm tempted to roll my hips forward or lean up and kiss him. But I'm just too anxious to hear his reply.

"Huh," he finally murmurs, nuzzling his chin against the top of my head. "I hadn't even thought about that, but you're right. You were my last."

Pride surges through me with his confession.

I was his last. *And now I'm his only.*

"We don't need condoms unless you want to use them," I repeat. I was pretty sure that was what I wanted before. Now I know with certainty I can't settle for anything less than everything.

"I don't," he grunts. "I want to be as close to you as possible."

I climb up his body and connect our lips in a searing kiss as the sun warms my back and my man heats me up from below. I let myself get lost in the rhythm of his mouth as my heart hammers out a confession I wasn't expecting to feel.

I want to be as close as possible to him, too.

Chapter 25

Cory

We spent most of the day by the pool, in another private cabana Jake reserved for us. He participated in the afternoon water slide races again and has made friends with every person age six to ninety-six at this resort. I was relieved when he suggested we stay in and order room service tonight. Taking him back up to Cousteau's would be a guaranteed multi-hour experience, given his extroverted-ness and instant popularity with the other guests.

Now we're back in the villa. Showered and clean. Full and satisfied. We both know exactly what comes next.

There's nothing hurried or frantic about tonight, though. There's this thread of tension and want buzzing between us, but it's not desperate or needy like before. It's solid. It's confident. It's sure. Which is exactly how I feel when I look at my husband.

I'm watching him strip out of his clothes, reveling in the way he keeps looking over like he's going to eat me alive as he unbuckles his belt and peels off his shirt.

Fuck, I want him so much.

And I get him. I get all of him.

He's standing in nothing but a pair of white Calvin Kleins, with a bottle of Oak and Cane rum in one hand.

Where the hell did he get that? And why does he look even hotter while holding it?

"I got your favorites right here," he teases as he grips the neck of the bottle and runs his other hand down his dick.

I don't bother arguing. Florida rum and his cock really are two of my favorite things.

"Less talk, more action. Get your dick inside me, Jake."

His eyes light up at my crudeness, and this time, I make a mental note of his reaction. For as filthy as his mouth is, I'm starting to think my man loves to be on the receiving end of dirty talk just as much as he likes to dish it out.

He approaches the bed slowly, making me ache for him a little more with each drawn-out step.

"Get naked, baby. I want you completely stripped down and on that bed, ready for me," he rasps.

His wish is my command. I can't get my clothes off fast enough. I kneel toward the middle of the mattress and can't help but clench my ass in anticipation.

He must notice, because he chuckles as he joins me. He mounts me and straddles the top of my thighs, his body weight pushing me forward in the most delicious way.

"Hold on to the headboard," he murmurs in my ear as he runs his hands up and down my naked form. After all the ways we've teased and played today, I'm surprised he doesn't want to at least kiss me. Maybe he's just as anxious as I am.

But then I notice he's still holding the bottle of rum, along with a jar of something else. And that's when I realize this *is* his foreplay.

He kisses me across the shoulders as he smears something up and down my spine.

"What are you doing?" I ask, craning back and get a better look.

He holds the jar in front of my face so I can read the label. It's coconut oil in solid form, but when exposed to the heat of my body, it melts into my skin. That's what he's spreading all over me.

"I'm a bartender, baby. And you've got these two perfect little back dimples that have been taunting me all weekend. I'm mixing myself a double shot back here."

My cock throbs in response to his words.

Fuck. Yes.

His hands glide over the ridges of my back in hot, demanding strokes. The slickness created by the coconut oil is mesmerizing. With each caress, he travels lower, digging his hands into my muscles until he's kneading my ass. I'm holding back a moan with each and every touch, feeling so desperate for him to hit home.

He works the coconut oil along my crack, but doesn't pay any attention to my hole.

"Tease," I grunt when he goes back to his ministrations without so much as a brush against where I'm aching for him.

"What was that?" he asks impishly. I don't have to turn around to know he's grinning. "I'll give you a tease," he mutters on his next breath.

Suddenly his hands are off my back and spreading me wide. He cups my balls in one hand, then digs his nails into the flesh of my ass with the other. I practically buck off the bed when I feel the warmth of his breath skim my hole.

He licks up and down my perineum, my body quivering in anticipation of where he'll go next.

His mouth is warm and wet as he licks and nibbles all the way around my hole. I want him so fucking bad it hurts, and I'm about to tell him as much when he spreads my ass cheeks wider, spits on my balls, laps that up with his tongue, and continues the line up to my puckered hole.

He works his spit into me with the tip of his tongue, the slight intrusion sparking an insanely intense reaction through my core.

Holy fucking shit.

I'm lucky I didn't just come on contact.

I'm about to start begging when Jake speaks first.

"I think you're just about ready for me, baby."

I scoff at his blatant understatement.

"Just let me take these shots, and I'll give you everything you want."

I feel the liquid hit my back and pool in my Apollo dimples. I can't resist peering back to watch him over my shoulder. He makes a show of running his tongue down the length of my spine, then finally slurps up the rum. Instead of swallowing, he swills it in his mouth, crawls up the bed, and tilts my chin to face him.

I know exactly what he wants without him asking. I greedily seek his mouth and suck in half the rum, savoring the burn and the warmth, tasting the sweetness from the coconut oil and the saltiness of my skin blending together on both our tongues.

He keeps it up, kissing me senseless, until I'm just about ready to flip over and demand he fucks me.

"Tell me what else you want me to do," he asks earnestly.

I don't think he's actually asking for instructions. But I remember how his eyes gleamed when I talked dirty earlier. He doesn't need directions; he wants my words.

"Kiss me like you want me. Mark me like you own me. Tease me, taste me, fuck me because you're mine."

He groans in response, resting his head on my shoulder and whispering "goddamn" right in my ear. "Say it again."

I reach back and grip his head, holding his face near mine. "Mine. You're fucking mine, Jake. This marriage may have been your idea, but now that we're in it... I own you."

He moans again, then kisses me in reverence. The kiss is everything. It's power and it's submission. It's loyalty and wanting. It's his acceptance of my claim. It's permission to accept what we're both feeling.

"How do you want me?"

"Take me from behind," I answer without a hesitation. It's all I've been thinking about since he fingered my ass last night. Him taking control and thrusting into me until we both see stars.

"Hands and knees, baby," he whispers in my ear as he smacks my ass with his free hand. He gives me one more pornographic kiss before he retreats.

I can hear him lubing himself up as he works a finger into me. The initial burn is there, but I'm already so worked up from the rim job, I easily relax under his touch. He starts strumming me like a fine-tuned instrument. I practically mewl when he brushes my prostate, but he doesn't linger long.

He works another digit inside, running his free hand over my ass and circling around to grab my dick. He kisses the length of my spine as he preps me. "I got you, baby. Relax for me. You're doing so good."

When I'm thrusting back on his hand, he knows I'm ready for more. A minute later, he's notching his dick in my ass. The burn is nothing to the fire that's being stoked in my belly. Fuck, do I want this—want him. It takes everything in me to hold still and let him work his way in.

When he's finally sheathed in my ass, he moans. "Co-ry." My name is glorious, drawn-out devotion. "Baby, you feel so good. You're so fucking tight."

I blush at his praise, then fold forward with that first thrust. The man is huge—I've never been this full in my life. He rolls his hips forward, driving into me with so much force my body jolts, and I scramble to grab the headboard again. I fucking love it.

I reach down to wrap my hand around my dick, but don't make it that far.

"Mine," he growls possessively as he fists my rock-hard length. "If you get to own me, then I'm staking my claim, too."

He fucks me and strokes me, building me higher and higher. Every time he moves inside me, I feel a part of my soul blend with his. A sheen of sweat coats my skin, making me feel animalistic and needy. The way he's hitting just the right spot without any sort of instruction has me lost to the sensation like I've never been before. I want more. I want everything. I want to stay lost in this all-consuming state of bliss. In minutes, my toes start tingling.

"Jake," I choke out.

"Thank fuck," he grits. "I'm so close, too." He presses one hand on my low back for traction, then goes wild, thrusting and jacking me to completion. I clench around his length right before we both fall. The tightening of my channel sends him over the edge; my name coming out of his mouth in reverence has me following a moment later. I feel his cum spurt in my ass as my own release pools in his hand.

We collapse on the bed, panting. We're a mess of cum and sweat, truth and vulnerability. I don't dare speak the words out loud, but that was the most intimate and satisfying sexual experience of my life. I don't ever want this feeling to end.

Chapter 26

Jake

There's nothing quite like Northeast Ohio in the fall. It's still warm enough during the day to walk around without a coat. Then it cools down to this delicious crispness every evening.

We got home from our honeymoon on Monday, Clinton's and The Oak officially became mine on Tuesday, September first. Cory started classes on Wednesday, then I held my first staff meeting last night. Now it's finally Friday, and I'm more than ready to experience my first weekend as a business owner while also enjoying some quality time with my man.

I woke up this morning to that biting cold nipping at me outside the covers, but I had a warm, solid body next to me to keep me warm. We fell into a routine so fast, it's stupid. We got the rest of Cory's things moved into my condo—*our* condo—and we've taken to having coffee together at the kitchen island each morning. He likes his espresso iced, so I make it for him the night before, then let it chill overnight. I've had to run over to

Acme every day this week because I keep learning about new things he likes. He never asks me to, but I'll do anything to earn one of those grins.

I enter The Oak and exhale. No other place has ever felt like home. The walls are covered in old pictures and sports memorabilia from both Archway Preparatory Academy and Hampton High School. Fitting, really, since I attended each school for two years myself.

Cole and Teddy are both behind the bar, working through our morning prep list. The transition to owner feels foreign and yet simple at the same time. I hired this staff. I trained them all. They know my expectations, and we all work well together.

"Morning, boys," I call out over the music. We play 80s, 90s, and early 2000s exclusively, which, according to my nieces, is technically the oldies. My favorite Incubus song is blasting through the speakers. It must be one of Teddy's favorites too, based on how he's giving Brandon a run for his money as he belts out the chorus.

Instead of joining them like I usually would, I circle around to the end of the bar and setup my laptop. There's an office in the back of Clinton's that I could use, and maybe someday I will. But just last week, I was a manager and bartender. It's feels too soon to be holing up in an office and pretending to be some big shot owner.

I typically spend Fridays making schedules and setting up the specials for the weekend. Now I have to worry about things like payroll, tracking business expenses, and setting up meetings with the health insurance rep so I can get my staff full benefits.

It's not the smartest financial move—Clinton's makes steady but slim margins, and The Oak has only been open for just over a year. Despite being packed every weekend, we're very much a new business. But I watched one of my oldest friends work her ass off, desperate to graduate from college and get a job with benefits so she could get the risk-reducing surgeries she needed. I'm in a position to make sure my staff never have to face something like that, so I'm doing something about it. Besides, Cory and I both work here now, and I want to make sure he's covered and taken care of, too.

I'm still toiling away on next week's schedule when Cole unlocks the front door at four. He greets our first customers, and I don't even have to look up to know who just walked through the door.

Tommy's staggered around this town his whole life. He's mostly harmless, and we've shared enough conversations across this bar that I've grown to genuinely enjoy his company.

"Tommy," I call out, lifting one hand in greeting. "How's it going, man?"

He grunts as he climbs onto a barstool a few seats down from me. He's got a leg that gives him trouble.

"You doing all right?" I push.

He finally settles in his seat and turns in my direction. "Fine, fine," he insists with a wave of his hand.

Teddy sets a whiskey sour in front of him without any prompting, and Tommy gulps down a mouthful, then sighs contentedly.

"I hear congratulations are in order."

I freeze at his comment. I'm sure word has gotten around. When you've lived in the same town your whole life, your business is everyone's business, always. I just don't know which life achievement he's congratulating me on.

My eyes divert to my wedding band, noticing the way it shines under the pendant light where I'm sitting. Most of the time, I don't even remember I'm wearing it, because it just feels right.

"It's been a crazy week for sure," I reply. There. That seems open-ended and safe.

Tommy takes another sip of his drink. "I didn't think I'd live to see a day when Mike Hobbs wasn't the owner of Clinton's Family Restaurant. Or of this place too, I guess. But he made the right call, selling them to you."

I smile and accept the compliment, relieved I don't have to delve into details about my sudden marriage. Not because I'm ashamed or because I don't want to talk about it. But my relationship with Cory is something I want to protect. I don't want to talk about my marriage with a casual acquaintance, because it's nothing like I expected. It's sacred. It's not for anyone but us.

"Well, I heard even more congratulations are in order." The shrill voice has me slow-blinking and taking a deep breath before I look farther down the bar.

Skippy Baker-Brooks is perched on the end of a barstool smack in the middle of the bar, swirling an ice cube in her glass of white wine. I do my best to smile and feign interest—she'll be here all night, and I'm not about to piss off a customer who's one day tab will cover half my payroll expenses for the weekend. "Oh yeah? What's that?" I ask indifferently.

Skippy was friends with my dad in high school—which tells me everything I need to know about her. Now she's a realtor who "makes her own hours" and ends up sitting at my bar more afternoons than not.

"Don't try to deny it, Jacob. I see the ring on your finger."

I wasn't denying anything. I just wasn't offering up my personal life for speculation. I brush my thumb along the smooth platinum on my left hand.

"So who's the lucky lady?"

I can't help but scoff. I've been out so long that it rarely comes up in conversation anymore. Most of the douche bags who gave me a hard time in high school have long since moved away. Most everyone else who lives in Hampton is either accepting or ignorant. I have no shame about my bisexuality. I'm confident in who I am. But this heteronormative bullshit always grinds my gears.

"Who said I married a lady?" I retort.

At that, Cole sucks in a sharp breath as he turns around and beelines for the opposite end of the bar.

It's like the universe wants to support me in my efforts to put Skippy Baker-Brooks in her place, because at that exact moment, my husband walks through the front door. He's coming right from class, dressed in khakis and a deep green button up that fits his frame like a glove. I can't help but admire how hot he looks today: his hair perfectly styled, as always, and he's got his messenger bag slung over his arm. And then the real kicker: he's wearing his glasses. I fucking love it when he wears his glasses.

I watch him scan the bar, then look around at each of the booths against the back wall. When his eyes finally land on me, I feel an almost Zen-like sense of calm. I grin and cock my head, urging him to get over here. He gives me a half smile and walks over to join me.

Cory says hi to Cole and Teddy, then turns to face me.

"Hi, baby," I greet, running my hands on either side of his waist and pulling him closer to where I sit on my stool.

"Hey," he replies feebly.

"Hey, yourself," I reply in challenge, smoothing one hand over his jaw and tilting his chin. I assess him, dread twisting in my gut as I realize something's wrong. I don't even bother asking if he's okay.

"Talk to me, baby," I urge.

He drags his messenger bag off his shoulder and sets it at my feet. Then he leans in, letting me hold him as I run both hands up and down his back.

"Co-ry..." I can be strong. I can hold him up. But I have to know what we're up against.

"It was just a shittastic day."

I smirk at his choice of words. I taught him that.

"Tell me about it," I encourage as he takes a seat on the barstool next to me. "You want a drink?" I add as an afterthought, an idea sparking in my mind.

Cory nods and gets comfortable.

"Yo. Cole. Pour me an Oktoberfest, and mix up a mojito for my husband, please."

"You got it, boss."

I know I should be fully focused on Cory right now, but I can't help glancing past his shoulder to witness the shock on Skippy's face. The joke's on her, really. There's no way she didn't know I was bi. She just chose to assume that if I got married, it would be to a woman. Serves her right for doling out microaggressions in this day and age.

"Remember how the registrar's office unenrolled me from all my classes because my tuition was late?" Cory asks.

I give him a pointed look as Cole brings over our drinks.

"I remember how the school dicked you around when they canceled your assistantship and didn't even give you a chance to pay the tuition before unenrolling you, yeah."

He takes a sip of his mojito and smiles. I don't know if he can tell or not, but I started stocking Oak and Cane, his favorite, as our house rum this week.

"Well, most of my professors were super understanding, and I got back into every class."

"That's great!" I encourage before he hits me with a look.

Oh. Too soon.

"Except now I'm the odd man out in my practicum cohort. Everyone's already paired up for this big assignment, and it counts for half my grade. Since I technically wasn't enrolled, I wasn't accounted for when everyone partnered up, so now I'm stuck in a three-way with my arch enemy, Jared, and his best friend, Simone."

"You better not be having a three-way without me, baby," I tease.

He shakes his head sadly. "Believe me. There's no part of this project that I'm going to enjoy. Jared is always trying to push my buttons. I have no desire to be stuck with him all semester. The alternative is dropping the class and taking it later, but it's only offered in the fall."

"That's bullshit," I huff, slamming my beer glass down on the bar top. "They screwed you over, Cory. You shouldn't have last pick for a project that's so important."

"It doesn't work that way." He shrugs, defeated. "It'll be fine. I'm just bummed."

"Hey, at least it's already Friday," I try to assure him. "I'm really excited to celebrate our one-week wedding anniversary," I tease as I rub one hand up and down his back.

He scoots his seat closer to mine, then rests his head on my shoulder and sighs. I wrap one arm around him, nuzzling in to kiss him on the forehead without giving the action a second thought.

I chance a glance across the bar to where Skippy is blatantly ignoring me, her back turned as she guzzles her wine and plays on her phone. My eyes land on Tommy for a moment, only to find him staring.

This is my bar. This is my husband. But I am acutely aware that Tommy could react like Skippy to my clearly fluid sexuality. I'm amused by her getting huffy with me. But I would hate for him to be uncomfortable.

Our eyes lock over Cory's head, and he smiles. He lifts his glass in our direction as I breathe out a sigh of relief. "Good for you, buddy. Good for you."

Chapter 27

Cory

I roll over and seek him out, my hands searching and my body needy in the dark of night. I have no idea what time it is or why I'm awake. My body woke of its own volition, craving his touch. His comfort. His affection. I woke up craving Jake.

But he's not lying next to me. I brush my hand across the still-warm fabric where I know he fell asleep in my arms. It's not until my eyes adjust that I see he's sitting up, perched on the end of the bed.

"What's wrong?" I ask, my voice groggy and disjointed from sleep.

"Shit," he mumbles as he turns to me. His face is illuminated by the blue-light glow of his phone. "I didn't mean to wake you, baby. Go back to sleep."

I shake my head and try to make sense of what's happening. He didn't answer my question.

"Jake. What's wrong?"

He sighs, then rises out of bed and rolls out his shoulders twice. "Dem's got a problem at the bar. Young kid who's plastered but refuses to call a ride share. I think I need to go down there and help him."

I nod, even though I don't really understand.

"Why don't they just call the police?" I ask through a yawn.

Jake makes a noise of contrition as he fumbles around to pull on his pants. "I'd like to avoid that if the kid's just having a tough night. There were probably lots of times someone wanted to call the cops on *me* when I was his age…"

I yawn again and slump back onto the pillows. A glance at the clock tells me it's only one thirty, meaning I've only been asleep for half an hour anyway. "Want me to go with you?" I offer. Not because I want to get out of this comfy bed. But because it seems like the husbandly thing to do.

"No, baby." Jake leans across the mattress and cups my face in one hand. "You stay here and rest. If I know I've got you waiting for me in bed, I'll get this sorted that much faster."

He kisses my forehead as my eyes drift closed.

Even in sleep, my body knows something isn't right. I don't know if I wake up because of a noise or because I can sense he's not there. But it's four thirty, and I'm staring at Jake's empty spot in our bed.

I stumble out of the bedroom and check around the condo, just in case. But he's not in the kitchen or living room, the bathroom or the workout room. He's not here.

We live less than five minutes away from The Oak. He said he'd be right back. Where the hell is he?

I send him a text to check in, then another a few minutes later. Both go unread.

He left more than three hours ago. He promised he'd come home as soon as he could. What if something happened? What if the kid he was trying to help got belligerent and lashed out? What if some drunk asshole ran a light or swerved and hit him?

I lean against the quartz countertop of the kitchen island, hissing when my skin touches the cold stone. Jake loves fall—so much so that the heat is off and the windows are wide open. The condo is frigid. I didn't mind waking up to chilly fall air all week because I had him to keep me warm. But everything feels colder when he's gone.

I don't want to be that person. But my mind is playing tricks on me now. Coming up with worst-case scenarios. Picking at my sensibilities because of sleep deprivation and old insecurities.

I unlock my phone and just do it.

The phone at The Oak is behind the bar, right in the middle of the action. Even if Jake is occupied, Dempsey or one of the guys will answer and give me an update. They wouldn't leave Jake alone to deal with an unruly customer.

Each time the phone rings, chills tickle down my spine.

Once.

Twice.

Three times.

Then four.

I'm shivering uncontrollably by the fifth ring, a perpetual freeze settling in my gut.

No one's answering. I don't know where my husband is. Something could be very wrong.

I blow out a long breath and try to center myself. I know I'm doom spiraling—jumping to conclusions and making baseless assumptions. But he promised he'd be home as soon as he could. Without any updates or any way to reach him...

I huff out a sigh and pace the kitchen, annoyed at myself for the level of anxiety I'm letting grip me right now. But that's the thing about anxiety—I can't pick when it flares up or how high it decides to climb.

Coming off a stressful week certainly doesn't help. And being exhausted isn't doing me any favors, either.

I peek at the kitchen clock—4:44 am—and consider my next move. I desperately need some advice right now. Someone outside the Jake Whitely bubble who could help me put this in context. But Tori is probably asleep. Abuela is still at work. And Lia has been giving me the cold shoulder since she found out about our marriage via text, which really sucks, because I know for a fact she's awake at this hour.

I tried to talk to her at work on Thursday after Jake announced the buyout. But she just wasn't having it. She's upset about me keeping secrets: about Jake, about Clinton's and The Oak—lying by omission, she dubbed it.

I'm so lost in my own head that I don't hear the door open. It's not until he's strolling through the kitchen, spinning his keys on one finger and whistling softly, that I realize he's home.

He freezes when he sees me.

"You're up?"

I scoff and shake my head. "Of course I'm up, Jake. You left hours ago, and I haven't heard from you since."

His eyes flare, his expression softening in the next breath. "Shit. I figured you'd go back to sleep and forget I even left."

Shame and something akin to anger blends in my belly. He thought I'd just go back to sleep? He was counting on me not noticing or remembering he was gone?

"Where were you?" I whisper. If I let myself speak any louder, I'll yell.

He cocks his head and raises one eyebrow. "I was at The Oak, just like I said."

I shake my head and avert my gaze. He wasn't at The Oak thirty minutes ago when I called. And we only live five minutes from downtown Hampton. Four, if there's no traffic, which there shouldn't have been at five on a Sunday morning.

As embarrassing as my confession is, I still feel compelled to call him out.

"You weren't at The Oak when I called there a little bit ago."

His eyes widen to saucers. He takes a few cautious steps into the kitchen but doesn't circle the bar to close the space between us.

"You called the bar?"

I turn to stare at the fridge before responding, suddenly fascinated by his collection of magnets. Las Vegas. Myrtle Beach. Orlando. Boulder Springs. When I look back to meet his gaze, I've built up just enough courage to lash out.

"I woke up and you weren't here. I texted you a few times. I was worried, Jake. I was worried something happened to you, or the kid you went to help was causing more trouble than expected. I called The Oak to check on you. I'm entitled to know my husband's whereabouts in the middle of the night."

"Maybe you should put a tracker on me," he quips. The remark is snide, although his tone is playful.

But I'm not interested in letting him get away with shit right now.

"Maybe you should have enough respect for me that I don't need to *track* you," I bite back.

He's around the bar two seconds later.

"Baby," he croons, trying to pry my arm off the counter and pull me into a hug. I let him—reluctantly—but even with his arms wrapped around me, I don't return his embrace.

"I'm sorry," he starts. At least he knows he fucked up.

I peer up at him—he's a few inches taller than me—and wait for him to go on.

"When I got to The Oak, it was worse than I thought. The kid was ranting and raving, wasted and probably high. Dem had his keys, but he wouldn't give up his phone or give them any information on who to call to pick him up. We *could* have called the police—but when I looked at his ID, I realized it was a fake."

My eyes widen in horror. "Who…"

"Cole," he replies before I ask the question. "If someone opens a tab, we hold their credit card and ID, just to make closing out easier at the end of the night. Cole didn't know it was a fake, which happens. I get that. But honestly, it was a really bad fake. Dem knew right away when he saw it, hence why he called me."

Jake shakes his head before continuing. "It's not even about the fine against The Oak—I just hated the idea of calling the cops and the kid getting arrested. He was having a bad night."

"Clearly," I interject.

My sarcasm is met with an unappreciative glare.

"Here's the thing you have to understand. I *was* that kid. He obviously had some demons to deal with. He wasn't there with anyone, so he wasn't doing it for attention. I didn't get his story, but pain recognizes pain. I couldn't stand the thought of the cops dragging him back home and telling his parents what he did."

"So what did you do?" I snake my arms around my husband's waist and let him hold me a little tighter. He releases a breath and drops his shoulders a couple of inches now that I'm letting him in.

"The kid pushed over an entire stack of clean glasses and broke about a dozen of them. I convinced him to come with me, buckled him in and put the Jeep's child lock on. Then I drove him home and helped him sneak back into his house."

He shrugs like there aren't a dozen things wrong with that situation. The hooligan breaks the law, puts The Oak's liquor license at risk, and destroys his property, and Jake's response is to help him get away with it?

"Once that was handled, I circled back to The Oak. The guys were still cleaning up glass. When they finished, I offered to make them breakfast, so we locked up and went over to Clinton's."

Understanding settles in. At least now I know why no one answered when I called.

"I'm sorry I worried you," he insists, placing one finger under my chin to lift my head, forcing me to meet his gaze. I don't doubt his story. Or that he's sorry. But my anxiety wasn't the only problem tonight.

"You have to treat me like a partner, Jake. You told me you'd be right back. It's okay that everything took longer than expected. But you should have texted me to give me an update."

"I thought you were asleep! And I didn't do anything wrong!"

He stiffens in my arms, clearly on the defense. I inhale through my nose and try to steady myself. I know he's got to be exhausted, too. But this whole scenario could have been avoided with better communication.

"Imagine if you woke up and I was gone. I wasn't answering your texts. I didn't pick up when you called."

His jaw ticks as he stares down at me through hooded eyes.

"I'd be pissed. And worried. But mostly pissed."

I nod slowly. "I'm responsible for my reactions and emotions, which, I'll admit, got the better of me tonight. But being in a relationship means that when you have the ability to meet the other person's needs, you meet them. I won't play the role of the nag. It's on you to communicate with me."

"I'm sorry, baby," he says, much more fervently this time. "I wasn't thinking about anything but taking care of business. I should have kept you updated. It won't happen again."

Fair enough. I'm not interested in harping on him or holding grudges. I yawn and rest my cheek on his chest.

"You tired, baby?"

I nod against him, letting the weight of exhaustion consume me now that I know he's safe.

"Want me to tuck you in?" he asks as one hand massages the base of my scalp while the other slinks down and presses into my low back. The way he says it makes it sound like we're about to do a lot more than sleep.

"Yes, please," I quickly reply, looking up at him with a smirk.

"I really am sorry," he whispers in my ear. With the way he's holding me, I know he means it.

"I know. I'm not upset anymore," I reassure him.

"Good. But I still need to make it up to you. Come on, baby. I'm going to tuck you in and make sure you get a *really* good night's sleep."

Chapter 28

Cory

"Nieto!" she cries when she sees me in the doorway. "Come in, come in!"

I exhale a sigh of relief. I haven't been back to my abuela's house in almost two weeks. Between work and school and Jake, I've been overwhelmingly busy. I haven't done a great job prioritizing her, but she seems excited to see me anyway.

I make my way into the living room and wrap her in a hug. As soon as I've got my arms around her, she starts jabbering in Spanish about how I never visit, and I don't even call. What's the point of having a cell phone if I can't be bothered to send her a text? Did I forget where she lives? Did I forget who raised me?

Ah. There it is.

I can't even be defensive about what she's saying—I *have* been wrapped up in my new life. Plus, I've never been in a position like this before: It's different having to make time to drive out to Cascade Falls to visit. Until a few weeks ago, we'd lived together my whole life. Even when we had opposite schedules, we'd at least catch each other coming and going most days.

"Lo siento, lo siento. Life has just been... crazy lately," I admit. "I promise I'll be better about coming over. We should plan a standing weekly visit at minimum so I don't lose track of my days again."

Satisfied, she smiles, then pinches my cheek harder than necessary. "Are you hungry?"

"No," I insist with a firm, pointed look. If this woman starts cooking for me, I'll be here for hours. Literal hours. She loves to feed me but always overdoes it and insists on making everything from scratch. I have to be at work by four p.m. today, so although I have plenty of time to visit, I do *not* have time to pay the respects required when Abuela whips up a five-course meal.

She *tsks* at my rejection, then sits on the couch. She finds the remote and mutes the soap she's watching before patting the cushion beside her.

"Sit down, nieto. You have a lot to tell me, I am sure."

That I do. Where do I even start?

"Tu esposo—es bueno contigo?"

"Abuela." I level her with a pointed look. "He's *so* good to me. So, so good. He's thoughtful. Funny. Charming. And that inheritance I told you about already came through. He's been spoiling me nonstop."

She grins at my enthusiasm.

"But this marriage—what did you call it? For convenience? Why are you smiling like a lovesick fool?"

Her question reminds me of just how far we've come in so little time.

Why *am* I smiling like a lovesick fool? And even if I think I know what this is—what's brewing between us and growing stronger each day—how do I explain it to her?

I gather my thoughts for a moment, tracing the brown and gold floral print on the couch that's been in this living room for as long as I can remember. I decide right then and there I'm going to buy her a new couch as soon as possible.

"What Jake and I have now... it's not what we started with," I confess. "It's so different from what I thought it'd be, Abuela. He's different. I'm different. It's better than I could have ever dreamed."

She assesses me through squinted eyes, her serious gaze searching my face and looking for my truth. I appreciate her concern. But it's so unwarranted it isn't funny. For as much as she loves her telenovelas and fairy tales, my abuela is a cynic when it comes to real life love.

I'm not sure there's anything I can say to make her believe me. She'll just have to see for herself. Jake keeps bugging me about coming over to meet her. I make a mental note to plan something soon. But until then...

I pull out my phone and open the camera app. "Look," I tell her, swiping through to the pictures we took in the airport before our honeymoon.

I hand her the phone and watch her eyes grow wide as she swipes through the dozen or so selfies Jake took of us showing off our rings. The first few are cute and smiley. But it's the next several when he's kissing me and making me squirm that tell the real story: we're into each other in ways most people dream of. The pictures radiate happiness. Those selfies encompass the best parts of my life.

"Nieto..." she whispers, looking up and handing me back the phone. "Estás enamorado."

It's not a question. It's a statement.

And for the first time ever, I admit to myself that what my abuela sees so clearly on the screen is true. What part of me has known since that night at Clinton's when things shifted between us. What I've wanted more than anything for my entire life.

I am in love.

--

Tori: Rhett just told me Jake bought you a Tesla. CORY!

I grin as I read her message and unlock my new ride. Jake keeps insisting I just have to walk up to the car and open the door, but I'm used to having to physically insert a key into the handle to unlock it. It'll be a while before I'm comfortable with every bell and whistle on this thing.

Cory: Can confirm.

I snap a picture of me in front of the car and shoot it off with the message before climbing into the driver's seat.

Tori: Stop. STOPPPPP. Of course it's black. And he got one too? You and your husband have MATCHING CARS? Why do I feel like every time we talk, you tell me the bare minimum about your "fake" marriage, then Rhett tells me something Jake said or did that makes me swoon?

I cringe at the word "fake" in quotation marks. I get where she's coming from, though. All she knows is what I've shared. Well, that, and what Jake tells Rhett, which Rhett then tells her. Maybe that's something Jake and I need to have a conversation about. I trust his judgment, and I know Rhett is his best friend.

But he may not realize that anything and everything he says will be repeated to Tori, which inevitably makes its way back to me.

I think about how I want to respond, considering I haven't talked about the surprising and profound depth of our relationship with anyone. Or I hadn't—until I spilled all the tea to Abuela over the last few hours.

For as much as I feel protective over our marriage and what it's transforming into, I don't think I can keep it all to myself any longer. It's not fair for me to get defensive when people inquire about my "fake" relationship if I haven't given them a clear picture of how it's evolved.

Cory: The last few weeks have been incredible, Tor. Jake is just... he's everything. It started casual for sure, but it quickly turned into more. There's so much more to him than I realized. He's done more for me in the past month than anyone has ever done. It's nice to be taken care of... to be wanted. I think I'm falling in love.

Her reply comes through immediately.

Tori: CORY!!!!

Cory: I know. I KNOW. Ugh.

Tori: Not ugh. I'm so happy for you!! I want to hear every juicy detail, but I'm about to go into a meeting. Call me this weekend so we can catch up?

Cory: Okay. Can you do me a favor, though?

Tori: Anything

Cory: Maybe don't tell Rhett I said that? Everything is amazing with Jake... but it's still so fresh and new. I haven't even said those words to him yet.

Tori: I won't. I promise.

I blow out a breath, dock my phone, then put the car in drive to head back to Hampton.

A pit of concern rolls through me when I think about what I just confessed.

But it doesn't feel as horrible as I thought it would.

Probably because it's true. And the truth always feels right, even when it's hard.

I'm falling in love with Jake Whitely.

--

I pull into the parking lot behind Clinton's with just a few minutes to spare before my shift, which means I can't avoid her when I see Lia in the parking lot.

I get out of the car and accept my fate. There's no way she didn't see me pull in.

"Nice car," she quips over her shoulder as she walks toward her pickup truck without breaking pace.

"Thanks," I offer amicably. I meet her gaze and smile, trying to reach out and connect with my best friend. We've barely talked in weeks, and I miss her.

"Did your husband buy that for you?"

I drag in a long breath and put on my proverbial button covers. Lia and I have been friends for five years. I know all her defense mechanisms. But I refuse to let her push my buttons about this.

"He did," I reply honestly. "Listen, I have to get in there now, but do you think we could hang out and talk this—"

She stops in her tracks and hits me with a look that makes me cower. "You have to get in there?" she challenges. "Being married to the boss isn't enough of an excuse to show up late to work?"

Her vitriol shocks me. I knew she was annoyed, but I didn't expect her to be hateful about this whole thing.

"That was low, even for you," I lob at her. "I understand that you're upset, but you don't know the first thing about—"

"You're right," she spits out as she takes several heated steps toward me. "I don't know a damn thing about what's going on with you, because you won't talk to me!"

My eyes widen as I process her words.

"Wait. You're not upset that I'm with him?" I've spent the last few weeks worrying about marrying a man I'd originally sworn off because of her. On the surface, I didn't do anything wrong—but deep down, it feels like a betrayal.

She rolls her eyes and crosses her arms before hitting me with an unamused glare. "I couldn't care less that you're letting Jake Whitely get it in."

Heat explodes like napalm in my chest, coursing through my veins and rushing all the blood to my head. "Watch it," I warn, taking two steps of my own so we're standing toe to toe. "That's my husband you're talking about."

She smirks and shakes her head.

"That. That right there. *That* reaction is what I'm upset about, Cory. Somehow, in the blink of an eye, you went from secretly marrying Jake for what—money? Tuition payments? To somehow getting dick-drunk and sappy over a man you've crushed on for years."

I blink in slow motion as her words sink in.

"Did you forget how he dropped me without any warning or context? Or how he acted like nothing ever happened between you two when you stopped taking his calls? He may be your husband, but we both know Jake's a hell of a piece of work. But you've let his charm blind you from that. I'm worried about you, Cor. Worried you're in too deep... that he's going to hurt you."

My body was on fire a moment ago. But now it feels like she's doused me with a five-gallon bucket of ice.

"Look," she tightens her messy bun and rolls out her shoulders, "I miss you. I hate this. I would love to get together soon and catch up. But you have to understand where I'm coming from. This whole thing is crazy. I don't want to see you get swept up in something that isn't going to last. It's Jake, Cory. Jake. He needs something from you right now, and I know that probably feels good. But he won't need you forever. And I just worry about you falling for someone who's clearly using you."

That shocks me into silence, and I'm left standing in the parking lot in a daze. Lia stands there and stares right back at me, willing me to reply. Willing me to dispute her argument.

It's not until my phone vibrates in my pocket that I realize I'm officially late for work.

Jake: Hey, baby. Where are you? Mitch said you haven't shown up for your shift yet. I just wanted to make sure you're okay.

"Gotta go," I murmur as I lift the phone in her direction. "The man who's supposedly using me just checked in to make sure I'm all right." I level her with a glare, then turn on my heel to head inside.

Jake's message was filled with nothing but genuine concern—I know that. I *feel* that, even through a text. But with an attitude like that, there's no way Lia can be convinced of the depth of what I'm going through. It's a lost cause.

"Cory," she calls out as I walk away. But she was out of line. And I'm already late for work. I raise one hand over my head dismissively and keep walking.

Chapter 29

Jake

Tonight, The Oak is on fire. Not literal fire. This kind of fire casts a spell over a room and makes a place just feel good. This is why I love what I do. It's the energy. It's creating an atmosphere where people can let loose and have fun.

The whole place feels like a party. Every seat is filled, every high top claimed. The booths along the back are overflowing. I've done a physical head count twice so far—we're really that crowded, and I have no interest in having the fire Marshall show up. The guys are working their asses off but having fun with it, and it shows. The whole room has this higher vibration. It'd be impossible to walk into my bar right now and not smile.

I've been on my feet for hours, but I have no interest in slowing down anytime soon. I get so energized by nights like tonight. I wish I could bottle up this feeling and sell it as an energy drink.

Some people find their calling in medicine or teaching, in ministry or the arts. But this right here is my domain. Creating a space where people want to be is my passion.

I worked behind the bar for a while, but now I'm clearing cups and wiping down tables. That's one of the things I love most about being the boss: I can lean in to my natural tendencies to make the rounds and move from one task to the next instead of being stuck in one place.

We've got a killer playlist going tonight, and there are already a few people on the dance floor, even though it's not even eleven. I'm going to check in with my staff and see if they're okay pushing last call back an hour. There's no way this place will be cleared out in an hour.

Speaking of the time… that's my second favorite thing about being the boss. I get the final say in the schedules. And lately, I've been coordinating mine and Cory's shifts so he works at Clinton's on nights I'm here at The Oak. Not only does that mean our days off are aligned, but it also means he can come hang out with me after he closes.

Someone calls me from behind the bar, but I can't tell who. I grab my rag and spray bottle and make my way toward the front, stopping to say hi to a few regulars as I snake through the crowd.

"Oh my God, I love your shirt!!"

I freeze where I stand when a woman about my age wearing a pink tiara and sash waltzes right into my path. I assess her from head to toe, noting the penis emblem on her sparkly crown as well as the stiletto heels she's carrying in one hand.

Bachelorette party. Yikes. By the looks of it, they've been at it for hours. And I just walked right into the line of fire.

"Seriously. This looks sooo good on you," she croons, running her hot pink nails down the front of my V-neck. I bite back a laugh and push down the urge to tell her there's half a dozen other guys behind the bar wearing the exact same shirt. What can I say? I picked a universally flattering style when I selected the black V-neck uniforms for The Oak.

"Jake! Seriously."

Saved by the bell. Or, in this instance, the Teddy. He's leaning over the bar and waving me over, desperate to get my attention.

"Congrats on your impending nuptials," I tell the bride-to-be, winking as I walk away.

She lets out a little pout, but I'm grateful I escaped before her friends could zero in on me, too.

"We're out of peach schnapps," Teddy informs me when I get within range.

"Seriously?" I can't even remember the last time I poured a drink with peach schnapps...

Realization sets in when I hear a high-pitched chant start up across the room. "Sex on the Beach! Sex on the Beach!"

"Say no more," I assure him, rapping my knuckles on the bar. "I'll be right back."

Before I can turn around, a hand glides over my shoulder. The touch is smooth, familiar. Recognition comes when I hear the voice in my ear on the next breath.

"Small business ownership looks good on you, Jake Whitely."

I drop my rag and spray bottle and pull him into a hug. "Drew!" I exclaim affectionately. "It's so good to see you, man."

He returns my embrace but lingers a bit longer than is comfortable. "Ditto," he murmurs in that low baritone that used to make me shiver.

When he finally pulls back, he gives me the proper once-over that makes me inexplicably squirm. "How have you been?" he asks, running that same hand up and down my bicep a few times before letting it rest on my shoulder.

I shrug him off as subtly as I can, but he notices. He's always been perceptive.

"I've been great." And I really mean it. I do a quick scan of the bar. Everything that I ever wanted—plus a few things I never knew I'd have the privilege of calling mine—have fallen into place over the last month. I'm not exaggerating when I say this is the happiest I've ever been.

"I hear congratulations are in order?"

He scans the bar, then glances at the logo on my V-neck. This shirt's getting an above-average amount of attention tonight, that's for sure.

"In more ways than one. I bought Mike out, so now I own Clinton's and The Oak, which you probably heard," I explain with a sweep of my hand. "Got married recently, too." I hold up my ring finger and grin, loving the way the platinum band has this vibrant blue shine to it in the low lighting of the bar.

Drew's eyebrows shoot up in surprise, then draw together in momentary puzzlement. "Huh." He rubs his chin and regards me once again, but this time, it's like he's seeing me in a new light.

"And now I know why you didn't reply to my texts when I got back into town a few weeks ago." He gives me a friendly wink, but it's a bit more suggestive than I'm comfortable with.

Actually, I didn't respond to his texts because I deleted all my old hookups from my phone. Anyone who wasn't a platonic friend or coworker got the boot. It took... an embarrassingly long time. But it was the quickest way to draw the line. Now, when unknown numbers text or call, I delete and ignore them—or block them if they're persistent.

I like Drew—he's in his early thirties and has this phenomenal body that's all smooth edges and hard lines, like polished marble. He travels a lot for work, and he was never the clingy type. Plus, he was always up for sharing a joint and cuddling after sex. But he's never been subtle or passive. When he sees something he wants, he goes for it. That makes him great at business and bossy in the bedroom. But I know for a fact he's not used to hearing no. I feel compelled to make sure he understands that I'm married, and that it's a big deal to me.

But before I can open my mouth, Teddy's on the other side of the bar, yacking in my ear.

"Peaches, Jake. Peaches," he whines, holding out the empty bottle of schnapps and reminding me of my intended destination. A flurry of bachelorette party attendees are circling the bar like vultures.

Right. Stock room. Peach schnapps. Now.

Technically, Dempsey's the manager tonight, and he should have a key to the liquor cage, but a glance down the bar confirms that Dem's doing what he does best: charming the pants off our customers and keeping the other guys on task. I smile and feel a little surge of gratitude for Dempsey Haas. He's like all the best parts of Rhett and me rolled into one person. His life sorta sucks these days, but you wouldn't know that from looking at him tonight.

I turn back to Drew and smile apologetically. "Sorry, man. We're slammed. But it was good to see you. And hey, next one's on me, okay?" I beckon Teddy back over, his eyes practically bugging out of his head when he sees the still-empty bottle in my hand. "I'm getting it," I insist, before pointing to my former hookup. "Get my friend here whatever he wants; on the house."

Teddy nods, and I turn to take my leave, clasping Drew on the shoulder as I move around him. "Take care of yourself," I tell him in passing. No point in saying any more than that. We were only ever sex and good times.

I grasp the neck of the bottle in one hand and pull my keys out with the other. It's more crowded in here than it was ten minutes ago, but I manage to navigate through the sea of bodies without getting stopped again.

That is, until I see him.

My man. My lover. My hot-as-hell husband, leaning against the back wall near the lineup of Hampton High football teams from the late seventies.

I take a sharp left and make a beeline for him. I missed him so damn much today. He didn't have class, but he went to visit his abuela, then we didn't have a chance to catch up before his shift.

"Hey you," I say when I'm finally close enough for him to hear me. I lean in to give him a quick kiss, but falter when I see his steely expression.

"Hey," he offers coolly, crossing his arms over his chest and making it impossible for me to wrap him in a hug.

I shift over and stand next to him instead, our arms brushing as I lean into the wall, too.

"You okay, baby?" I ask, tuning out the antics around us and trying to create some semblance of privacy. I creep my hand across the wall until my pinkie brushes his. He doesn't recoil from my touch, but he doesn't relax and hold my hand, either.

"Co-ry..." I brush my hand against his, willing him to look at me. I turn my head slowly in an effort to connect with him.

When he finally meets my gaze, his scowl is surprising. There's fire behind his glare, but he also looks uncomfortable, like he's in pain. My heart beats double time at his expression. Something's seriously wrong.

"Hey, come with me. I've gotta get into the liquor cage, but we can—"

"I'm good," he interjects. He pushes off the wall and turns to face me completely, that guarded look still dancing behind his chocolate brown eyes. "It looks like you have *a lot* of people to take care of tonight. I'll just see you at home."

Oh.

Ohhh.

This isn't a blip of attitude or a random bad mood.

This has to be a direct reaction to whatever he saw—or thinks he saw—over the last few minutes. I glance at the clock on the wall behind the bar: it's already after eleven. Cory got off at ten, and even if it took them a while to close over at Clinton's, he's probably been here for at least ten or fifteen minutes. That means he saw the bachelorette run her nails down my chest. And my former hookup with that lingering, all-too-comfortable hand on my arm.

He saw things. But he didn't hear my replies. I would be all fired up too if there were multiple people pawing at my man.

I have to fix this. Now.

"Come with me," I insist, grabbing his hand and catching him off guard so he has no choice but to follow. I push through the crush of bodies toward my original destination—down the back hall to the liquor cage. I can't tell if he's trying to pull out of my grasp or just getting swallowed up by the crowd, but I refuse to drop his hand, despite the tug of resistance.

I push into the back but don't slow my pace. It's not until we're right outside the cage that I swing my arm around and trap him in an embrace.

"Baby," I whisper huskily, weaving my fingers through the metal grates on either side of his head. "Look at me," I command when he tries to avoid my gaze.

"What's wrong, Cor? Talk to me."

He keeps his head turned to the side—my stubborn, beautiful man—but he severely underestimates my tenacity if he thinks he can wait me out.

I run my nose up the column of his exposed neck, nudging against his jaw to get him to face me.

"You feeling a little jealous, baby?" I nip at his earlobe, and finally, fucking finally, he reacts. His subtle sigh tells me I've hit my target. I breathe him in again, my heated breath inspiring a shiver that I watch tease through his body. Even after a full day of work, he smells incredible—this mix of citrus and sweetness, plus something distinctly him that always revs up the animal in me. I kiss along his jaw, then bring my lips to hover over his before whispering my reassurance.

"You don't have anything to be worried about. I only have eyes for one person: my husband."

He scowls, and I swear I can feel the air between us crackle. He's on fire right now: his rage kindling into full-blown flames because of the way I'm pushing him to open up. My man gets heated when he's worked up like this, that's for damn sure.

"I'm not jealous," he retorts. "I'm insecure."

I scoff at the cop-out. I don't discount that he may have been insecure when he was younger. But Cory has confidence in spades. He's just not as boisterous about it as me.

"No, you're not," I taunt him, nipping at that pouty lower lip he won't kiss me with. "Insecurity would be cowering in the corner and being too afraid to speak up. You were ice cold when

I found you tonight. And now I can practically see the steam billowing out of your ears."

I run my tongue along his top lip, tracing his cupid's bow with the tip. "You're not insecure," I whisper haughtily. "You're *possessive*. But that's okay. I like being possessed by you."

His resolve snaps with my call out. Suddenly, his mouth is on mine. He shoves me, and I push right back: our combined weight rattling the door of the cage at his back. He kisses me like he wants to battle this out and make me pay for stirring up his baser instincts.

I roll my hips into his, tightening my grip for leverage until I'm crushing him into the metal. Our dicks press against each other with every shove.

The push. The grind. His fire. My desire. It's the most incredible cocktail of sensations every time our bodies collide.

He moans when I press my cock into his, so I do it again.

And again.

And again.

With every thrust of my hips, our bodies fight for dominance. That's the thing though—I don't want to fight with him. I want to give him everything.

"Take my dick out," I command as I grind against him. I can't get enough traction like this. I need more. When it comes to him, I need it all.

"Jake, we're at work," he pants before his lips seek mine once more. Every kiss, every lick, every moan into my mouth tells me he needs this just as much as I do.

"Yeah? And who owns this place?" I grunt as I whip off my belt. If he doesn't want to cooperate, I'll do it myself.

"You, husband dearest," he mocks.

"That's right," I tell him through gritted teeth. I've got my fly down and my jeans hanging open. Now I just need him to follow suit. "And you know who owns me?"

I grip his chin between my forefinger and thumb.

"You. You own me, Cory."

He stares, wide-eyed and panting, before he spits out, "You're not going to use sex to distract me, Jake Whitely."

I literally laugh out loud. "Oh yes I am." I'm hard as granite. We both need this, and we need it right now. I move to undo his pants, pausing to make sure he knows my intentions. His eyes blow out when I cup him over his jeans, telling me all I need to know.

I work his cock free in a matter of seconds.

I grip my fist around him, then shift my body forward until I'm holding both our dicks in one hand.

"You feel that? You feel how hard I am right now?" I squeeze his shaft against mine, then spit on the crowns of both our cocks. I smooth my palm over his swollen head first, then swirl it over my own dick, alternating back and forth at a frantic pace, working us into a frenzy.

He feels so fucking good.

On my hand.

Against my cock.

In my heart.

"Feel how hard I am for you right now. That's all for you, baby. Only. You."

His breathing hitches when I stroke us faster.

"I spent the whole night waiting for you to show up. Waiting around like a lovesick fool, desperate to see your smile."

He's thrusting into my grip now, every roll of his hips driving his length into mine as I continue to fist us in tandem.

"The girl who stopped me back there? I've never seen her before in my life. But her friends have spent hundreds of dollars here tonight, so I wasn't about to embarrass her."

I bow my head and spit on our dicks again, jerking us harder in the process.

"The guy I was talking to at the bar? He and I used to hook up."

Cory lets out a growl so fierce I almost break pace. Keyword: almost. But he's straining in my hand, and I know that look in his eye. My man's getting close. Nothing can stop me when I'm chasing his release.

"You go ahead and growl, baby." I kiss him hard to drive home my point. "Let it out. I know you're pissed. My perfect, possessive king. But you don't get to say you're insecure. You don't get to doubt me, to doubt *us*. I was giddy to show that fucker my ring and tell him I'm married."

His eyes flutter shut as his head falls back and rattles the cage. He's right there. His release is mine.

"You." I grip us with both hands now, determined to make him fucking feel how deeply my devotion goes.

"It's fucking you, Cory."

I thrust against him and yank on our dicks, desperate to prove my point.

"No one else."

Thrust.

"Not now."

Yank.

"Not ever again."

Thrust.

"Only. You."

He climaxes in my hand like I willed the cum out of his body with my words alone—crying out and shooting pulse after pulse until he's wrung out and panting. Once I know he's satisfied, my body topples over the edge after him. I seek his mouth and kiss him hard as ropes of cum combine with his release. I rub it in and massage us both, just to make myself clear.

Cory slumps against me, lifting one arm and wrapping it around my neck while he settles his chin on my shoulder. He sighs contentedly, then lets me support his weight and hold him.

There he is.

"Do you want to talk about it?" I ask as I tuck him back into his pants and do the same for myself before wiping my hand on my boxers and fully wrapping him in a hug. He slumps back against the metal locker, pulling me with him.

I've got him captive again, but it's a totally different vibe. Before, I was pushing him to let me in. Now he's clinging to me like he never wants me to let him go.

"I just... I saw Lia in the parking lot before my shift tonight. I let her get to me."

I narrow my eyes and try not to jump to conclusions. "When you say she got to you... do you mean she was talking about us?"

He nods, then pulls me close again, nuzzling into my chest like he needs reassurance that I'm not going anywhere. I rub one hand up and down his back, desperate to be what he needs.

"I'm getting pretty tired of her shitty attitude," I mumble. She's been even more cutting and sarcastic than usual since we got back from our honeymoon.

"Jake..." It's meant to be a warning. But the way he sighs—defeated, like he's been through enough today—that just pisses me off. I hate to see him like this. I won't stand for it.

"I'm serious, baby. If you get to be possessive, then I get to be protective." I kiss the top of his head and squeeze him tighter. "If she's got you twisted and worked up like this, she needs a wake-up call. Tell me what happened. Tell me how I can help."

He sighs again, this time craning back to look me in the eye.

"I just... I feel like I keep having to defend it. Our marriage. Us. I keep insisting this is real. But the more I dig my heels in, the more I worry that I'm wrong."

I scowl as he speaks his unease about what we've become. No way is Lia or anyone else going to make him doubt what I feel with every fucking beat of my heart.

"Tell me I'm not crazy, Jake. Tell me you feel it... that you're in it, too."

"Cory." I slam my fist into the cage above his head, startling us both. But fuck, it feels like words aren't enough right now. He has to know. He has to fucking feel it.

"It's real," I swear, my words a solemn vow. "Every breath. Every moment. Every day. I live for you, baby. I wake up thinking about you. I fall asleep with you in my arms, and it still doesn't feel close enough. I ache for you when we're apart."

I bow my head and brush my lips against his.

"This is the realest thing I've ever experienced. It's so fucking real it scares me. But it's worth it. *You're* worth it."

I seek his lips again, kissing him once, twice, a dozen times until he's smiling against my mouth.

"Be real with me," I whisper.

He nods, and something passes between us then. It's more intimate than anything else we've shared; more serious than the wedding vows we recited a month ago. It's deep. It's true. It's me and him. It's us, doing this together. And it's everything I never knew I wanted.

Chapter 30

Jake

It's probably one of the last nice days we'll have this year, so I've got the girls at the splash pad for the afternoon. Not that the temperature matters to them. It could be sixty degrees and breezy, and they'd still beg me to bring them here.

Ashleigh was invited to some sort of women's alumni luncheon at Archway Prep. When she texted and asked if I was free, I was ecstatic—I see my nieces way less frequently during the school year, so a little bonus Saturday fun was an instant yes from me.

"Hey, Uncle Jakey!" Amelia screams, even though she's only about ten feet away.

"What's up, Meemers?"

She giggles at one of her many nicknames, then jumps up and runs at me, flinging her wet body around my legs.

"Wait a second!" I laugh, reaching for her Jack Skellington towel to use it as a buffer between us. Too late. My shorts and my shoes are soaked. I couldn't care less. Not when she's looking up at me and smiling like that.

I wrap her up like a burrito, then lift her upside down until she's giggling so hard I'm afraid she'll pee on me if I don't right her.

"Wanna hear a joke?" she asks once she's settled on my lap.

"Hit me."

Her eyebrows scrunch together in the cutest way.

"That means yes, tell me," I explain as I tickle her again.

"What's a pirate's favorite type of pants?"

What the heck? Kids are so weird.

"I don't know," I finally relent. "What *is* a pirate's favorite type of pants?"

"Arrr-gyle!" she screams, before bursting into a fresh fit of giggles.

Fiona joins us then, scowling. "She always mixes that one up," she explains with her hands on her hips.

"I do not, Fifi!"

"Hey, hey, hey. Be nice," I scold, trying to keep a straight face as I point from one to the other. After two seconds of silence, they both start laughing.

That's fair. I'm not exactly the stern disciplinarian type.

"The joke's supposed to be—what's a pirate's favorite type of sweater?" Amelia explains.

Oh. Argyle. That makes more sense.

"Then for their favorite pants, it's supposed to be 'carrr-go shorts.'"

"Cargo shorts?" I exclaim, rising to my feet and spinning around with Amelia's towel-clad body in my arms. "I've never seen a pirate wearing cargo shorts! His peg leg would stick out!"

Both girls are laughing while Amelia squeals at a deafening pitch. She's screaming so loud I almost don't hear the words spoken over my shoulder.

"What the hell is this?"

It's low and haunting. A voice that instantly inspires dread in my gut.

"Daddy!"

Amelia is squirming out of my arms as Fiona shoots past me at a sprint. I watch, horrified and frozen, as my older brother stands menacingly on the edge of the sidewalk.

Fiona leans in to hug her dad, but Julian takes a long stride back, lengthening the space between them and holding out one arm. "Stay back, please. You're soaking wet, and I'm wearing three-thousand-dollar Italian leather loafers. You'll ruin them."

Asshole. I cross my arms over my chest, feeling defensive on Fiona's behalf. It's not until I feel a little tug on the hem of my T-shirt that I realize Amelia's still by my side.

Her eyes are as wide as saucers, none of the glee from earlier left in her expression. I squat down on instinct, unsure of what she needs but ready to soothe her.

"Uncle Jakey." As soon as we lock eyes, her bottom lip quivers. "Did I ruin your woafers?"

She's focused on my sneakers now, which are, in fact, soaking wet from spinning her around and chasing them through the splash pad. I grind my molars so hard I wince as I try in earnest to keep from reacting.

"No way, Mimi," I tell her cheerfully, booping her on the nose so she has no doubt about my answer. "You couldn't ruin anything, even if you tried. You make everything better."

She grins down at me, then skips over to join her sister near their dad.

I rise, sobering once again, and face my brother.

"Where's Ashleigh?" Julian demands, looking from me to his kids, then back again.

Damn. This sucks.

I choose my words carefully, knowing that no matter what I say, it'll rub him all the wrong ways.

"She had a lunch event at Archway, so I offered to watch the girls."

His brow furrows just a hair. "You're *watching* my kids?"

Fuckin' A.

I don't know if it'd make this better or worse if I admitted to my brother that I've been spending time with his kids on an almost-weekly basis for the last four years. It wasn't supposed to be a secret. He just never cared enough about their lives to ask.

"I am. I try to help out Ashleigh when I can."

I trace the outline of my phone in my pocket. I'm itching to pull it out, to text her, to *warn* her. She needs to know that Julian knows. I've got to talk to her before he does.

"I didn't realize you knew I even *had* kids. I was driving to the office when I passed by and saw Ash's van. No way in hell did I expect to find my children here with *you*."

There's something sickeningly familiar about the disgust he doesn't bother to hide—it's in the tone of his voice, the glower he casts my way. Standing before him now makes me feel inexplicably small, even though we're about the same height. It's his menacing aura, the way he carries himself. It's the way he reminds me so much of our dad. I shudder involuntarily under his scrutiny.

The girls, thankfully, are oblivious to the tension coiling between us. That is until he pulls them right into the middle of it.

"Fiona," he snaps. "When's the last time you saw this man before today?"

Fiona looks at me in amusement, probably because of the way he didn't use my name. I offer her a quick smile meant to reassure her before taking a few steps forward and setting my sights on my brother.

"Don't do this," I murmur. Loud enough for him to hear. Soft enough for them not to worry.

"Answer me, Fiona," he demands, ignoring me completely.

His dismissal hits like a punch to the gut. I fist my hands by my sides in anguish.

"Well..." Fiona sticks one hand on her hip and screws her face up in concentration. "I think it was the day after I lost my tooth."

Julian side-eyes me before turning back to his oldest daughter. "And when did you lose your tooth?"

Stupid fucker. She lost it last Wednesday, during art class. The school nurse gave her this tiny little tooth box to keep it in, which made Mimi extremely jealous. Fiona FaceTimed Cory and me last week to tell us the news. Then I went ahead and ordered a twenty-four-pack of those tiny tooth boxes on Amazon and had them overnighted. We took the girls out for ice cream after school the next day while Ashleigh got her nails done.

But Julian doesn't know any of that. He's not around. He's not interested. It doesn't directly benefit him and Whitely Enterprises, so he's fucking clueless.

"She lost it the day before we went to get ice cream with Uncle Jakey and Coco!" Amelia chimes in.

My heart bleeds out as Julian shoots her a glare. She's five years old, for crying out loud. She's trying to be helpful.

"Who's Coco?"

Fiona is starting to pick up on the tension. She looks at her dad, then back to me. Her expression is a blend of confusion and concern. Meanwhile, Amelia is blissfully unaware of everything that's happening around her.

"Oh, father," Amelia sing-songs as she plops down on the grass and plucks out the tiny little budded weeds she thinks are flowers. "Coco is Uncle Jakey's boyfriend."

"Nuh-uh!" Fiona interjects, momentarily abandoning her concern when the temptation to correct her sister hits. "Coco is his *husband*." She puts that second hand on her hip and gives me a proud smile.

I smile right back at her, desperate to make sure she knows she didn't do or say anything wrong. She's a kid, and she has no context for why my relationship with Cory would be cause for concern. I'll be damned if anyone—Julian included—inserts some heteronormative bullshit narrative in her mind.

"This is wild," Julian guffaws, breaking away from his typical brooding and shaking his head. "Get your things, girls. I'm taking you home."

Both girls snap their heads to look at me, seeking permission. I'm grateful Julian's too focused on stalking toward me at that moment to see their reactions.

"You have a husband?" he sneers, stopping a few feet away and leveling me with a pointed look.

"I do," I respond coolly, before adding, "I figured the estate lawyer would have notified you by now."

I knew better. I fucking knew better. But I couldn't help it.

I watch as disbelief morphs into realization. Now he's getting it.

Instead of calling me out about my inheritance, he circles back to the topic of my man.

"Has Ashleigh met him?"

"Of course she's met him. Do you really think Ashleigh would let your kids spend time with someone she doesn't know?"

"She lets them be around you."

I don't bother with a rebuttal. There's no version of this I want the girls to see. If Julian wants to pick a fight, he knows where I live. I refuse to take the bait and give him a valid reason to keep me from his kids.

Because that's the heart of what's at stake here: I don't give a shit about my brother with his absentee parent vibe and stupid Italian loafers. But I do care about the two little toe heads sprawled out in the grass bickering about whose weed-flower bouquet is better.

My heart catches in my throat as I accept defeat. There's a familiar prickle of unease nudging at my subconscious, but deep down, I know I have nothing to be ashamed of.

This isn't ten years ago. Julian isn't Joe. I'm not cowering in fear and letting him win to try to protect myself from his wrath. I'm letting him win because I care about *them* too much to lose them over something as inconsequential as my brother's dislike of me.

"It was good to see you, Julian. Do you want me to drive the girls back home or…"

I trail off and leave it up to him. He's their father, after all. And if Julian is anything like what I remember—*like the man who raised us*—I know right now he's desperate for control.

A wrinkle forms between his brows as he stares. Then, without replying, he turns on his loafer-clad heel and stalks toward the girls.

"Fiona. Amelia. Let's go."

Fiona hops to her feet but keeps a measured distance from Julian. Amelia grumbles something unintelligible and moves into a kneeling position but doesn't take her eyes off the grass.

"Amelia Marie Whitely. *Now*."

I cringe at his tone while Amelia acts unaffected. The only way a scolding like that doesn't land is if you're numb to it. I know from experience. I hear her mutter "yes, father" under her breath as she drags her feet and follows him toward the car.

I stand stock still and watch them go, but Fiona and I must be thinking the same thing at that moment. She's just brave enough to voice it.

"Wait, Dad. What about the van?"

And then Mimi chimes in. "Yeah, wait! Your car doesn't even have car seats!"

Fuck. She's too smart for her own good.

I try not to stew in judgment of my brother's lack of parenting prowess. But given what just happened and knowing the ego behind the man, I take off across the parking lot at a clipped pace. He's not stupid. But I wouldn't put it past Julian to buckle them up in his back seat sans car seats just to prove a point.

"Here's the van key," I assert, shoving it into his hand. "Ashleigh's event ends at two. She has my car, so I'll wait here. When we swap back, she can drive your car home."

I don't give him time to respond. I assume Ashleigh has a key for his car, and if not, he can leave it on the dash. All I care about is getting the girls home safe.

I turn away and head back in the direction of the splash pad, then think better of it. Without the girls with me, it's creepy as hell for a guy in his midtwenties to be hanging out at the playground. I look both ways, then jog across the street, striding up the hill that sits at the edge of the skate park.

I pick out a secluded spot and plop down on the grass, stretching out as I stare up at the sky.

I type out a text to Ashleigh, detailing everything that happened with Julian and the girls. I try to give her just the facts. I want her to be informed—she needs to be prepared.

Once Ashleigh replies, I send off another message.

Jake: Hey Bro. Any chance you can call me?

My phone is vibrating in my hand ten seconds later.

"Hey," I answer miserably. If there's anyone I can be real with about what the hell just happened, it's Rhett.

"Hey, yourself. Why do you sound weird?"

I hold in a laugh. Leave it to my best friend to call me on my shit right out of the gate. This is why I called him in the first place.

"Just had an epically horrible afternoon," I confess.

"Uh-oh. You got boy problems, buddy?"

I don't bother holding in a chuckle at that one. Although I do correct him. Rhett hates being wrong.

"Bro. When have I *ever* had boy problems? Seriously? It's like you don't even know me."

I can hear his grin through the phone. "I mean, do you blame me for questioning it? You *did* go from proud relationship virgin to married man in less than a week. Being a husband is a lot harder than being a fuckboy."

Oh. This isn't playful banter anymore. He's actually concerned about my relationship.

"Things with Cory couldn't be better," I assure him.

"Seriously?"

Well, now I'm just insulted.

"Yes, Rhett. Seriously. I mean, it's not perfect, and we're still learning and figuring each other out. But..."

Fuck. This isn't why I called him. But I can't help but want to gush about my husband.

"Things with Cory are incredible. I thought it would be easy with him, fun, even. But it's so much more than that. There's so much more to him. My life feels more vibrant with him in it. It's like I've leveled up in ways I can't even explain. There's BC—before Cory—then there's the now. And the now is fucking incredible."

I pause, feeling the weight of my words as I confess my heart. "You there, Bro?" I've been rambling without any response from Rhett for so long, I'm worried the call may have dropped.

"Uh, yeah. I'm here. I'm just sort of... speechless."

"Yeah, right. I can't remember a time where you didn't have something to say."

"Ha ha. Believe me: Tori and I have had plenty of conversations about your marriage with benefits thing. Which, by the way, kudos to you for coming up with a relationship category that's even more screwy than what she and I did for all those years."

I smirk at his shrewd assessment of my marriage and his own relationship.

But that was then. This is now.

"I really like being married," I confess, willing the sincerity in my voice to hold steady. "I really like being married to *him*," I clarify.

"I'm just so happy when we're together. I can't wait to get back to him when we're apart. We have fun, and the sex—*fuck*—I didn't realize all you people in committed relationships were having sex like this."

Rhett chuckles in response.

"But it goes beyond fucking and having someone to come home to. He sees me in ways that I don't even see myself. He pushes me. He forces me to be real when I'd much rather crack a joke or brush something off. He makes me feel good, but he makes me want more, too. More intimacy. More authenticity. More of him. I want to be a better person for him."

Eventually I stop talking, but Rhett stays quiet. I inhale the biggest breath I can manage and let the sun warm my skin as I bask in the truth of the words I've spoken.

"Fuck, Jake. I was not expecting this from you," he finally sighs into the phone.

I can't help but grin. "You and me both, bro."

"Wait. You said you didn't call to talk about Cory. So what's really going on?"

I toy with the idea of telling him about Julian like I had planned. He knows more about my history than anyone. But after gushing about Cory the way I did, I feel this urge to talk to my husband about the situation instead.

I've relied on Rhett for years. But he's not the only one in my corner anymore. And in that moment, I realize I *want* to talk to Cory first.

"Eh," I feign indifference. "Something came up, but it's really no big deal. I guess I just wanted to talk to my best friend."

"I feel that. I'm glad you called. Hey, listen. I've gotta get going. I promised Tori I was just running out to the store, and I've been sitting in the parking lot talking to you instead."

Normally, this would be when I'd heckle him for being pussy whipped or tied down to an old ball and chain. But for the first time, I get it.

"I wanted to start talking Thanksgiving plans soon, although V says it's too early to worry about that just yet."

I shake my head at his type A tendencies. Some things never change.

"Originally I thought we'd go up to the cabin, but if you need to stay in town, we can just do it in Hampton at my parents' house instead."

My heart flutters at the idea of celebrating my first holiday with Cory. I freaking love Thanksgiving. The food. The drinks. The movie marathons. The way I get to slip into my gray sweatpants and complain about overeating for hours before committing to a steady diet of leftovers and pie for the rest of the weekend.

"Thanksgiving in Hampton sounds perfect, bro. Just let me know how your schedule is shaking up, and we'll figure it out. I'll keep the same hours Mike used to keep for that weekend, and I'll check in with Cory about his schedule, too."

We hang up, and I exhale. I'm totally out of my element when it comes to counting on anyone besides myself and the few people who have been there for me my whole life. But this feels right. Different but right.

I shoot off a message to Cory to let him know I'll be home in a few hours. Then I stare back up at the cloudless, boundless sky.

Chapter 31

Cory

Things have been touch and go all night. Jake came home upset after the run-in with his brother at the park. I've spent time with his nieces, and I've met Ashleigh, too. But Julian is an enigma.

I feel out of my league right now—how can I support him through this? Does he need comfort? Does he need to vent? Is he interested in problem solving? In my defense, I don't think he knows, either. So I've relegated myself to the kitchen and am focused on making my man some tried-and-true comfort food with what we have on hand.

"That smells amazing," Jake says as he saunters into the kitchen and heads for the fridge. He grabs himself another beer, then throws his empty bottle in the recycling bin under the sink.

"Anything I can do to help?" His arms are around me the next moment, two strong tethers that link us together and promise to withstand any storm.

I lean back into his touch, letting myself savor how it feels to be wrapped up in him.

"I've got this," I murmur as he brushes his big hands up and down my ribs with featherlight touches. It's the chaste kiss on the exposed skin along my neckline that really does me in. It is so easy to get lost in him. But I feel compelled to keep him from relying on sex to distract himself from what's really going on here, so I quickly change the subject.

"Do you want to watch a movie tonight?" I ask as I sprinkle more cheese on the Johnnie Marzetti. My dad used to make this for me all the time. It's not the most complex recipe, but it tastes like pure comfort. That's what I want to give my husband right now: a huge hug, a full belly, and a night to switch off and focus on taking care of himself rather than everyone around him.

"You know I never say no to movie night and a good cuddle."

He kisses my neck again, then leaves me to it.

An hour later, we're devouring bowls of cheesy pasta in front of the TV.

"This is freakin' delicious," Jake declares through a mouthful of food. "Did your grandma teach you how to make this?"

I scoff at the notion of Abuela ever making a dish like this. "Johnnie Spaghetti-O," she called it the one time I brought leftovers back from my dad's house. The woman's a food snob.

"No, my dad is the king of casseroles. He'd whip up something like this on Friday, then we'd eat off it all weekend."

Jake gives me a closed-mouth smile that doesn't quite reach his eyes, then nods thoughtfully as he chews. "I'd like to meet him sometime. Your dad. I want to meet your whole family."

"You will," I assure him, leaning over to rest my head on his shoulder.

Maybe I shouldn't have brought up my dad so casually, given what he went through today. But maybe this is my opening.

"Do you want to talk about what happened?" I ask, nudging my jean-clad knee against him.

He came home and changed into light gray sweatpants and a fitted navy T-shirt. I spent the better part of an hour glancing at the drawstring and crotch of those babies. It's sort of ridiculous, really. We have sex most nights and sometimes in the morning if we're not rushing out the door. I know what's behind those pants. And yet I'm still mesmerized by the sight of him.

Jake finishes his food and sets the empty bowl on the coffee table. When he sees that my bowl is empty, too, he takes it from my hands.

"You want more, baby?"

I shake my head. He sets my dishes beside his. He'll wash them later, just like he does every night, regardless of whether he cooks.

"Today was eye opening," he starts. "That's for damn sure. Seeing Julian interact with the girls confirmed about a dozen things I always suspected but didn't know for sure."

He told me the logistics of what happened at the splash pad as soon as he got home. But this is what we haven't talked about yet—his reaction to interacting with his brother for the first time in years. And the fact that our not-so-secret marriage was exposed.

"Everything about watching him with them stirred up old shit for me," he continues. "Julian isn't outwardly cruel like my dad. But maybe that's how it started with Joe, and I don't even remember. It just sucks to see a walking, talking clone of the most awful person I've ever known, and to know my girls are stuck with him…"

He slumps back on the couch, defeated.

I reach out and take his hand. "Are you worried he won't let you see them anymore?"

Jake sits up like a shot, his eyes frantic as he searches my face. "What? No! Why would you even say that?"

I keep my composure, fighting the urge to recoil and smoothing my thumb over his knuckles in hopes of easing the sting. "He's their dad, Jake. If the situation today was as volatile as you say it was..."

"It was," he insists through gritted teeth.

I'm not questioning him. Just trying to put things in perspective.

"I believe you. I do. But if Julian doesn't want you around them..."

"What's he going to do?" Jake spits out. "Declare himself Father of the Year and suddenly be in town for more than a few days each month? They may be his kids, but those are *my* girls."

I am so out of my depth here, it's not even funny. I know he's not mad at me. It's the shitty situation, woven together with his big old heart and protective nature.

"Did you think he wouldn't find out?"

He blows out a long breath and relaxes into the couch once more. That subtle shift tells he feels safe enough to work through this without censoring himself.

This is Jake being real. And as hard as it is to watch him struggle, I'm so damn proud of him.

"Honestly? Yeah. I sort of did. Ashleigh wasn't about to tell him. And although we've never told the girls not to mention me to him, I get the impression that he rarely, if ever, has any sort of meaningful conversation with either of them. I didn't overthink it because it seemed improbable that he'd ever find out."

"That makes sense. But now that he knows, things can't go back to how they were. You know that, right?"

He glances at me through his peripheral but doesn't interrupt or rebuke what I'm saying.

"I know this isn't what you want to hear..." What had been a skeptical side-eye has transformed into a full-on glare. "But I think you're going to have to make amends with Julian if you want to maintain your relationship with the girls."

He blows out a sharp breath, like I've sucker-punched him. And maybe I have. But there's no point sugarcoating this. He loves those kids. He hates their dad. Only he can decide which of those realities he's willing to bend on.

"There's nothing you can do about it tonight," I remind him, brushing along his knuckles again before giving in to the urge to bring his hand to my mouth and kiss it. The movement has him scooting closer, positioning himself so the sides of our bodies are pressed into each other.

"And I'll support you through whatever you decide to do."

His only response is a long, low hum.

"How about that movie?" I suggest. There's no point in pressing the issue. These things take time. It's okay to sit in discomfort for a while. I just want him to know he doesn't have to sit in it alone.

"You gonna let me pick, baby?"

The lilt in his voice tells me I'm in for another late-nineties cult classic. For some reason, the man loves that era of film: the darker and campier, the better. Last weekend we watched *Donnie Darko* and *Armageddon* back-to-back. A few weeks before that I was subjected to an entire Brendan Frasier marathon: *The Mummy*, *Blast from the Past*, and *George of the Jungle* all in a row. In the six weeks we've lived together, I swear we've watched *Match Point* at least three times.

"You can pick this time," I relent, swatting him on the ass when he hops up to grab the remote. "But don't get used to it. This is supposed to be an equal partnership. I call dibs on the next two movie nights to even the score."

Chapter 32

Jake

Memories of the way Fiona cowered and Amelia disconnected around Julian replay in my mind. It twists my gut to think about my girls like that. I fucking hate that they have that kind of relationship with him.

But as awful as things feel, it's not hopeless. Cory made a lot of valid points tonight. With his help, I'm going to figure out a way to work through this for the girls' sakes.

I'm so fucking raw right now. Every memory, every thought that crosses my consciousness... it's all more intense than anything I usually allow myself to feel. And the emotions—they're lingering. Or maybe they're clinging. It's like now that I've opened up and let myself get real with Cory, I can't shut off the worry, shame, frustration, and anger coiling through my body.

I towel off my hair, throw my gray sweats back on, and make my way into our bedroom to find him sitting up in bed. He's propped against the headboard, wearing those adorable glasses I love, staring at his iPad intently. He likes to read at night. I always try to linger in the bathroom or take my time turning lights off and making his coffee for the next day. Just little things to give him a few extra minutes. Because as soon as I crawl into bed, all I want to do is get lost in him.

We fuck every night. Well, that's not entirely true. Sometimes we fuck. Then other times we make love. I've never experienced sex like this before. It's like we create our own personal oasis each time we connect. Sacrificing ourselves to one another, savoring every inch of affection, making promises with our bodies. I could spend hours getting lost in him: learning what makes him tick, unlocking his pleasure points. I'm intimate with him in ways I've never connected with another person.

And Cory always gives as good as he gets. The way this man works me over and burrows into my deepest desires: He's not just focused on my body. It's like he's casting a spell on my soul.

I make my way over to him and hover on his side of the bed. I'm still deep in my feelings: not totally present but desperate for our connection.

"Baby," I murmur, leaning over to rest my forehead on his. Abandoning the screen, he seeks my gaze immediately. He wraps his arms around my neck; kneads his hands into the tight muscles of my shoulders. His touch calms me as much as it turns me on.

I inhale deeply, letting my senses become overwhelmed by his delicious and oh-so familiar scent. I close my eyes and take in another steadying breath, preparing myself to ask for something I didn't know I needed until a few minutes ago.

"Will you fuck me tonight?" I whisper.

I scan his face, searching for reluctance or hesitation. We haven't done this yet. We haven't even talked about it. But tonight... I need him to take control.

Our foreheads stay pressed together as his Adam's apple bops up and down.

"Do you... I mean, are we..."

I can see his wheels turning. He's questioning the timing. But this isn't just about what happened today. It's about how deeply I'm in my feelings. My emotions are wreaking havoc on my mind, and suddenly I'm desperate to feel him everywhere.

"I want it. I *need you*."

I know he's done it before. So have I. We just haven't done it like this together.

"Jake."

My name is a vow on his sweet, kissable lips. An acknowledgment of what's grown between us over the last several weeks. An oath of what our future holds, even if we haven't clearly defined what comes next.

"Cory. Please..."

I trail off and turn my head, feeling so damn vulnerable that he's making me beg. A hint of shame prickles down my spine as the threat of denial lingers between us.

"Hey." He sits up straight and takes my face in both hands.

"Look at me," he commands.

I slowly turn my head back in his direction, my eyes downcast until he uses two fingers to tilt my chin.

"I see you," he declares, studying me through reverent eyes. "I've got you," he adds solemnly before shifting forward and rising to stand.

I watch, transfixed, as he blows out a long breath, runs one hand through his hair, and gingerly sets his glasses on the nightstand. When he turns back to me, his eyes are ablaze.

"Get undressed and get on the bed."

His words are strong and authoritative. I hurry to pull off my sweats, then perch on the end of the mattress in just my boxers.

I watch him dig through the nightstand drawer and arrange a few pillows. When he looks back at me, my heart jumps into my throat.

"Naked, Jake. I need you naked if you want me to fuck you."

Goddamn.

I scramble to slide down my boxer briefs as I suck in a trembling breath. I'm so fucking needy right now, but I can't help it. I'm desperate for his touch. For his love. For his approval. I'd do anything for him.

I rest my hands on the tops of my thighs, tension coursing through my veins as I wait for what's next. I've been naked in front of him so many times. But never like this. Not until now.

His shadow blocks the light as he comes to stand between my legs. "Look at me," he instructs.

My head shoots up embarrassingly fast. When our eyes lock, my cheeks flush in response.

"I'm going to take such good care of you," he murmurs as he reaches out and runs both hands through my hair. "I'm going to fuck you until your dick weeps with pleasure."

Arousal surges through me.

"Scoot up on the mattress and lie down. Let me see you."

He juts his chin, and I position myself like he wants. He's still half-clothed, whereas I'm completely naked before him. He gives me a long, thorough perusal, slowly assessing every mound of muscle and inch of flesh. Heat creeps up my neck as he continues his unhurried, tantric appraisal.

When his eyes return to mine, he bites down on his bottom lip. "You're perfect," he praises. "You're so fucking perfect, Jake."

The way he says my name has my heart catching in my throat. He's on me a moment later.

His weight crushes me into the mattress as our mouths collide in a greedy, sloppy kiss. He climbs up the bed and straddles me, pinning me down as he puts all his weight on my abs. I relish the solidness of his body holding me down.

He sucks on my bottom lip, then thrusts his tongue into my mouth in hard, hurried strokes. I moan when he rolls his hips and matches the rhythm of our kiss.

He breaks away to scrape his teeth along my jaw, then he grabs my hair and pulls my head to the side. Once he's got me where he wants me, he bites and sucks on my neck, eventually working his way down my chest.

"You taste so good, baby," he croons. "You feel so right under my tongue. You're so fucking perfect for me, Jake."

Emotion overwhelms me as another pool of arousal gathers in my core. I realize I haven't uttered a word in response to anything he's said. I can't think of a single thing to say.

All I can do is feel.

He peppers kisses down my chest, lavishing each nipple and moaning against my skin like I'm his favorite dessert.

When he reaches my abs, he rises to his knees, then shifts back to climb off the bed and hover over me again. He waits for me to make eye contact before he slowly lowers his lips to my stomach: his moves are deliberate, his breath hot on my skin.

We're staring into each other's souls as he kisses the top of my abs.

"You are important."

I watch as he shifts lower, offering another kiss and more words.

"You are admirable."

I'm holding my breath now, trying to hold back my reaction.

"You are strong."

I realize what he's doing. My chest starts to ache with the pain of a broken rib. I track his movements and shudder. Three down. Three fucking more to go.

"You matter."

When he kisses the next segment of my abdominals, I turn my head to the side, desperate for this to be over.

"You are adored."

He pauses. We both know I'm on the brink of breaking down.

I can't swallow.

I can barely breathe.

I screw my eyes closed and try to keep still as my body trembles in rebellion.

"You are worthy."

He lets that kiss linger. His lips brush back and forth against my skin, leaving goosebumps in their wake. It's not until I feel him rest against my midsection that I exhale and open my eyes.

A tear I didn't give myself permission to cry tracks down my cheek. I turn my head to the other side to hide it. I don't dare brush it away and draw attention to it.

"Baby..." He swipes at the moisture with his thumb as I close my eyes in shame. He's never called me that before tonight. I don't think I've ever heard anything so sweet.

He traces the path of the traitorous tear as I keep my eyes closed tight and try to shut him out. "You *are* worthy, Jake. Worthy of love. Worthy of happiness. Worthy of receiving everything you so generously give to everyone else."

I choke back a sob.

I can't do this.

It's too much.

I can't let him see me like this.

His lips brush the side of my face before he whispers: "Let me in, Jake. Let me in and let me stay."

I shiver and nod, fighting with everything I am to steady my breathing. When I finally open my eyes, his face is just inches from mine.

"Do you want to stop? We don't have to do this tonight."

"Please don't stop," I rush out. If I thought I needed him before...

"Tell me how you want me."

I shake my head in earnest. "I want you to decide."

His eyes narrow slightly, as if he's emboldened by the challenge. He pushes up, and I can't help but appreciate his tan, defined arms and his trim, lean waist. The man's a masterpiece. *My* masterpiece. I find something new to love about his body every fucking day.

He runs both hands down my chest, brazenly teasing the V of my hips. He rubs me once, then again, letting his fingers trail along the crease of my thighs in the most tantalizing rhythm.

All it takes is a few more strokes, and my solid erection is standing up, begging for attention. He eyes my cock lasciviously before meeting my gaze.

"I'm going to take you right here. Just like this. You're gonna lay back on our bed and watch me while I fuck you, Jake."

My abs clench in anticipation.

He wraps one fist around my cock, squeezing me just hard enough to toe the line between pleasure and pain. "Eyes on me," he murmurs as he bows his head.

I watch, transfixed, as he stares at my length for two seconds, then spits on the crown of my dick.

I swear to God—my balls jolt of their own accord. Holy fucking shit.

"Oh, baby," he croons. "Look at you. Look what you gave me."

I can't look at anything except the devilish smile pulling at the corners of his mouth.

"As soon as that spit landed, your cock gave me the perfect little pearl. Watch me as I lap it up, Jake. Watch me take what's mine."

My breathing falters, but the feeling of his plush mouth encasing me jolts me back to life. I struggle to keep still as he sucks, bopping down on my shaft, then gingerly running his teeth up my dick.

"You taste so fucking good." His voice is husky now. He smiles against my pulsating head as he lifts just his eyes to make sure I'm still watching. "You love it when I suck you, don't you, baby?"

I can do nothing but nod.

Nod and try to breathe.

Nod and try to keep myself from combusting.

"I'm gonna suck your dick while I prep you. But you have to tell me if it's too much. If my mouth's full of cock, I won't be able to see you. Do you understand?"

I nod again.

"Words, Jake. Use your words."

"Yes," I croak out, my voice cracking with desperation.

"Good boy."

He reaches for the lube, coats one hand, then spits on my dick again.

"Eyes on me, baby. Don't let me look up and catch you not watching."

Not a chance in fucking hell.

He grips me with one hand, takes me in his mouth, then works his lubed hand between my cheeks. I tense on instinct, but quickly relax into his touch, letting my mind focus on the way his tongue is running back and forth under the head of my dick.

Fuck, does he give good head. Every time I think I've got his rhythm figured out, he changes it up. He's soft kisses and slow licks. Frantic pulls and the perfect amount of suction. I'm so lost in him I don't even flinch when he breaches my hole with a well-lubed finger.

He pops off my dick, looks up at me, and grins.

"You're doing so good for me, baby."

Desire flushes my entire upper half. He's barely touching me—but his words. His fucking words. He's undoing me from the inside out, and he doesn't even know it.

"Relax, Jake. Let me in." His brow furrows in concentration as he swirls one finger inside me. I can't help but buck my hips when he grazes my prostate.

His smile widens. "You like that, don't you? You like when I touch you there? I'm gonna hit that spot with my cock over and over again until you're spasming so hard your orgasm makes *me* come."

His mouth goes back to my dick. He works in a second finger, then eventually a third. I grimace through the stretch—through the fullness that borders on pain. But I know this is the only way through. This is the only way I can truly let him in and feel it all.

"You ready for me, baby?" he asks, removing his hand and reaching behind my head for a pillow. "Lift those hips for me."

I'm not even processing his words anymore. I just do whatever he says, immediately, on command. He owns me: mind, body, and soul. I've never felt more free than I do in this moment.

I lift up, and he moves the pillow beneath me. He uses his hands to spread my thighs, exposing me further. He stares between my legs: at my rock-hard dick, at my needy, ready hole.

There's not an ounce of trepidation between us. I want this. I want this so fucking bad it hurts.

I watch as he removes his pants and coats his dick in lube, then leans forward, notching himself at my entrance. But instead of pushing in, he bends down. And he kisses me. He kisses me until I see stars. He kisses me until I'm writhing underneath him. He kisses me until I beg.

"Cory," I plead against his mouth, bearing down with my ass as I try to take over.

"Mine," he asserts, finally breaching me and giving me all of him.

It's just the tip, but fuck, he feels so good. I bear down again, desperate for more.

"Cory, please."

"I've got you," he promises, pushing in another inch as his hand smooths up my chest and grips my throat. He kisses me once more, then peels back, gazing down to where his length disappears inside me.

"Oh, baby," he praises. His words are brimming with emotion. Admiration. Love.

"You look so fucking good stretched around my cock. You should see how perfect you look with my dick in your hole. You're doing so good for me, Jake."

I claw at the comforter as he works in another inch.

"So."

I buck my hips up and clench around him when he gives me more.

"Fucking."

I wince at the intensity of the stretch, running my hands through my hair as waves of pleasure crash over me with each word he says.

"Goood."

We both moan when he finally bottoms out.

I feel his balls hit my ass cheeks. My own sack tingles with need.

"Perfect. Absolutely fucking perfect."

I haven't taken my eyes off him. I'm hypnotized by his every word. When he finally looks up, he smiles.

It's not a smirk. It's not a sneer. It's a perfect, genuine, effortless smile.

"Fuck, baby. I love being inside you," he says earnestly.

A second later, his eyes darken.

"Now show me how good you can take it."

He finally pulls back and begins to move.

He braces himself on my thighs, using my body to get deeper, to give himself more leverage. He's got the angle figured out before I even have time to process what's happening. I can feel the head of his dick nudging at my prostate with each and every thrust. I had no idea it could be like this—that it could feel this fucking good.

"Fuck, baby," he hisses as he thrusts with a force that has me levitating out of my body. "There's no way I can do this for long when you feel this fucking good. I have to get you there. I need to make you come."

My eyes roll back in my head, and his face screws up in concentration. I'm mesmerized by the sheen of sweat coating his naked, gorgeous body. I'm so present—so fully in this, in every possible way.

"Cory," I groan. "Fuck, baby. Fuck... Touch me. Please touch me."

He grunts in response, then moves his hands from my thighs and wraps one hand around my aching cock. The contact is everything as he finds a rhythm that matches every rut into my body. He's ramming into me with brute force, and his balls are slapping my ass with each thrust.

But the way he's wrapping his hand around my dick is where I really feel our connection. He holds me tenderly, lovingly. He strokes me like my pleasure is his only priority.

"Give me what's mine, Jake. Show me how good you can take it. I want your cum to shoot out of you so hard you pass out. Give it to me, baby. Give it to me now."

Fuck. Fuck. *Fuckkk*.

I curse through my release: Bucking. Convulsing. Thrashing with his dick in my ass. I do just what he asks of me, orgasming so hard everything goes fuzzy, and my vision tunnels while I come. He growls his own release, his cock pulsating over and over again, emptying inside me. I bear down and clench him appreciatively, drawing out his pleasure as he collapses against my chest.

We both say nothing, instead clinging to each other's sticky, sweaty bodies, panting through what can only be described as an existential, soul-shattering, earth-shifting experience.

That was it. That was everything. That was love, in its purest, rawest, most carnal form.

More tears prick behind my eyes, but this time, I let them fall. Nothing hurts when he's holding me. Everything feels right when we're together like this.

Cory lifts me up. He sees me. He knows me. He gets me.

He's everything I never knew I needed. He's more than I ever thought I deserved. Now that I've found him—now that I've experienced this—I'm never letting him go.

Chapter 33

Cory

How did a night that felt so hopelessly delicate transform into something so beautiful?

I've been sleeping with this man for weeks, and yet I've never seen him respond and open up the way he did for me tonight. He unraveled at my words. He preened when I praised him.

It was profoundly intimate. And I'm already craving another round.

It wasn't just about the sex, though. I've never been wrapped up in another person like this. He may think he needed me tonight—that what I did was for his benefit. But the crest of emotions that finally came to a head was the most transcendental experience of my life.

This man letting me in: physically, emotionally, mentally—it's not something I take for granted. I know him well enough now to know just how huge this step is for our relationship.

We still haven't talked about what we're doing; what this new version of us means. I'm itching to know how things have changed and how he feels about the original parameters we set. But I'm so sated by his love, fortified by the confidence I feel when I'm with him. No previous relationship or partner ever felt like this. Nothing compares to Jake. Nothing has ever felt this good. This right. This special. This real.

I hold back a snort at the notion of being in the most "real" relationship I've ever experienced with a man who married me for money. A nibble of anxiety tries to pick at the edges of my bliss, but I silence the noise of my rioting mind and wrap him in my arms even tighter.

I trace the tattoos on the arm he's got slung across my bare chest as he sleeps. I do this often—watch him and just hold him while he sleeps. He's so animated and jovial when he's awake. It's a privilege to see him like this: Soft. Vulnerable. Not putting on a show or cracking a joke to make someone else smile. He's the most effervescent individual I've ever known. I love those things about him: but he's so much more than the mask he wears for the world.

I see it. I see *him*.

I think he's finally starting to see it, too.

I outline the familiar Route 8 road sign on his bicep, mindlessly drawing an infinity pattern over the 8 like I do every night before I fall asleep.

Infinity.

Forever.

That's what I want with him.

I want this to last forever.

Chapter 34

Jake

I sense him beside me, and my body relaxes. Eyes closed, I reach out in the darkness, grasping for something true. I don't have to reach far. I readjust his arms so he's holding me in an embrace, even in sleep. We always end up a tangle of limbs in the middle of the night. I wouldn't want it any other way.

I've never experienced anything like this. There's a primal longing and sense of satisfaction dueling for supremacy in my mind. I can't get enough of him.

He's a comfort I've unknowingly craved for years.

He's the reason I feel safe, seen, loved.

In a matter of weeks, the man I married for practical reasons has elevated my life in ways I never imagined possible.

I'm not alone.

We're in this together.

He's right there.

This thing that's been growing between us—it multiplied tenfold tonight. I don't just feel him. I'm tethered to him. Protected from the storm. Galvanized by his love.

There's no way to describe the depth in which he sees me.

And for the first time in my life, I want to be seen.

With Cory, I don't have to pretend. I don't have to fake it. I don't have to make myself larger than life to meet his expectations.

The way this man loves me...

Fuck.

He loves me.

At least, I think he does.

I never thought this would be an option for me. I don't even have to think about the words as they tumble out in a rush.

"I love you, baby," I whisper, pulling his arm around me tighter and willing him to feel my adoration. I'll have to work up to saying the words when he's actually awake, but for now, this is enough.

Nothing has ever felt so real to me. Nothing has ever felt so right.

I'm a mess and I'm broken, but I'm his. And he sees me and accepts me and loves me for exactly who I am.

Fuck.

Cory loves me.

And I love him, too.

Chapter 35

Jake

It's reasonably busy for a Sunday night, which is just the way I like it. I've been here since lunchtime because I'm trying to make Dempsey take a damn break. He closed Friday and Saturday night but refused to take off, even when I told him I had it covered. I know he's got a lot going on at home and that he uses work as an escape. But I'm worried he's starting to adopt some of my workaholic tendencies. The guy's financially set for life and only twenty-six. He does not need to be putting in sixty hours a week at my bar.

I don't let myself dwell on it. Cory worked tonight, but Clinton's closes early on Sundays, so he should be walking through the door soon. We slept in and had breakfast together this morning, but then he insisted on abandoning me to head to the campus library to study. I tried my hardest—a.k.a. I got down on my knees and made a direct plea to his cock in the shower—to get him to study at home so we could hang out a while longer. But he was adamant that if he stayed home, I'd just distract him. He had me there.

We haven't talked about last night yet: about what passed between us. About what feels like this new, enormous step in our relationship.

How he cared for me, how he inspires me to be the best version of myself all the time... *Fuck*. I just want him to get over here so I can kiss him senseless.

I'm wiping down the back bar when the front door chimes. I look up expectantly, but I'm disappointed to see it's just two men, boisterously laughing as they claim barstools near the entrance.

I watch them for a moment as they settle in, noting their expensive suits and general aura of snobbery. Julian would probably like their outfits.

I snort at my own joke, then hear one of them speak.

"So much has changed, but it feels good to be back."

A chill shoots down my spine.

His voice is familiar, haunting in a way. Goosebumps erupt on my neck as I try to shake off my bizarre reaction.

I peek at the pair again from the corner of my eye. They're not regulars, and they're perusing the bourbon list. There's nothing outwardly weird about their behavior. But I swear something's off.

My instincts are always right. And right now, my instincts say run.

I flag Dempsey over and give him the heads-up. "Hey, take care of those guys who just walked in. Try to chat them up and let me know if they say or do anything that seems off."

He nods and doesn't question me, instead moving over to greet them.

I busy myself with inventory and get started on tomorrow's orders. I'm surprised Cory still hasn't shown up—Clinton's must have been busy tonight, too.

A few minutes pass before Dem scoots behind me to reach for the Blanton's Reserve. He prepares the drinks and serves them, chatting up the new customers just like I knew he would.

I lose track of time tenthing bottles and updating my inventory sheets, eventually ducking into the back hallway and double checking a few things in the liquor cage. When I emerge from the back, Dempsey's rocking on his heels, waiting for me.

I cock my head and wordlessly call him over as I take a seat at the far end of the bar.

"Get this," Dempsey starts, leaning in close to keep our conversation private. "I actually know one of the guys who ordered the Blanton's. He was an assistant to the athletic director back when we were at Arch. His name's Ian McDowell."

What. The. Fuck?

My heart rips itself from my chest, plummets to the ground, and hits with a thud.

Ian McDowell.

Ian *Fucking* McDowell?

The man who roofied me—the man who tried to assault me when I was sixteen—is currently parking his no-good predatory ass in *my* bar? I scramble to my feet on instinct, desperate to not be in a compromising or submissive position. I feel a sharp pain along the crown of my head before I realize I'm pulling on my own hair.

My body feels weightless. Like I'm empty. Like I'm nothing. All I want to do is evaporate into a mist and be anywhere but here. I try to inhale and feel my chest burn in objection. I'm gonna fucking hyperventilate if I don't get it together. Fast.

Either Dem doesn't notice that I'm short-circuiting or he knows better than to ask. "He says he just moved back to town. He's been named director of admissions at Arch."

Without thought, I let out an audible groan. I didn't even realize I did it until I heard it. I swear to God I have no control of any of my faculties right now. It's like I'm having an out-of-body experience, watching myself spiral from behind the bar. I'm sure I look manic. I can't even look at Dempsey for fear that he'll see me: that he'll connect the dots, that he'll *know*.

I have to get out of here.

I snort out a chortle at the absurdity of running away from my own bar—from my own life—because of Ian McDowell. But even though the logical part of my brain knows that my reaction is absolutely asinine, I can't control it.

I don't have words. I don't have thoughts. I just have shame.

And right now, that shame feels like nitrous-oxidized fuel burning through my veins.

Chapter 36

Jake

Fight or flight is real, and I was fueled up and ready for takeoff.

I don't remember leaving. I can't believe I just ran out of my own bar and abandoned my staff without a word.

I don't remember making the decision to come here, of all places.

What the fuck am I doing?

The pool is covered, and most of the outdoor furniture is put away. I must have dragged a lounge chair from somewhere, though, because I'm flat on my back, staring up at the cloudy Hampton night sky.

I'm appalled that I didn't recognize him the second he stepped into my bar. For all intents and purposes, he looks the same. Older, with thinner hair and more of a smarmy vibe. But the Ian McDowell who walked into The Oak tonight is the same man who tried to take advantage of an overly enthusiastic teenager ten years ago.

I scoff at the notion: *tried*. What happened that night changed the trajectory of my life. It corrupted my sense of self. It demolished my already-shitty relationship with my dad. It altered my entire future.

All because of what he tried to do. *All because of what I went back for.*

I'm such a fucking coward.

I turn my head from side to side on the lounger, feeling the strips of plastic shift under the weight of my skull.

It's stupid that I came here, of all places. I never even told Rhett what really happened that night.

He knows a lot of it. My best friend came to my rescue. I called him the second I realized something was off, then I ran like hell until my body gave up in the school parking lot out near the salt shed. Rhett and I were so attuned to each other back then that somehow he found me.

It was his idea to let me drive. He thought being behind the wheel and having some sense of control would calm me. He didn't realize how far gone I was. Hell, neither did I.

That wasn't the only plan he concocted that night. He also forced me out of the driver's seat so I wouldn't get in trouble after I crashed the car.

Sitting in his Audi with the airbags deployed while Rhett's arm hung limp at his side is a core memory. Not because it was so gruesome or scarring, which it was. But because it dragged on for literal hours.

He refused to call for help until he was sure the Rohypnol had worked through my system, giving me the autonomy to decide who I told about what happened that night.

He was the one who sustained the injuries. Yet he sat in the driver's seat cracking jokes and sweating through the pain, offering me sips of water and words of reassurance as I came in and out of consciousness.

He waited. *He fucking waited.*

Then, hours later—after we'd both gone to the hospital to get checked out, after he was taken back for surgery and I was taken home to be spit on by my dad—after it should have been all said and done...

I went back.

I can't even think about it without feeling nauseous. It's a secret that's festered inside me for more than a decade. My deepest regret. My greatest shame. By the time I made my choice, my mind was clear. I had all the information I needed to stay away and keep myself safe.

But I didn't.

To this day, no one knows that in the early hours of morning, when the sun was rising and I was at my all-time low, I swiped a bottle of gin from my dad's bar cart, picked a random set of keys for one of his dozen cars, and willingly drove myself back to campus to be defiled by the man who had tried to assault me hours earlier.

There's so much hatred rotting inside me. I don't even bother turning my head as I cough and dry heave over the memory. Nothing ever comes out. I wish I could vomit and make the feeling pass. But even after ten years, the burning hasn't subsided. I keep this one shoved down deep—I rarely think of it anymore, instead replaying other parts of that night in my mind to distract myself from the worst decision I've ever made. But when I do let myself go there, it feels like the worst heartburn in the world raging through my body.

I close my eyes and see his face. Hear my name. Taste the gin. Feel the pain.

There's no escaping the demon that haunts me. Because the real demon is me.

It's not until I hear my name again—for real this time, not just in my head—that my eyes fly open.

I shoot up like a shot, running a hand frantically through my hair and trying to stop the world from spinning as the blood rushes from my head. The pool lounger shifts under me, and for a second, I worry I'll topple over.

"How'd you find me?" I croak as I steady myself and plant my feet on the ground.

Cory takes two steps forward and holds up his phone. "I asked for help," he whispers.

He looks—*fuck*. He looks horrible. Forlorn. Like he's in excruciating pain.

"I've been out to the Ledges, then on a wild goose chase through the maze of storage units off Carnegie. This"—he gestures around the Wheelers' backyard—"was Tori and Rhett's idea. And, honestly, it was my last hope."

He crosses the yard slowly, focused on me the entire time. His expression is filled with so much concern I have to turn my head and look away.

When he's finally standing in front of me, he stops, then slowly sinks to his knees.

I can feel his eyes boring into my temple and jawline as he searches my face. But I refuse to look at him. He places both hands on my quads, creating friction against the fabric of my jeans as he runs them back and forth.

"Jake." He then crosses his arms on my lap and lowers his head to rest on my thighs. "Dempsey told me someone showed up at the bar tonight. That you got upset and took off."

He can't see me with the way he's resting in my lap, but I nod.

"When I couldn't get a hold of you, I made him tell me everything he could remember. Dem thought it had to do with two guys who came in for a drink. He said one used to work at Archway Prep. I didn't push him for more information, but was it—"

"Yes," I rush to reply before he can say the words. I can't bear to hear who he thinks Ian McDowell is to me. A villain? Yes. But also the source of shame that's metastasized in my body over the last ten years. The root cause of why I'm so damn good at compartmentalizing, shutting down, tuning out, and pushing people away.

Cory sighs again, nuzzling his head into my lap, willing me to let him in.

My gut clenches in regret: For what I did. For what I can't bring myself to do now.

I want to crumble.

I want to beg him to hold me.

I want to tell my husband the truth.

I want to show him my darkest demon and have him tell me that it's okay. That it doesn't change things. That what I did ten years ago doesn't define me.

But I can't.

I just can't.

I won't risk everything we've built over the last few months by letting him see me at my worst.

If Cory finds out what I gave up so easily, and for no good reason besides wanting to prove to myself that I was capable of feeling something beyond Joe's disappointment that night...

"I think it would help if we talked about it," he urges, peering up at me before pushing to his feet. He brushes off his jeans, then reaches out a hand.

I let his arm just hang there and keep my head turned away, ignoring him completely.

"Jake... please. You're allowed to be upset right now. I know you're hurting. But you don't have to hurt alone. This is what a relationship is. When you're at your lowest, you can count on me. Please talk to me. Let me be here for you."

"You wouldn't understand," I mutter, running my hand down my face to prevent myself from having to actually look him in the eye.

"Try me," he whispers.

I huff out my self-loathing. "No. I can't explain it. Not to you, Cory."

Hurt flashes in his expression at my rejection. But he's not done.

"Let me in, baby."

My defenses soften slightly at his insistence—at the way he's looking at me so ardently. But then I snap back to reality and remind myself what's at stake. *That*. That right there. The way he's looking at me now: I can't lose that. I won't.

"Leave it alone, Cory. I'm not doing this with you."

A flurry of emotions plays on his face as I rise to my feet without taking his hand. He doesn't move as I brush past him. He isn't backing down. I pivot on my heel and pace. He needs to go. I'm about to tell him that when my phone vibrates in my pocket.

I mindlessly pull out the device, scrolling past the dozens of missed calls from Cory. How long have I been out here?

Dempsey: Ian McDowell and his friend are still here after last call. I've got it under control—just wanted to give you a heads-up.

I see red. Then yellow, then pink, then black. Every color of the rainbow flashes before my eyes as I read Dem's message over and over again.

There's a threat in my home. A predator on my turf. Ian McDowell is lingering in my domain. I may never have a shot like this again.

Dempsey's not some young, naïve kid. I'm not worried about him.

But I still feel compelled to get to the bar. Now. I know an opportunity when I see one.

I assess my husband up and down, shaking my head in frustration.

Fuck.

I wish he hadn't come here.

"The man who tried to sexually assault me as a kid showed up at the bar tonight."

Cory's eyes bug out of his head as he processes my words.

"He's still there, actually. He's still sitting at my bar, roosting in my nest, refusing to take a hint that last call means *get the fuck out*. So I've gotta go."

"Jake," he hisses in warning.

I knew he wasn't going to make this easy.

"Did you talk to him? Does he remember you?" he frantically asks.

The seconds tick by as I stare at the lock screen of my phone. I don't have a plan. But I need to do this. I just have to figure out how to make Cory loosen his grip so I can get away.

"I didn't speak to him. He has no idea he's sitting in the bar of the kid he took advantage of." I pause before making my intentions clear. "But he's about to."

"Wait, what?" He closes the space between us and tries to wrap me in his arms. I spin out of his hold and take two measured steps back.

"Let me go," I choke out, turning my head in shame.

He doesn't respond. He just comes at me again with open arms.

"Cory! Stop!" I holler, pulling out of his hold and crossing my arms over my chest to fend off any other attempts. This isn't some kumbaya moment where we're just going to hug it out and everything is going to get better.

"No, Jake! I'm not going to stop. Not until you let me in and let me help you!"

And there's the rub.

I can't let him in.

Not now.

Not when it comes to this.

His arms are still outstretched, an invitation I ache to accept. What I wouldn't give to let him hold me right now. But I can't. If I let him get a grasp on me again, I'll admit everything. And right now, I need to go.

"Jake, look at me," he demands with an urgency I've never heard from him. "Promise me you won't engage with him or reveal your identity."

There's a part of me that wants to get wrapped up in his protectiveness. But I tell that part to sit down and shut up. I don't have time for those kinds of feelings tonight.

I shake my head and steel my expression. "I can't promise you that. I've gotta go."

He reaches for me, but I shrug him off.

He moves in front of me, but I sidestep and evade him.

"Don't do this, Jake."

I ignore his words and make my way through the side yard. There are enough fallen leaves littered on the grass to punctuate each step with an audible crunch. I focus on that sound—concentrate on the rustling of dead leaves underfoot—to distract from anything but my desire to get to The Oak.

Cory's hand encircles my wrist, halting me in my tracks.

"I know what you're trying to do. You're trying to shut me out. You're trying to punish yourself. But that's not acceptable. It's not just you anymore, Jake. If you get hurt—if you do something reckless and rowdy—those consequences aren't just yours to bear. Please. I'm asking you to stay."

I can't.

I want to.

I wish I could.

But I can't.

"Don't ask me to do that," I huff out defensively, "unless you want to be disappointed."

He glares at my rebuttal. Like he doesn't believe me. Like he's not giving up.

"I'm serious, Jake. There's no good reason for you to go back to The Oak right now. None. You're just going to hurt yourself. You're going to hurt *us*."

I close my eyes and consider for one split second what it would feel like to stay. To give in. To lean on him. But it's a silly notion: a fool's game. He may think he knows what happened. But in reality, he has no idea. Divulging the depth of my pain—carving out the scar of my shittiest decision and showing him how deeply I can cut and how beautifully I can bleed—that's not going to happen. Not tonight. Not ever.

So instead of giving in, I push back. Hard.

"Drop the concerned husband act," I sneer. "This has nothing to do with you and me. This is something I have to handle on my own. Don't try to butt in where you don't belong."

He physically recoils at my rejection.

"Please don't do this," he whispers.

I turn on my heel and storm away. Too scared—*too sad*—too raw to look back and take in the pain I left in my wake.

Chapter 37

Jake

I don't even remember starting the car. Thank God for self-driving technology. As I coast through the familiar streets of Hampton, I'm on autopilot, too. Which is a good thing, since I'm completely distracted and trying desperately to keep Cory's expression out of my head.

I'm such an asshole. I regretted every word the second I said them, instantly wanting to suck them back in and swallow them down. But it was like I couldn't stop myself from shutting him out and cowering away from the situation.

I bolted. I wish I could say I'm surprised by my own behavior. But this is what I do best. Run away. Flee.

I just... fuck. I just couldn't let him see me like this. Not after everything has been so fucking good between us.

Except the truth is undeniable: all my attempts to hide my pain were in vain. He sees me. He fucking sees me more clearly than I see myself. He knows that something's eating me from the inside out. It was pointless to try to hide this from him.

What's it going to be like tomorrow? Next week? It's not like he's going to forget what happened. I can't erase the memories of what he just saw and how I reacted.

Fuck.

I can't tell him about Ian.

And yet...

Not telling him doesn't feel like an option anymore, either.

I groan as I ease the car to a stop at a red light and hear the train horn blast in the distance. Acceptance glides over me like a shroud as the weight of realization sets in.

I can't hide from Cory. I'm too far gone—too *in love*—to not open up to him now.

It was so stupid to think I could just—what? Ignore what happened? Pretend like there isn't this secret festering inside me?

Telling him might ruin everything.

But not telling him would be worse.

"Fuck!" I push down hard on the accelerator as soon as the light turns green. The momentum has my body slamming into the seat, forcing me to suck in a long breath and refocus.

I don't want anything to change between us.

But what he said—*"this is what a relationship is"*—he's right.

This isn't something I've been able to get past on my own. But maybe, if I open up to him and confess what I did, we can face it together.

I turn into the closest parking lot as I grab my phone from its mount. I take a moment to steady my breathing, the interior of the car illuminated by the glow from the Jersey Bagels sign in front of me. Ironically this parking lot is smack in the middle of Hampton. It's the halfway point from my condo to Clinton's and The Oak.

I shoot off an overdue reply to Dempsey first.

Jake: Thanks for the update. Just do what you have to do to get them out the door, then check the cameras to make sure he's really gone. I knew that guy in a past life. Not good people. I have to get home to Cory, but call if you need me.

His response comes through a moment later.

Dem: Got it, boss.

I flip my phone a few times and consider my options. I'm fucking terrified to slink back to my husband with my tail between my legs after the way I just acted. I could text him, or I could call. But both those options seem like cop-outs, given the enormity of what I still need to confess.

Fuck it. I can be back to the condo in less time than it's going to take to sit here and figure out my next move. I just need to see him—talk to him face to face. Once we're together, it'll be okay. When I'm in his arms, I can do anything.

I remount my phone and adjust my seat when the screen lights up with a notification. I glance at it as I put the car in reverse, just to make sure it's not Dempsey calling for backup.

The name on the display has me stomping on the brake.

I put the car in park again—this time all cattywampus in the middle of the Jersey Bagels lot—then quickly grab the device to accept the call.

"Hello?" I rush out.

"Jake. Thank God..."

Her panicked voice makes my heart rate spike.

"What's wrong?" I demand. There's no good reason for my sister-in-law to be calling me at eleven on a Sunday night.

"It's Fiona. I think she's having an asthma attack. I'm in Columbus because my sister is having a procedure tomorrow, and Julian, he... he was supposed to..."

I slam my fist against the top of the steering wheel in anger. She doesn't need to explain to me what kind of parent Julian is. I witnessed it firsthand.

"Are they at the house?" I ask, putting the call on speakerphone as I shift into drive.

"Yes. They're at the house. I have no idea how long she's been wheezing, but I can hear the rattle through the phone. Jake—"

Her plea undoes me. It's like my brain and my body and my entire existence have just one purpose now.

"I'm on my way. I'm literally in my car, Ash. I'll be at your house in... eight minutes, tops. Do you want to stay on the line with me? Or do you want me to call you when I get there?"

"Call me. Just get there as quickly and safely as you can."

"On it," I assure her. "I'll call you as soon as I get to her."

Her thank-you is barely audible as the line disconnects, and I whiz through the main intersection of downtown Hampton.

"Where is she?" I demand when my brother swings open one of the thick front doors to the Whitely Estate. This is the house I grew up in, so I know my way around. I push past him and stomp through the foyer, assuming she's either in the living room or upstairs.

"Through here," he grumbles as his wide stride overtakes mine and he passes me in the hall. "I told Ashleigh not to bother you." He sighs loudly, frustration radiating off him as I quicken my pace to keep up.

As soon as I spot her, I'm there.

"Feef," I murmur, scooping up her little body in my arms and sitting down on the couch in the spot where she'd just been curled up. She opens her mouth like she's going to speak, then sputters out a ragged, shallow cough.

Mimi's on the far end of the couch, playing on her tablet. She sets it aside and scoots closer to me, wrapping her hands around my bicep as I rub her sister's back.

"Hey, you," I greet, kissing her on the forehead quickly before turning my attention back to Fiona.

"You're okay," I murmur assuredly to my older niece. She blinks up at me and makes another grunting noise. It's like she can't even get a word out. Shit. This is bad.

"What have you given her?" I demand, my eyes shooting to my brother as I run one hand up and down her spine. I can fucking feel her lungs laboring under my touch as she tries to inhale, the wheeze making her whole body tremble.

"Nothing," Julian admits. "Ashleigh told me where to find the inhaler, but I can't get her to actually use it." He rakes a hand through his hair and points absentmindedly to where the red and white inhaler sits on the coffee table along with the bag of medical supplies.

"Meems, bring me that bag," I instruct before looking up at my brother. "Call Ashleigh and put her on speakerphone."

His face screws up in protest, but I cut him off before he can even start with me. "She's expecting my call. Either you do it, or I delay giving your daughter her inhaler even longer by going out to my car to get my phone."

Julian scowls and huffs, but he's not my focus right now. As soon as Mimi brings over the medical supply bag, I dig for the spacer, then shift forward to grab the inhaler off the table.

"Let's try it this way, okay?" I ask Fiona.

She nods weakly as I sit her upright on the cushions beside me.

I connect the two pieces, deciding to go for a full rescue dose instead of the two puffs she would normally get. "Breathe out first," I remind her, bringing the end of the spacer to her lips and tilting her chin up slightly.

I watch, anxious, as her face screws up in pain. She blows out, but the breath is so shallow it barely moves the little filter flap on the top of the spacer. Fuck. When she inhales, she coughs and sputters, but I see a good amount of the medicine leave the chamber. It's a start.

"How is she?" Ashleigh's panicked voice fills the room.

I don't bother responding just yet—at least not to her. "Good job, baby girl. Try again. Blow out again for me."

Fiona gets in another good dose of medicine, and it takes a few seconds before she starts sputtering this time. She repeats the inhalation a few more times until I'm satisfied she got as much in her system as possible.

"*Psst.*" I jut my chin toward Mimi, who's picked her tablet up again. I know she's watching us, taking everything in. Kid doesn't miss a thing. But shutting down is one of our shared coping strategies, so I know she's scared for her sister right now, even if she doesn't show it.

"I need some help from nurse Mimi."

She grins at the screen before looking up at me.

"Get me the finger thingy," I instruct, knowing she'll know exactly what I mean.

She searches in the bag as I wrap one arm protectively around Fiona, then finally turn to where my brother's pacing with the phone in hand.

"Can you hear me, Ash?" I ask, circumventing Julian completely. He scowls at being ignored but steps closer so I can hear his wife's response.

"Yes! Yes, I can hear you. How's she doing?"

I look down at Fiona, who just seems—fuck. She seems listless. I have no idea how long she was struggling before Julian finally called Ashleigh. But I know it was too long. I glance over to Mimi, who's sitting up on her knees beside me now, opening and closing the Velcro pouch that holds the portable pulse ox. I've never had to do this before, but Ashleigh showed me how to use it. It can't be that hard to figure out.

"She's just okay," I offer tentatively. I don't want to put anyone on edge, but I know things aren't good. "You're going to be okay," I whisper to Fiona before smoothing back her hair and kissing her on the forehead. "I did the full six puffs on her inhaler, and I'm about to check her pulse ox."

"Okay, good. Thank God." Ashleigh's appreciation doesn't feel warranted, and I can't help but notice how the wrinkles deepen between Julian's brows as he glares at his phone.

I hold out my hand, and Mimi places the device in my palm. There's only one button on the thing, so I push it, and the screen comes to life. I open the clamp, and Fiona sticks her finger out for me. She's done this a million times before, so she knows the drill.

"Just try to breathe normally," I encourage as we watch the red lines dance on the screen, reading the oxygen saturation in her system.

"I go next," Mimi whispers beside me.

I fight back a grin and nod in her direction.

When the number pops up on the screen, my stomach bottoms out. "It's eighty-seven, Ash."

Fiona's eyes widen at the number, and Julian's scowl deepens.

"Is that good or bad?" he asks, looking at the phone, then back to me.

"It's supposed to be between ninety-five and one hundred, Julian," Ashleigh snaps through the phone.

Fiona is suddenly overcome by another coughing fit, cranking the vibe of the room up another fifty decimals. I gently caress her shoulder, whispering words of reassurance.

Julian's pacing now, but he's close enough I know Ashleigh can hear me. "Ash—am I remembering correctly that six puffs is the max?"

"Yes," she answers automatically. "When did you give them to her?"

"Literally two minutes ago. What do you want to do?" My question is aimed at Ashleigh, but my gaze is fixed on Julian.

We're locked in an emotional stare down as I try to hold my temper but also wordlessly let him know I think he's a shitty parent. Sure, things happen. Fiona's had asthma attacks before. But I can't help but wonder if his lack of parental know-how contributed to what's turning out to be a traumatic ordeal.

"Take her to Children's," Ashleigh says.

I nod, assuming her words are directed at me, until I realize Julian's opening his mouth, a combative look marring his face.

"You got it," I chime in, cocking one eyebrow in challenge when Julian's head snaps up.

He can be pissed off all he wants: there's no way I'm letting Fiona out of my sight until I know she's okay. Hell, I'd take her to the hospital by myself if I didn't think it'd complicate things with all the HIPPA laws and insurance crap.

"Why don't you go potty real quick, okay?" I tell Mimi. I rise to stand, then turn to scoop Fiona up in my arms. Her color looks better now than when I first arrived. But she's still not herself.

"I'm driving," Julian declares as he storms out of the room.
Okay then.

"You're coming with us?" Fiona manages to whisper as she wraps one hand around my neck. I've got her cradled in my arms, even though she'd probably be fine to walk. I snatch up the medical supply bag and grab Mimi's tablet with my free hand.

"Yep," I confirm, popping the *P* to lighten the mood. "Looks like we're having some late-night Uncle Jakey time."

She giggles, and Mimi comes scurrying back through the kitchen to join us. We head to the garage together where Julian's already waiting.

Chapter 38

Jake

I'm bone tired, but I don't dare close my eyes. All I can do is stare at the monitors displaying Fiona's vitals.

They admitted her when we arrived, just like I knew they would. Now I'm pressed up against my brother on this miniature plastic couch with a sleeping Mimi sprawled between us. He's let out more sighs than seem reasonable over the last few hours. I'm shocked as shit when he actually opens his mouth and speaks.

"I'm sorry she called you."

This fucker. I can't even imagine what would have happened if she hadn't. I physically shudder at the thought, then smooth back Mimi's hair mindlessly to ground myself. I can't lay into him in the middle of his daughter's hospital room. Doesn't mean I'll let him get away with shit.

"I'm not," I huff.

Julian leans forward and rests his elbows on his knees. He turns to me and watches as I stroke Mimi's hair. "How did you…" he starts, trailing off before he can actually ask a question. "Never mind," he mutters, tenting his hands and resting his forehead on his fingers.

"How did I what?" I push.

He's quiet for a moment, but I'm not in a rush. It's not like we're going anywhere anytime soon. I can wait him out for hours if that's what it takes to get him to open up. I learned that trick from Cory.

"How did you know how to do all that?" He glares at me, but I don't think he's mad that I intervened and administered Fiona's inhaler. He's probably feeling inferior, which I assume is a foreign feeling for the formidable Julian Whitely.

I fight the impulse to rag on him or give him a hard time. Things feel more fragile than hostile between us at the moment, but I'll be damned if I give him any excuse to keep me away from the girls.

"Ashleigh taught me all about Fiona's asthma and Amelia's strawberry allergy before she left me alone with them the first time," I explain. "She made me get a CPR certification at the Holt State rec center, too."

He looks at me with a mix of skepticism and wonder, almost like he's seeing me in a new light. "I had no idea…" he mutters as he trails a hand through his hair.

I'm over his inattentive parent bullshit. If he's not going to step up and try harder with them, they're going to need me more than ever.

"There's something you should know, Julian."

He sits up straight and shifts back to meet my gaze.

"I love these girls. They're seriously some of my favorite people in the world. I would do anything, give up anything, sacrifice everything, for their health and happiness. Nothing can keep me out of their lives." I pause for a breath before throwing down my decree. "Not even you."

His nostrils flare in challenge, but he doesn't utter a word. We sit there, glaring at each other for what feels like hours. Finally, he blinks and looks away.

He inhales deeply, then sighs. When he speaks, I'm stunned by the words that come out of his mouth.

"I'm sorry about what happened at the splash pad yesterday."

My eyes go wide as I wait for him to pull the rug out from under me. But he doesn't follow up with anything else. Did my brother just—apologize?

"Okay," I reply hesitantly. "I appreciate that."

He continues. "I was in shock. I felt like a fool. I drove by, spotted Ash's van, and thought I'd surprise the girls. I was home earlier from my business trip than planned. I was jet-lagged, and I was unnecessarily short with you and them. And then to find out you're married—"

"Don't," I growl out in warning.

"Don't what?"

I grind my molars and try to keep my cool. "Don't even think about casting judgment or making a remark about my husband," I warn. "He's a good man, Julian. An *amazing* man. I love him, and for the first time in my whole damn life, I think I might be genuinely, truly happy."

My words come out harsh and rushed. But they needed to be said. He can think anything he wants about me. But there's no way in hell he's allowed to talk shit about my man.

Julian scoffs defensively. "I wasn't going to—"

I cut him off before he can make his case. "Yeah, you were. I know how your mind works. I know what you think of me. But you can keep that shit to yourself. There's too much love in my heart to let your hate taint my marriage."

We sit in heavy silence then, both scowling, lost in our own heads.

"Jake," he says softly, almost like he's struggling to get through to me. "I wasn't upset at the splash pad because you married a man. I'm not Joe," he sneers. "I was upset to find out that you got married and I had no idea."

The room's too dark for me to search for the lie in his eyes. But the weight of his words feels genuine.

Still.

"Just like how I had no idea you had kids?" I mock.

"Fuck," he mutters. "I deserved that. I'm sorry about that, too. I'm sorry about so much when it comes to our relationship. Truth be told, this isn't how I thought my life would go. That I'd work myself to the bone every day. That I'd barely spend any time with my family, that I'd have no idea how to take care of my own damn kids. Yet here I am. I'm just like him."

I've barely had time to process his confession before I'm taking the open shot.

"Then do better," I insist.

Mimi stirs in my lap, rolling over so she's facing away from me now, one hand thrown over her eyes and forehead. I can't help but smile when I look at her. She's so docile and sweet when she's sleeping. It's a noticeable shift from her day-to-day sass.

"It's not hard to show up and be there for people when they need you, Julian. Just because you're CEO of Whitely Enterprises doesn't mean you have to be like him."

"You think I *want* to be like him?"

I did. And part of me still does. It would take monumental effort on his part for me to change how I view my brother in comparison to our dad. I can tell he resents the idea, though. And I don't blame him for that. Joe Whitely was a vile, despicable excuse for a father. I choose my next words carefully.

"I think that you and Joey are more than happy to perform the roles he assigned to you."

"And what about you?" he asks, turning the conversation back on me. "How have you managed to exist outside the shadow of his demands?"

I guffaw at his oversimplified assessment of my relationship with our dad. Does he really think I just skipped along through adolescence, completely unaffected by the monster who spawned me?

"Well, when you tell your only living parent that you were drugged and almost raped, and his response is to spit on you and say you were probably asking for it, you tend to lose the ability to care about his demands."

The air grows thick between us and the temperature in the room ratchets up a notch. I hadn't planned to share that with him—now I'm spiraling in a mix of fear and shame while I wait to see how he'll respond.

"You were sexually assaulted?"

My jaw ticks as the truth itches to break free. Yes isn't the wrong answer. But it's far from the whole story.

"In high school. There was this assistant athletic trainer at Arch who was in his early twenties. I... I met up with him with the intention of hooking up. But things got way out of hand. He drugged my drink, then he started to get really aggressive with me." I swallow past the lump of emotion that forms each time I recall the first part of that night. "I shouldn't have been there, I know. But yeah. A guy named Ian McDowell tried to sexually assault me when I was sixteen."

"Ian McDowell?"

Those two words sound like a vile curse on my brother's tongue. His disgust is evident, although I'm almost positive it isn't directed at me.

"Yeah. Friend of yours?" I scoff, desperate to lighten the mood.

"Hold on," Julian mutters, pulling his phone out of his pocket and swiping aggressively across the screen. I watch as his eyes narrow further with each swipe.

After what feels like an hour of silence, but in reality is only a few minutes, he explains what he's doing. "Ashleigh and I are both on the alumni advisory committee at Archway. We just signed off on the hiring of an Ian McDowell."

Rage and adrenaline course through my veins with the reminder. My body flushes with hatred when I think about that man, both in terms of what he did back then, as well as what he could do again now in an administrative position at Archway Preparatory Academy.

"That's him," I manage to say through gritted teeth.

Julian's head snaps over to look at me. I can see the shock and disgust mapped across his face in the blue-light glow of his phone.

"How do you know?"

"Because he came into my bar tonight, and I recognized him. One of my employees chatted him up, and he mentioned he'd just been hired."

"No fucking way," Julian sputters, his outrage tangible. "Not on my watch."

"Wait..." I muse, starting to connect the dots. "Can you do something about him?"

He holds my gaze and smirks. "You bet your ass I can. He's gone. He hasn't even started, but he's done. I'll have to make a few calls tomorrow, but there's no way in hell that predator will be on the payroll or anywhere near students at any institution ever again."

A tsunami of emotion smashes into me, assailing me from all sides. There's relief and redemption, shame and unhealed pain. A spiral of self-loathing twists in my gut, but it's replaced by something lighter. Something brighter. Something that feels a lot like hope.

I suck in a frantic, ragged breath when I finally snap out of it. I never, in a million years, thought that my brother—who I have dismissed for most of my life because of the similarities he shares with Joe—would be in a position to right this wrong.

I think I'm still in shock, but Julian's regarding me with his brows raised.

My words come out forced but steady. It's like I'm too afraid to ask him to do what he's already offering. "I think if you have the power to remove him, you should. You don't want someone like that working at Arch when the girls are old enough to attend."

I grind my molars and hold my breath, desperate for his confirmation.

"Jake," he admonishes in a way that has me doing a double take. I stare into his eyes as he shatters the last wall between us. "It's not just about them. I'm doing this for you."

For me?

Julian wants to do this for me.

This was so not how I expected this night to go. And yet here I sit, my leg pressed up against my big brother's, his daughter cradled in my arms. For the first time in my life, at least where my family is concerned, I feel the power of giving—and receiving—unconditional love.

Chapter 39

Cory

I sit alone at the kitchen island, staring at the natural stone until I see shapes in the quartz. I chance a glimpse at the clock on the microwave—again. The digital display mocks me as it reveals that less than two minutes have passed since I last looked.

3:52 a.m.

He isn't here.

He hasn't called.

He isn't coming home.

I scoff as I think about the last time I sat up all night, waiting for the man I married. Was that really only a few weeks ago? It feels like we've lived a lifetime together since then.

We've grown.

We've changed.

We've blossomed.

And yet, here I sit. Alone. Again.

I've called his phone a dozen times. I've called The Oak, and Clinton's, too, just in case. I've resisted contacting anyone else. It's not like I didn't see him tonight. I know exactly where he was planning to go.

I just don't know where he is now.

I sigh out his name in anguish. I'm just so... defeated. Frustrated, angry, pissed off, and disappointed, too. But mostly defeated.

To watch him grapple with the decision, then *still* shut me out after I gave him chance after chance to stay...

It's heartbreaking. And eye opening.

The entire situation is made worse by the fact that I finally know what it feels like to be let in.

Just last night, he opened up. He let me in, and he let me stay.

Tonight, he shut it all down. He put a hard and fast halt to everything that's grown between us.

My heart aches for him, but it also beats out a familiar rhythm of self-pity. The throbbing is painful, but it's not foreign. Deep down, I know I did this to myself. My pain is self-inflicted. That's the curse of loving too easily.

I flick my ring on the countertop, watching it spin until it loses momentum, falters, and falls.

I always do this.

I fall first. Fall harder. Think a relationship is deeper than it is. It's like I want to believe in love so badly, I've got blinders on to what's actually happening.

But every other time I thought I was in love, there was always a nagging voice in the back of my head, questioning my feelings and planting seeds of insecurity. I've grown used to doubting my own judgment over the years.

I didn't realize it right away, but over the last few weeks, I haven't had to silence my self-doubt or tell my intuition to back down. Because I never felt it with Jake.

I thought he was different. I thought *we* were different. That things had shifted between us, especially over the last week.

I thought wrong.

I knew better than to fall for him. He's always affected me in a way no other man ever has, and I knew I was taking a risk by giving him my heart.

I knew it all along.

I wanted to love him. I wanted him to love me, too. I wanted to live happily ever after.

I wanted the fairy tale.

I've never done this before. It's embarrassing, really. I've been in a number of long-term relationships. But I've never broken up with anyone. Ever.

I'll uphold my end of the agreement; I don't want to mess up our arrangement. But things can't go on the way they have been. This time, I have to choose me, even if I break both our hearts in the process.

Jake pushing me away last night proved I'd let myself get too close.

Now I have to shut it down.

As I watch the clock change to four a.m., I accept my fate.

Jake made his choice. It was selfish, and it hurt. But he did what he had to do to protect himself.

Now I have to do the same.

I slide off the bar stool and scan the now-familiar kitchen. We made so many beautiful, poignant memories in such a short amount of time. When things were good, they were so damn good. I'll never regret basking in the all-consuming glow of Jake's affection.

But healthy love doesn't hurt. Not like this. I have to accept that I deserve more than "what could have been" from a relationship. I have to choose me.

I leave my wedding ring on the counter and make my way back to the bedroom to pack.

Chapter 40

Jake

I slip through the front door and guide it closed so I don't wake him. The second I heel off my shoes, I sigh. The cool hardwood panels soothe my aching feet through my socks.

Exhaustion is tightening its grip on me—I'm physically, emotionally, and mentally drained. All I want is a hot shower, my bed, and my man.

When I turn the corner into the kitchen, I realize there's no need to be quiet. Cory's up, sitting at the breakfast bar.

He's right there.

My heart flutters when I see him, my nerves instantly settling as the adrenaline drains from my body. I'm so comforted by his presence. Being close to him feels like coming home.

We have a lot to talk about... fuck. I know I have to apologize and explain. Even in the light of a new day, I'm still committed to telling him the truth about what happened with Ian McDowell. He deserves to know. I want my husband to know everything about me: the good, the bad, and the ugly. Before last night, I wasn't willing to accept that, but now I can finally admit my truth: I trust Cory. I love Cory. And I believe that no matter what I confess, he'll love me anyway.

But as I try to meet his gaze, his posture throws me off. He looks... withdrawn? Like he hasn't slept? Maybe he's more upset about what happened last night than I realized. I blow out a long breath; I've got some groveling to do. That's okay: he deserves an apology. I want to give him what he needs so we can move past this.

"Hey," I cautiously greet him before pulling open the fridge for water. What is it about hospitals that makes people so thirsty?

He whispers his reply, his voice so low I barely hear him over the hum of the fridge. "Where were you?"

Fuck. I'm embarrassed as hell about how I acted last night. It was immature and selfish to push him away when I needed him most. I know I owe him an apology. And an explanation. I exhale and hold up my arm so he can see the bright orange band.

"I was at the hospital all night."

He's up and out of his seat a moment later.

"What? Are you okay?"

I'd left my phone in my car, then Julian drove us to the hospital. In all the chaos of the night, followed by my heart-to-heart with Julian, I hadn't even thought to text Cory and let him know what was going on.

"Oh, shit. Yes, I'm fine. Really. It was Fiona. She has asthma, and she was wheezing pretty hard last night. My dumbass brother doesn't even know how to administer her inhaler, let alone check her pulse ox. Ashleigh called me in a panic, so I ran over to their house to help."

I down my entire glass of water and let out a satisfied sigh.

"As soon as I saw her, I knew she needed medical attention. I went with them to the ER, then they admitted her overnight for observation since she'd been in respiratory distress for so long. I stayed with Julian since Mimi was with us, too."

I can't help but smile at the memory of her sprawled across us on that hospital couch.

"I probably should have taken her home, but my brother…. he was so fucking out of his element. I felt like I had to be there in case he needed help. Thankfully Fiona's vitals all stabilized, and they discharged her this morning."

His next words come out a choked whisper. "You were at the hospital all night and you didn't even think to tell me?"

His question is full of judgment and indignation.

I take two steps forward, desperate to close the space between us and make this right.

"I'm sorry, baby. I wasn't thinking about anything but Fifi last night."

His eyes double in size. I don't understand why he's so upset about the hospital. He shakes his head, sticks his tongue in his cheek, and mutters "unbelievable."

"Cory, talk to me. I said I'm sorry. What's wrong?"

"What's wrong? Seriously, Jake? What's *wrong*? You left me standing in Rhett's backyard without telling me where you were going. You made it sound like you were going after the man who sexually assaulted you as a kid! I begged you to stay, and you left anyway. I've been sitting up all night worrying about where you went, what you did. I've been worried to death about what you might do, about what he might do to you if you …"

Oh.

Shit.

"Last night was the worst night of my life." Cory fists his hands at his sides as he paces the length of the island. I've barely processed his words before he continues.

"I was worried about you. I was worried about *us*. I've been here all night, helpless, resigned to the fact that you were out making shitty decisions and regrettable choices. You have no idea the kind of scenarios I came up with in my mind."

Fuckin' A. Last night I texted Dempsey that I was going home to Cory. My husband has no idea that he *did* get through to me: that I pumped the brakes on my impulsive plan to go after Ian McDowell and that I had every intention of coming home to him before Ashleigh called.

He has no idea because I fucked up and didn't tell him any of that.

I circle the bar to meet him and open my arms.

"Baby, I'm so sorry. Let me explain…"

"No."

What the hell?

"No?" I question, like maybe I didn't hear him right. But he says the word again.

"No."

Dread settles in my gut as I realize just how much weight those two little letters hold. Not gonna lie—it hurts. It fucking burns. His rejection stings in a way I've never felt before. I'm tired and on edge and so desperate to not fight with him right now. But all I can seem to do is push back in defense.

"So what?" I spit out. "You're just going to shut me out? Not even let me apologize?"

"It's not that simple, Jake."

"It can be! I said I'm sorry! I was at the fucking hospital with my niece! I meant to text you, but I was so determined to get home and just talk to you instead. Then I left my phone in my car, and I didn't realize... I didn't mean..."

I'm doing a shitty job of explaining myself, and I'm getting even more flustered because I can't make the words make sense.

Cory shakes his head and averts his gaze. "Last night was the worst night of my life," he repeats. "I owe it to myself to never have to go through something like that again. I can't give you that power over me."

I blink in slow motion as his words chip away at my tattered, tired heart. He won't meet my eyes; he's shutting me out just like I did to him last night. I'm desperate for him to just let me explain, but he won't even look at me. I follow his gaze, my eyes landing on the ring sitting smack in the middle of the island.

What the fuck?

That ring's supposed to be on his finger.

I run a hand down my face in anguish, grasping for any sensible thing to say to put an end to this madness. There's a pulsing ache in the pit of my stomach as his intentions become more and more clear to me. He's standing right in front of me, and I already miss him.

"You can't just—"

He interrupts me before I can even object. "I have to."

The look in his eye... the weight of his words... without consent, my body begins to shake.

"Cory, no. Please. Let me explain. I was coming home to you last night, I swear. I even told Dempsey I wasn't coming to The Oak because I needed to get home to you."

"You had time to text Dempsey?" he asks accusingly.

Fuck! I put my hands on my head and grip my hair, racking my brain for the right thing to say.

"I know that sounds bad, but I didn't think—"

He cuts me off again.

"We can stay married, but only on paper, until the two years are up," he offers resolutely. "This? Whatever this was?" He points to himself, then to me. "This is over."

I choke back a sob as the gravity of it all slams into me.

"Cory, please..."

He shakes his head, closes his eyes for a long moment, then opens them again. And all I see in his expression is resolve. "Let me go," he begs.

But I can't do that. I won't.

"Baby, you can't leave," I plead. "What we have? How I feel? This is real. This is more real than anything I've ever felt before. What I didn't tell you is that I—"

"Don't," he hisses, shutting me down before I can utter the words I've been too hesitant to say to his face until now. Fuck. Why did I wait?

"Don't say it," he repeats. "Don't you dare."

I hate fighting with him. But I have to try.

"But I do. Cory, I swear to you, I do. I've known it for a while now; I was just too chicken to say it out loud. This is the most real thing I've ever experienced in my life, but I had to admit it to myself before I could tell you. You can't leave, because I need you. You can't leave, because I *love* you."

His face twists up in pain. In agony. In total and utter anguish.

And all I can think about is how I did that.

I caused his pain. I'm responsible for everything he's feeling. I'm the asshole who messed this up and hurt him in inexplicable ways.

I bury down my own hurt and reach out for him.

But instead of letting me hold him, he meets my gaze and slaughters me.

"If that's all true, then let me leave."

He takes a tentative step toward me. And even though I know I should move out of his way, I can't make myself budge.

I swallow past the lump in my throat and make my final plea.

"I don't want you to go."

He brushes past me without making eye contact.

"Now you know how I felt last night."

Chapter 41

Cory

She knew I was coming, yet she still looks shocked to see me on her doorstep. Maybe not shocked to see me—but taken aback by the state I'm in, perhaps.

"Hi," I choke out, my voice cracking pathetically as I push down the tears that have been threatening to spill since the moment I pulled out of the garage at the condo and started the solo drive to the airport.

Tori's expression softens, her eyes full of sympathy as she reaches across the threshold and pulls me into a hug.

"Cor," she soothes as she tightens her hold on me.

I exhale and soak in the empathy emanating from her.

Coming to Virginia like this is beyond out of character for me. But I didn't know where else to go. My abuela and my parents know about Jake, but they don't know how things have evolved or just how deeply I was in it. Lia and I have been on rocky ground since the confrontation in the parking lot a few weeks back, so I can't open up to her, either.

I need a friend. And yeah, okay. Maybe I want a friend who knows Jake better than most people because I know she'll understand what I'm going through without me having to explain just how magnetic that man really is. It would hurt too much, honestly, to have to try to capture his essence in words.

"Come on," she instructs as she pulls me through the doorway. "Let's get inside so we can do this properly."

I nod, then follow her into the expensive, modern apartment. I'm not two steps in the door before Penny is scurrying through the kitchen and yipping at my feet. Tori laughs at her dog's overly enthusiastic reaction before looking back over her shoulder at me. "Looks like I'm not the only one who missed you."

The first genuine smile I've felt all day breaks across my face as I crouch down to greet the pug mix. I questioned my choice to come here about a dozen times on the flight, but now that I'm here, I know this is right.

--

"I'm just so mad that I let myself believe it was real," I bemoan for probably the tenth time. We're splayed out on Tori and Rhett's enormous sectional couch, our takeout containers still littered all over the coffee table.

Tori sits up straighter, leans forward, and reaches for my hand. "I hate this for you. I wasn't sure where things stood when you showed up here today. But now I'm even more conflicted."

"What?" I demand. "What do you mean?"

She gives me a sad smile and scrunches her nose, pausing for a minute before she answers thoughtfully.

"Do you really want to hear this?"

Ugh. Do I? I mean, I do. I desperately do. But I thought I'd at least have a few more hours to wallow before she started dishing up her signature style of pragmatic advice.

"It sounds like this relationship has taken you both by surprise. Jake isn't the boy he used to be. He's what I worried about most when I moved here. But when I talk to him lately, or when Rhett gives me an update... I can tell he's changed. He's different these days. I think he's different because of *you*."

She pauses and gives me a pointed look.

"Jake went from being a rowdy boy who could barely tolerate himself to being this man with so much love to give. I know you don't want to hear this... but what if what you had *was* real? Is *still* real?"

I swallow past a lump of emotion clogging my throat. This was so not what I expected. This is a woman who held the man she loved at arm's length for six years. Tori's not the hopeless romantic; I am. But if she thinks there's hope... *Dammit*. I don't want her to encourage my traitorous heart. I want her to see the sensible side of this and tell me I did the right thing by walking away.

I mindlessly scratch Penny behind the ears and consider her words. I know I'm being melodramatic. What we had was real; I feel it in the very core of my being. I know because my heart won't let me forget it. That doesn't mean I was wrong to walk away.

"I know what we had was real, or at least on its way there," I admit. "But that makes it worse. I hate that it was real, and he just threw it all away."

Tori purses her lips and studies me warily. "Did he, though?"

I narrow my eyes and assess her. Is she really taking his side in this? I've spent the last several hours telling her everything, multiple times. We've analyzed our whole relationship up, down, and sideways. How we were really falling for each other. How good things were between us. I went into thorough detail about the night he left and didn't come home or even bother texting. I told her all about how he put me through emotional purgatory the other night when he fled, wouldn't answer my calls, pushed me away, then stayed out all night without so much of a courtesy text to tell me he was okay.

"He did," I insist. "He should have known I would be sitting up all night worrying, but he didn't think of me once. I can't play games like that, Tor. I've been someone's afterthought too many times to let myself fall for it again."

Silence thrums between us. She doesn't agree with me—I can practically feel her dissent—but she at least has the courtesy to let me sit in my pain for a few minutes before pushing back.

"I know this might not be what you want to hear—"

"Then don't say it," I deadpan.

"Just let me get this out," she pleads. "You and I are best friends, but Jake and I go way back. Let me say this, then I'll leave it alone. I'll support you no matter what you decide; I promise."

I nod, resigned.

"Based on everything you told me, do you think there's a chance he just... made a mistake? And I know, I know." She holds up both hands for emphasis. "I know what he did was hurtful. He handled it all wrong. But given the timeline, I can't help but wonder if he just got caught up in everything happening that night. I guarantee you Jake's not used to being accountable to anyone. He's spent his whole life on his own. He *should* have known better than to leave you in the dark all night long, especially since you've already gone through that situation with him before. But what if he just—forgot?"

I consider her words, letting my mind feel out that explanation. The problem is that every point she touched on sounds like a broken record of excuses that I've supplied for every guy I've ever dated. What Jake and I had was so special and exhilarating and real—and yet I'm left feeling just as forgotten, unworthy, and unimportant as I did in the past.

Tori continues. "He's like a toddler when it comes to understanding the expectations of being a partner, Cor. I'm not saying you have to accept that behavior. But I can't imagine Jake not actively trying to grow and improve if given the chance. That's the thing about him: he loves hard, even if he doesn't always get it right. I can't help but wonder if you just need to give your relationship more time."

I want to pick apart each statement, but at that second, Penny jumps off the spot where she was sleeping between us and barks frantically as she runs to the door. She's going so fast she slides the last few feet, right into the waiting arms of Everhett Wheeler.

"Cory!" He beams in greeting as he rises to full height after doling out a few belly scratches. He shucks off his suit jacket and drapes it over a kitchen chair as he makes his way into the apartment. He's wearing a light blue gingham button-down with perfectly tailored navy dress pants and an expensive-looking light brown belt. He looks every inch the part of young, hot, millennial CEO.

Rhett strides into the room, dipping his head to greet his wife with a tender kiss that has me aching with jealousy. "Hi, beautiful," he murmurs.

I watch as he works a hand onto the nape of her neck, tilting her head up slightly so he can kiss her again.

"I missed you today," he adds when he finally pulls away.

How those two managed to stay broken up, then live apart for years, has always been baffling to me.

Rhett straightens back up before turning his attention to me. "It's really good to see you, man. Although I have to admit, I was pissed to find out you were coming to visit us by yourself. Next time, bring that husband of yours with you, okay?"

His comment is obviously in jest. I guess Tori didn't tell him the actual reason for my last-minute visit. She snaps her head up and gives him a look, then suddenly Rhett's brows draw together in a grimace.

Ah. There it is.

"I'll, uh, I'll leave you to it, then," he offers hastily, turning on his heel to walk out of the room.

We sit awkwardly for a moment as Rhett takes his leave, although I can hear him unloading the dishwasher in the kitchen a minute later, so I know he didn't go far.

Tori sighs and turns back to me. "Where were we?"

"I believe you were trying to convince me that Jake Whitely is capable of love," I jibe.

"Cory..." She smiles sadly at me, and I know this is it. She won't push it if I'm not open to discussing the possibility of what-if.

And honestly? I don't think I am. As much as my heart wants to—as much as my soul aches to justify what he did and make a plan for how we could possibly move forward—my brain just won't allow it. I've compromised too many times before.

"I think I just need to be sad," I admit. "And a little salty. He tried to use that against me, you know. He told me he loved me to try to get me to stay."

I've barely closed my mouth when Rhett pops back into the room. "I'm sorry. I know I shouldn't have been listening. Or butting in now—"

"Everhett," Tori warns.

"I have to." His words are barely a whisper as he grimaces apologetically at his wife. When he sets his gaze on me, he's all business.

"Jake told you he loved you?"

I nod as my face flushes. I'm embarrassed that Rhett overheard my confession. And I'm completely mortified that he's calling me out on it now.

"Like, he used the three words together, 'I love you,' and not as a joke?" he pushes.

"Yes," I huff out, too uncomfortable to even make eye contact with him now.

"That fucker..."

Rhett turns away from me—thank God—and paces from one side of the living room to the other. He's got this haughty, put out air about him. I sneak a glance at Tori, who's eyes are also on her husband. But her expression is calm, almost serene. She tracks his movements, but her vibe is nothing like his right now. He's an anxious, ticking time bomb wearing a path in the carpet. I have to hold back a laugh when Penny joins him, dancing at his feet as he continues his pacing.

"Is he...?" I mutter to Tori out of the side of my mouth, unsure of what I'm even asking.

She waves a hand nonchalantly in his direction. "He's fine," she assures me. "Just let him get there."

We sit in silence, cross-legged on the couch, as Rhett continues to swirl up a cloud of emotion with his pacing. He pulls out his phone and swipes through it at one point, then shoves it back in his pocket and mutters under his breath.

"Are you sure—"

"Just wait for it," Tori whispers.

After another minute, he halts.

He strides to where we sit on the couch, squares his shoulders, then brings his hands to his hips. I can feel the intensity of his emotions as he levels me with an unwavering glare. I'm a little scared, if I'm honest. And a little turned on.

"Cory, I know you and I don't know each other that well. But Jake's been my best friend since kindergarten. I've seen him at his worst... at his lowest... I know everything there is to know about him."

I nod and avert my gaze. Rhett doesn't need to tell me how close they are. I'm aware, and I really don't need another reminder of how little I know about the man I married.

He continues. "I tell him I love him on a regular basis. Monthly, at least. Sometimes even more than that. I've been saying it to him for years. He has never once—never once in our goddamn lives—said it back to me. That's okay. I don't need to hear it, because I know the truth. He just doesn't say it. Like, ever. I can only think of one exception. I think maybe he said it to Tori once?"

She nods. "On the morning of our wedding day," she whispers dreamily. "But that's it. That's the only time he's ever said it to me."

"So if you're here because something happened between you two... and Jake said he loved you..."

My eyes go wide as Rhett's confession unravels the narrative I've woven about the last forty-eight hours of my life.

Mierda.

"I'm sorry. I feel like an asshole for intervening, but now that I know what's at stake..." Rhett blows out an extended breath as I try to make sense of his words.

My mind is at war with itself as the enormity of Jake's confession expands and takes on a life of its own.

He loves me.

But he doesn't know how to love me.

He loves me.

But loving him will only end in heartbreak for me.

Rhett interrupts my spiraling thoughts. "If Jake put that out there, I can guarantee you that he wasn't trying to manipulate you or smooth things over. He wouldn't even think to use those words against you, because it's just not something he says. If Jake said he loves you... Fuck..."

He turns on his heel and resumes his pacing, pulling his phone out of his pocket again before pounding out a message on the device.

"He cusses a lot for a CEO," I mutter, desperate to cut the tension.

Tori giggles beside me before wrapping my shoulders in a hug. "He really does." She rests her head on my arm as we watch her husband process our conversation.

As if sensing our eyes on him, Rhett looks up and gives us an apologetic glance. "Excuse me. I've gotta make a few calls." He steps forward and reaches out for Tori.

She lets him grasp her hand in his, then he lifts it to his lips and kisses it.

"Beautiful, I'm probably—"

"I know," she cuts him off. "He needs you. Go."

Rhett gives her this deep, emotive look, then turns to me and nods once before walking out of the room.

"Wait." I pull back so I can look her in the eye. "Is he—"

"Yeah. Yeah, he is."

What does that mean for me? For Tori? For this visit?

"So are you—"

"Oh, no." She chuckles, stretching her arms overhead and smiling. "Running back to Hampton to save the day is Rhett's MO. He'll go. He'll make sure Jake's okay. He'll help him figure his shit out and keep us updated."

My eyes widen at her explanation. How does she know all that from the three words he uttered?

She squeezes my arm once and offers me a sympathetic smile. "I'm staying here with you. Our only job is to sit on this couch, eat ice cream, and feel our feelings. Because at the end of the day, it doesn't matter what it means for Jake to say I love you if you don't feel the same way."

But that's the true heart of the issue: I do.

Chapter 42

Jake

The pounding on the door matches the pounding in my head. Jesus fucking Christ. If that's one of my tenants, they're about to regret waking up and choosing violence today because I'm fully prepared to match their rage.

I swing the door open, ready to tell them off. That's what work orders are for. There's no fucking reason for someone to be interrupting my drunken wallowing.

But when the door opens, it's not a tenant on the other side.

My mouth gapes as I stare into the piercing gray-blue eyes of my best friend.

"Expecting someone else?" he taunts as he pushes past me.

"Bro... what the fuck? What are you doing here?"

He turns on his heel and gives me a pointed look. I don't miss how he side-eyes my messy-ass kitchen before appraising my sorry, unkempt state.

"You told Cory you love him," he declares matter-of-factly, as if that answers my question.

My eyebrows shoot into my hairline. What the fuck? How does he know that?

"How'd—"

He cuts me off before I can even formulate a question.

"Where do you think he is right now?"

Realization sweeps over me. I saw the airline charge on our account. But I figured he went somewhere warm, somewhere fun. Somewhere to get away from me.

"He's in Virginia?" I run a hand down my face as things click into place.

"He's wrecked, bro. He needed a friend."

My gut twists at the reminder of how I hurt him.

"What did you do?" Rhett demands.

I narrow my eyes as I pick up on the judgment in his tone. This bossy fucker thinks he can just come in here and accuse me of fucking up? Never mind that he's 100 percent right. This is all my fault. But I still have enough self-respect to get defensive. I've been itching for a fight all day. Looks like it came knocking at my door instead.

"I let him get too close." I shrug, burying every real emotion trying to flare up inside me.

Rhett chuckles—he fucking laughs at me—shaking his head slightly in the process.

"No. No way," he declares. "You don't get to retreat into yourself and act like there hasn't been some cosmological shift in your life because of that man. Own it, Jake. Stop pushing people away and pretending like you don't deserve love."

My heart clenches as my brain scrambles to recover. He's not going to make this easy. I've been wallowing in my own bullshit for the last forty-eight hours. I haven't slept. I haven't eaten anything except pizza rolls. I haven't even gone into work because I couldn't stand the thought of anyone mentioning his name.

He's gone. I drove him away. And I was dead set on making myself pay for my transgressions with self-hatred and poor choices before Rhett showed up at my door.

Truth be told, I'm fucking tired. Tired of replaying the whole thing in my mind. Tired of wishing I'd done things differently. Last night, I lay awake for hours, honest to God Googling "what to do when you fuck up your marriage."

After scouring the internet for most of the night, here's what I learned: men are fucking stupid, and what happened between Cory and me isn't as horrible as it could have been.

Except...

It really was. The hurt in his eyes. The resolve in his decision. I fucked up. Then he fucking ended it. I honestly didn't even have time to process what was happening before he was out the door, the wedding ring he left behind mocking me from the kitchen island.

My hand immediately goes to the chain around my neck as I finger our rings through the fabric of my T-shirt.

"I feel like I should take your picture right now," Rhett mocks.

I cock my head and level him with a glare. "Don't you fucking dare." "The great Jake Whitely, looking mopey as fuck. I need photographic proof that you're not always Mr. Brightside."

Shame prickles through me as his teasing sinks in.

"Rhett, this isn't a joke." I tent my arms and slump against the quartz countertop, hanging my head in shame. "I fucked up. I fucked up big time."

"Yeah," he agrees, coming over to stand next to me at the bar. "You did."

What. The. Hell? Did he fly all the way back to Hampton just to make me feel shittier about myself? I've mastered self-loathing; no assistance needed.

He clasps my shoulder as he continues.

"You fucked up, but you're not a fuck-up, and you know it. You're *so* fucking close to having everything you never knew you wanted. Clinton's and The Oak? Someone you're crazy about, who loves you in return? Revenge on Joe as you spend that sweet inheritance?"

I smirk at the call out. He's not wrong.

"But you're the only one who can decide if you're going to chase the life you deserve, or if you're going to roll over and give up."

I scoff at the very notion. Then I can't help but smile: Rhett's my best friend for a reason. He knows exactly how my mind works—exactly what to say to force me into action.

He's still got his hand on my shoulder when I finally look at him. "I don't know how I can come back from this," I admit. I shake my head a few times to expunge myself of the heartache when I think of Cory's expression the other day. "You should have seen him, Rhett. He wasn't even mad—just sad. And determined. He said he couldn't do it. He said it was over, that it was too late. Then he just walked out the door."

"Bro." He cocks one eyebrow in challenge.

Judging by the amused assessment he gives me, I must look pathetic.

"I don't want to downplay what happened... what you did or how it made Cory feel. But I can promise you this. If you're meant to be—if you feel about him the way you said you did—you'll find a way back to each other."

I stare at him, annoyed with the cosmic bullshit. Where's the advice on how to fix this?

"You don't get it. You didn't hear how angry he was with me—" I start to explain.

"And you haven't been in a relationship before," he counters. "You're not the first person on the planet to disappoint your partner or not communicate something clearly, bro. You fucked up, but you didn't fuck it up forever. You haven't been through this, but shit like this happens to everyone. But step one is deciding that what you have is worth it. You have to decide that you want to fight for your marriage. It might not happen the way you want, or as fast as you want, but these things tend to work out in time."

"Yeah, okay," I mutter. I don't totally buy it, but if Rhett thinks there's hope, I owe it to myself to try to figure this shit out.

"How'd you get so wise?" I tease, batting his hand off me and mock-punching him in the arm.

He smirks as he ducks out of reach before I make contact. "You're talking to the king of regrettable fuck-ups, bro. I've messed up, too. Plenty of times. But I had the best people in my corner who never gave up on me."

A moment of understanding passes between us as his words take root. I've always prided myself on being the best friend, in supporting him through anything. I guess now it's my turn to be on the receiving end of that support.

He steps forward and pulls me into a full-body hug. "It'll work out, bro. I can't tell you how, but I promise it will," he murmurs. He hugs me for longer than necessary, all up in his feelings and trying to work his emotional intelligence magic on me. When he finally releases me, he leans back and grimaces.

"You smell like beer and pizza rolls," he groans. "You're done wallowing, by the way. Go get changed and grab your sneakers. We're going for a run."

I balk at his bossy-ass instructions, about to argue that he can't possibly run in his stupid collared shirt and fancy work pants. But then I see the overnight bag at his feet. Huh. So this isn't just some stopover pep talk.

I retreat from the kitchen, reach behind my back, and pull off my shirt as I make my way to my bedroom, resigned to the fact that I'm about to be on the receiving end of that special brand of Everhett Wheeler tough love. My calves are already cramping at the thought. I can't fucking wait.

We're sitting side by side on the top row of the bleachers, dripping sweat and panting after what has to be our tenth round of stairs. My best friend's crazy cardio-loving ass made us jog all the way out to Hampton High, sprint a mile around the track, then race up and down the risers until my vision went fuzzy. Maybe he thinks he can exhaust some sense into me this way.

It's not a particularly warm day, but we're both drenched. I don't need to look over at him to know his cheeks are bright pink, his brow furrowed in satisfaction from the crazy-hard workout he just subjected us to.

"Fuck, it feels good to run outside."

I smirk at his enthusiasm. Then I sit up straighter, mentally preparing to share what I've been thinking about since we made our way under the train bridge on our jog out here.

I don't bother with context or platitudes. If I don't just come out and say this, I never will.

"There's more to the Ian McDowell story than you know." I keep my gaze set on the field. He shifts beside me; I can feel his eyes boring into the side of my face.

"Everything you know is accurate," I clarify. "I never lied about how it all went down. But the version of the story you know... that's not all that happened that night."

When I glance over to gauge his reaction, he's got that Rhett-Wheeler jaw-ticking thing going on.

"Care to fill in the blanks?"

I do. But I won't. Not yet, at least. I want to tell Rhett what happened—I think I need to, in a way, to finally come to terms with what happened and how it affected me. But I can't tell him yet.

I shift to face him head-on, to ensure he can see the sincerity in my promise. After another few seconds, I swallow past the hesitation and just say it. "I will. I swear. But I need to tell Cory first."

His questioning expression transforms into a full-blown smile. He wraps one arm around my shoulders and shakes me. "There it is," he says smugly.

"There *what* is?"

"What you just said about Cory. That's it. That's literally all I needed to know about your marriage."

I cock one eyebrow in question, trying to make sense of how my refusal to tell him something has anything to do with my relationship.

"Bro, you just explained that you can't share something with me—something that I literally went through with you years ago—because you need to tell your husband first. *That* is a big fucking deal. Whether you realize it or not, he's become your number one. As he should be. That's what a relationship is, Jake. It's putting someone first time and time again; putting their needs on par and sometimes even above your own."

"Fuck." I shake my head in frustration. "I suck at this."

"Watch it," Rhett scolds. "That's my best friend you're talking about."

I smirk and nudge his shoulder, gripping the edges of the metal bleachers and blowing out a long breath now that I've stopped panting from his cardio torture.

"But I really do."

"But you don't want to," he counters. "The fact that you *know* you've got a long way to go, and you want to do it anyway? That's more than half the battle, bro. You want this to work. You want to be better for him. I honestly had no clue what I was coming back to when I showed up here unannounced, but you've shown me all I need to know."

"I have no idea how to fix it," I lament. I squeeze the edge of the bleachers tighter, vulnerability gripping my insides with the reminder of how badly I fucked up and just how hard this is going to be.

"You fight. Figure out one small step forward, and start there. Fight for your marriage. Fight for your man. Don't stop until he forgives you and you figure it out, together. Even when it's hard—even when it hurts—you can't stop fighting."

I nod resolutely, letting his words galvanize me and pulling strength from his belief in my ability to do this. I may not have a clue where to start, but I do know one thing for sure: I'm not giving up. Not now, not ever.

Chapter 43

Cory

He's everywhere.

We've never been in this airport together, and yet reminders of him follow me from the security checkpoint, through the terminal, and to my gate.

The TSA agent cracked a joke, and whereas Jake would have been all over the witty banter, all I could do was stammer through a halfhearted response.

Two little girls who looked like brunette versions of Fiona and Amelia were behind me in line for coffee, begging their mom to buy them cake pops.

Even the weird middle-of-the-airport jewelry counter mocked me with its overhead lights flickering ominously over the glass displays.

It's like everywhere I look, he's there. Even when I'm trying to forget—willing my heart to be reasonable and move on—I can't shake him. This is going to be so much harder than I thought.

I only stayed in Virginia for two nights. Tori had to get back to work, and I refuse to get further behind in my classes.

I still don't know what I was looking for by coming here. If anything, I'm more conflicted than when I first arrived.

Or maybe conflicted isn't an accurate description, because there's no question about what I have to do.

I'm not conflicted. I'm heartbroken. I feel like a shell of a human, just going through the motions, knowing that when I get back to Hampton, I have to move out of the condo and put an end to every version of us.

I can't even think about him without tearing up. How the hell am I supposed to face him?

I cycle through the indisputable facts every time I doubt what I have to do.

Jake isn't a good partner for me.

He hurt me not once, but twice, in the exact same way.

He didn't even realize he'd fucked up until I laid it out for him: that's how emotionally immature he is.

It was only going to last two years, anyway.

The last excuse is shaky at best—my heart knows we were on our way to much more than the messy "marriage with benefits" arrangement we started with. But repeating all the practical reasons loving Jake Whitely would have ended in heartache softens the blow.

After a day of silence, the calls started to come. He called me at least a dozen times yesterday, and he's already tried to reach me a few times today, too. I haven't answered a single one. I don't want to give him false hope. And I can't say what I have to over the phone.

I still care about him. I care about him so much I ache. But I can't be his salvation if I can't even put on my own oxygen mask when we're together.

I owe it to myself to protect my heart and be proactive, instead of sitting back and waiting for the other shoe to drop. I just wish that stupid bleeding organ in my chest would catch up.

I'm going to break up with Jake.

I glance down at the boarding pass in my hand and double-check the gate number. I sit down on the edge of one of the awkward interconnected plastic seats and stick my bag on the chair beside me to fend off any fellow travelers looking to socialize.

When I lift my hand from the bag, the lighter band of skin where my wedding ring used to be catches my attention. If that isn't the saddest, most perfect analogy for our relationship.

It doesn't matter if I try to block him from my mind or tell myself this is the right thing to do: there's a part of Jake Whitely that's branded on me in a way I can't escape. Hopefully in time, like the tan line from my ring, it'll all fade away.

Chapter 44

Cory

Dread washes over me as I push through the front door of Abuela's house. I called her to tell her I'd be out of town for a few days, but beyond that, she knows nothing. I don't know how the hell I'm going to explain this. If I hadn't come over here gushing like a schoolboy weeks ago, I'd probably feel less ashamed.

I'm not two steps into the house when I'm hit with a wall of mouth-watering scents. All worries dissipate when I breathe in the fragrant aroma of sancocho simmering on the stove.

"Abuela," I call into the house as I kick off my shoes and drop my bag near the door.

I listen for her response, but am met with the sounds of her deep, robust laughter instead. She says something I don't catch, and I realize she's either on the phone or not alone.

I'm another two steps through the living room before I hear it. Not it: *him*. The unmistakable cadence of his laughter wraps me in a tingly embrace before my brain catches up and reminds my body that we can't let him affect us like that anymore.

What the hell is he doing here?

I shuffle into the kitchen as quietly as possible, turning the corner just in time to see Abuela pinching Jake's cheek affectionately as he doles out one of his adorable, dimpled smiles.

Seriously. *What the hell?*

I clear my throat to garner their attention. Abuela turns her head and beams, rushing over to wrap me in her arms. I let her hug me as I lock eyes with Jake over her head.

"I didn't know you would be here," I open, leveling him with a stare that says *don't fuck with me right now*. He has some nerve inviting himself over like this—inserting himself into this part of my life I hadn't shared with him yet.

At least he has the decency to look sheepish. I tilt my head, daring him to tell me he said anything about us to Abuela. His brows draw together before he gives me a quick shake of his head.

I blow out a long breath as I debate how to play this.

"Tu esposo called me yesterday, nieto. He was asking about your favorite foods, and told me he wanted to surprise you. He did not believe me when I said I did not have a recipe for sancocho. I insisted he come over and learn it himself!"

She's radiating joy as she peels out of my arms and returns to the stove. She looks back at me, then to Jake, still smiling. "You two must have missed each other while you were gone."

"Like you wouldn't believe," Jake murmurs, raising one bulging, tattooed arm to scratch the back of his neck. He looks at me with the most earnest expression—like I didn't just catch him trying to use my abuela to weasel his way back into my heart.

"Can we talk?" he asks softly.

"Go, go," Abuela insists. "This will not be done for another hour, and I still need to make the rice. I will call you when it is ready."

I huff out a sigh, fuming that he dragged her into the middle of this.

"This way," I relent, cocking my head so he'll follow me down the short hallway that leads to the bathroom and two bedrooms on the other side of the house.

I softly open the door to my bedroom, then move out of the way to let him enter before shutting it behind him.

The room feels smaller than I remember. Most of my belongings are still at the condo. I pace halfway across the room and plant my feet firmly at the foot of the double bed.

"You shouldn't have come here."

His head snaps to attention, pain blossoming in his expression as he takes in my stance.

"I didn't expect you to show up," he tries to defend.

"Dammit, Jake! I don't know why I'm even surprised at this point. How dare you think you can introduce yourself to the woman who raised me and charm her into loving you just to manipulate me!"

"Baby," he pleads, taking a step forward that has me glaring in warning.

"Cory," he corrects.

Ouch. I hate that. But this is how it has to be.

"Fuck," he curses through gritted teeth, bringing both hands to his hair. "I'm sorry. I wasn't trying to... Fuck. I just wanted to... No. You know what?" he challenges, his tone shifting from despondent to determined. "I'm not going to apologize for this.

I mess up a lot, but this isn't one of those times. I'm here because I'm trying. I'm here because I'm fighting for us."

"There is no us," I remind him, glancing down at the worn floorboards to avoid his gaze.

"Oh, yes there is," he counters. "Or at least there will be. But you need to understand something. Nothing I do—nothing I have *ever* done—has been to manipulate you, so you need to strike that idea out of your mind."

I glare at him through narrowed eyes. He's pulled himself to his full height, standing his ground. I open my mouth to argue, but he continues before I can get a word out.

"Okay, wait—that's not true. The very first night, at Clinton's, when I got you to come over to my condo? That night, I had an agenda. But I swear to you, I haven't had one since. I respect you too much for that shit. I'm not trying to trick you or trap you. I've never once in our relationship tried to control you. So get that shit out of your head."

I'm completely taken aback by his words. This is not the man I left behind a few days ago. This version is determined, confident, and bossy as hell.

"I've been thinking about you nonstop since you left—about you, and about us. And I think I figured it out."

"Oh yeah?" I scoff sarcastically. I prepare my heart for impact, while secretly hoping he really *has* figured it out.

"You don't trust me. Whether it's because of your exes or because of my past, uh, lifestyle." At least he has the decency to look chagrinned when he alludes to his previous fuckboy ways.

"You don't trust me, and it's not fair of me to just expect you to. I have to earn your trust, and I know now that's going to take time. That's the one thing we haven't had yet, Cory—time. Everything else is there—the attraction, the friendship, the intimacy, the sex"—he wags his eyebrows at me, because of course he does—"but we haven't had time to grow together. We've been totally wrapped up in this relationship, going at warp speed. I realize now there are some things we just can't rush.

"So that's why I'm here. That's what I'm doing. I'm going to learn your favorite recipes so I can make them for you at home. I'm going to get to know your abuela so I can learn more about you, too. This is me trying. I'm going to try so fucking hard to love you how you deserve to be loved. I'll figure this out, I swear. I've already got other ideas written out on the Notes app on my phone. Whatever you think I need to work on, I will. You can even make me a sticker chart and put it on the fridge. I just need time to figure this out and get it right. I just need you to give me time."

He pins me with a look that cracks the outer shell of my emotional armor.

Everything I've felt for the last few days and the decision I've made to let him go feels unnecessarily rash as I stand before this man.

He's right. I don't trust him. And that won't change overnight. Just because so many other pieces of us clicked seamlessly in to place, doesn't mean the one thing we have to work at as a couple is reason enough to throw it all away. It was unrealistic for me to think that.

I quietly crack the knuckles on each hand as I war with myself over admitting I was wrong.

"That makes sense," I relent, ducking my head but gazing up at him to gauge his reaction. I don't miss the way his hazel eyes ignite with hope as he processes my words.

He doesn't gloat. But he does take two tentative steps toward me, closing the space between us so we're just a few feet apart at the foot of my childhood bed.

"I'm glad we're in agreement," he declares, pausing to see if I'm going to challenge him.

I'm not. I *do* agree with him. I'm just embarrassed to admit to him *and* to myself that I overreacted.

His tone softens when he speaks again. "I'm going to do everything I can to get this right. But you have to stop lumping me into the same category as your douchebag exes. First off, I'm way hotter than any of them." He smirks, and I roll my eyes. He's never even seen any of my exes. But he's not wrong. "And second, that's not me. You know me, Cory. You know me better than anyone ever has."

I level him with a pointed look.

"Even Rhett," he whispers, answering my unspoken challenge.

I gulp down the magnitude of his confession. My mind is racing, my baser instincts in overdrive. Part of me wants to come up with another reason to keep him at arm's length and double down on my plan to end things between us. Meanwhile, my traitorous heart is already doing somersaults in celebration.

He takes another step forward, then reaches out one hand. I lean in, seeking his touch.

He cups the side of my face and runs his thumb along my jaw. The way he's looking at me—*fuck*. I want him to look at me like this for the rest of our lives.

"Be with me. Grow with me. Teach me how to be the best husband I can possibly be—and give me time to prove my love." He leans into me until his forehead is resting on mine. I close my eyes and soak in the authenticity of his promises.

His lips tickle the shell of my ear when he speaks again.

"Because what I told you last time wasn't a trick, baby. It was so much more than just words. It was the truest version of how I feel: I love you, Cory."

Hearing him say those three words, and now understanding the gravity of what they mean, has me breathless in wonder.

"Jake..." I sigh, rubbing my forehead against his in frustration. I'm so overcome with emotion—so tempted to just give in and move forward—but there's still this conflicted, practical voice in my head, reminding me in excruciating detail about what drove us to this point.

"It's too much," I whisper. "It hurt too much."

When I open my eyes, he's staring back at me, a tortured look on his face.

"I'm sorry I hurt you," he starts, walking me backward until the backs of my knees hit the edge of the bed. He presses gently on my shoulders until I give in and sink onto the mattress. Once he's settled beside me, he takes my hand and continues. "I'm so sorry about everything that happened that night. I didn't think. I didn't prioritize you, or *us*. I know I messed up, but there's more to the story. I'm not trying to make excuses. But I want you to know what happened. Can I tell you?"

I squeeze his hand in confirmation.

"Here's the most important thing you need to know: I was already coming home to you when Ashleigh called me in a panic. I was literally in the Jersey Bagels parking lot, turning the car around. You were—you *are*—my priority. I was a mess that night, though. And I let myself get sidetracked because of Fiona. Between worrying about her and facing off with my brother, then being at the hospital... I didn't even have my phone with me most of the night. Literally every part of my brain was occupied just trying to get through it."

He rubs his fingers over my knuckles, soothing himself as much as me.

"I'm sorry I shut down on you in Rhett's backyard. And that I pushed you away. I've never been able to count on anyone. That's not an excuse. Because that won't happen again, I swear. I just want you to know that I was already on my way back to you. I was headed home. You're my home, Cory. You're where I want to be."

I swallow down the emotions raging inside me. It's a heady sensation, to be brimming with so many complex feelings battling for dominance in my mind.

I want him.

But he's not good for me.

I forgive him.

But he might hurt me again.

I love him.

But is love enough?

"There's something else I need to tell you."

How could there possibly be anything left? But there must be. I can feel the anger, resentment, and shame rolling off him in waves, so I adjust myself on the bed so I'm facing him directly, giving him my full attention.

"The night that Ian McDowell..." He trails off, blows out a long breath, then grips the edge of the mattress and sits up straighter. "The night that Ian McDowell drugged me and tried to rape me, I went back."

Time stands still as I try to make sense of his admission.

"What do you mean—you went back?"

His jaw ticks as he stares straight ahead. I stroke his forearm to get his attention and bring him back to me.

"After my dad laid into me that night, after he shoved me back into the closet and spit on me, I didn't know what to do. I was still trying to make sense of the situation, reeling from my dad's dismissal. Rhett was in the hospital because of me. Tori wasn't answering my calls because she was on a bus trying to get to downtown Akron to be with Rhett. It was all too much. I had no one. I felt like... I felt like I was nothing."

I squeeze his arm in support, desperate to convey just how much he matters.

He's never been nothing. *He's everything to me.*

"I was sleep-deprived. Exhausted. Distraught. I decided to do the stupidest thing I could think of, just to numb the pain. I called Ian, went back to Archway's campus, and... and did the thing I originally set out to do that night."

I'm digging my nails into the palm of my left hand to keep myself steady. That sick, predatory piece of shit hurt my husband more than I could have fathomed.

"Jake, did he...?"

"No. I mean, I guess not. I don't really know. I went back, Cory. I fucking knew what was going to happen, and I went back. Willingly."

"You were a kid," I remind him, stroking my thumb over the ink-covered veins of his forearm.

"Yeah, well, I knew what I was doing." He huffs a sardonic laugh. "I knew what would happen, and I did it anyway. That's why seeing him at The Oak was such a mindfuck. I don't feel like I can even blame him anymore. The first part of the night, sure. But the second part? Where I was a willing participant and just gave myself to him?" He shakes his head violently and shudders.

"You were a minor, Jake. He was an adult. In a position of power."

He nods wordlessly, like he hears me but doesn't agree. He's shutting down, clamming up and throwing away the key to his candor and vulnerability. I don't want to push the issue. But I don't want him to shut me out, either. I'm out of my league here, but I want to support him in any way I can.

"Thank you for telling me. What does Rhett say about all this?" I ask, gently nudging him to keep talking if this is something he needs to get off his chest.

He raises his head and looks me right in the eye as he admits: "Rhett doesn't know I went back. No one does. You're the only person I've ever told."

Mierda.

I can't hold back. I reach forward and wrap him in my arms, running one hand up and down his back. I palm the nape of his neck with as much tenderness as I can muster.

His confession is my undoing. It's the final string—the inevitable snap. The key that makes this all make sense. It's Jake showing me his darkest truth. He's handing over his power and opening up to me in a way he's never opened up to anyone.

And now his reaction that night makes even more sense. He wasn't just triggered by the attempted assault. He was facing down relentless waves of shame and self-loathing, reeling from a secret he's kept buried for more than ten years.

The power of the moment plucks at my heartstrings as this beautiful, vivacious man lets me hold him. I can't fix this, and we both know it. He could have kept this from me forever, and I'd be none the wiser. But giving me this truth—sharing the darkest secret he holds, that he's never let anyone else possess—it's a selfless act of genuine trust.

"It's okay," I soothe, holding him tighter, as if my strength alone is enough to get him through this. "You're okay," I whisper. "You're okay. You're okay. You're okay."

He's heavy in my arms, broken down and defeated. And he's letting me hold him instead of brushing me off or pushing away.

"Do you want to talk about it?" I ask after a few minutes of silence. We may not have spoken any words out loud, but I put everything I had into making him feel my love and support.

He shakes his head in the crook of my neck, a subtle indication that sharing this was enough.

"I just needed you to know."

His vulnerability speaks directly to my insecurity. His authenticity is a comfort and a balm. Every wall I've built to fortify my heart crumbles in that moment as the realization hits: I don't need to protect myself anymore. I don't need protection from him.

There were really no words that could have dampened my resolve to end our marriage.

But apparently, there were actions.

I inhale the heady scent of musk and vanilla as I breathe him in.

He's not perfect.

But no one is.

I'm not sure about this.

But that's okay.

I can be real—I can be uncertain—I can give my heart to this man. He might not always get it right. But what he said earlier is wrong: I *do* trust him. I trust him with my heart.

It was me I didn't trust.

I pull back as my emotions overwhelm me. We're sitting in a storm of vulnerability. Teetering on the edge of something terrifyingly beautiful and real.

I kiss his cheeks, tasting his tears, willing him to absorb all the comfort he needs.

"I owe you an apology, too," I confess.

He cocks his head in question.

"I started this arrangement on guard. You had the power to consume me—you always have, and I knew that." I shake my head at the admission. I didn't have context for our connection when we first hooked up—but looking back on it now, I know there's a reason I broke all my rules to be with him.

"For the last six weeks, I've been waiting for the other shoe to drop. Waiting for you to prove me right, that I can't trust you with my heart. I was so quick to cut you off as soon as things didn't go exactly like I thought they should because I was scared. I'm sorry. I know it won't always be perfect... And I don't want you to feel like you have to be perfect, or like you're walking on eggshells in this relationship. You're right: we need time."

He nods solemnly, scrubbing his tears away with the heels of his hands.

"I'll wait," he vows. "I'll wait for however long you need. A few weeks, a few months; I'll wait for years if that's how long it'll take for me to earn your trust and prove my love."

I smirk at the notion of either of us possibly fighting this connection for any significant length of time. Our relationship needs time to strengthen and grow, but he's out of his mind if he thinks I want anything to change or slow down.

Still.

I share my final ice-thin defense, just to ensure we're on the same page.

"I doubt you'd wait that long. This was only supposed to be for two years anyway."

He narrows his gaze, then comes at me so fast I fall backward. He pushes me into the mattress, straddles my hips, and pins me with his eyes.

When he gets in my face, I'm hypnotized by the intensity of his glare.

"It was *never* only going to be two years. I knew it the night before our wedding when I kissed you at Clinton's. And I think you knew it then, too."

Tension thrums between us.

After a dozen beats of my racing heart, we both move at the same time. Jake's lips meet mine and reaffirm every emotion we've just shared in a searing kiss. It's a kiss that consumes me, all frantic passion and reckless abandon—a kiss that mends the wounds we suffered to get to this place.

He pulls away first, but he doesn't go far. He whispers his truth against my mouth, making sure I feel the passion behind his plea. "I want more, Cory. I want it all. I want you forever. Stop fighting me, baby. I just need you to say yes."

I already know my answer. But I need him to understand how hard it was to get here.

"I'm so fucking scared," I mutter against his mouth.

"I know, baby. I am, too. But I won't intentionally hurt you. Ever. If you can be patient with me, teach me how to love you, if you can just give us time—"

"Okay," I interrupt, unable to wait one second longer to move forward with this man.

"Okay?" He's grinning from ear to ear, his eyes dancing with delight and that signature Jake mischievousness I love so damn much.

"Okay," I repeat, that single word a solemn vow.

He sighs contently, then closes his eyes before rolling to his side. "So what do we do now?"

I use my elbow to prop myself up and pull his hips into mine. After all those days apart, I can't stand to not touch him. "I don't want or need time apart," I declare. "I know we need time to learn each other, and more importantly, I need to be patient. But I'm not letting us go backward in this relationship. I just want to be with you."

"Co-ry," he groans, like I've just whispered the hottest dirty talk in his ear. "That's the best fucking thing you could have possibly said." He rolls his hips forward and wraps one arm around my low back, holding me tight. "I missed you so much, baby."

I revel in his words as our bodies reacquaint themselves. We're kissing again, grinding our dicks together, running our hands all over. There's this hunger and longing coursing between us that I swear I've never felt before. But all it takes is a quick glance around the room to remember where we are and what we probably shouldn't do here.

I pull away and sigh against his neck. "I want you to take me home and fuck me so hard I can't walk straight tomorrow."

I feel his pulse spike as he pulls back and looks at me.

"Well, let's fucking go!"

I laugh and lovingly tousle his already messed-up hair. We're both going to need a few minutes to get ourselves sorted.

"We're not going anywhere anytime soon. I hate to break it to you, but you doomed us by coming here today."

His eyebrows pinch together in question.

"If you got Abuela cooking, we're going to be here a while. Maybe even all night."

Chapter 45

Jake

We barely make it into our bedroom before I've got him pinned against the wall. I've got this hunger burning inside me that I've never felt before.

Words aren't enough for moments like this.

I need to make him feel my love; everywhere, and in every way.

I ravish his mouth with mine, our bodies grinding against each other as heat, passion, and longing rise between us. There's a charge that sparks every time we kiss: a hunger that will only be satisfied once I've thoroughly fucked him into our mattress and slowly made love to him, too.

I hope he's well-rested. We're gonna be at this *all* night.

I knead his traps with both hands, then cradle his head so I'm not grinding his skull into the wall as I continue to work him over. His hands are everywhere as he matches my desperation to be close in every way.

He tugs on the hem of my T-shirt, then rips it over my head, breaking our connection for a single second that stretches into eternity. But before I can kiss him again, he places both hands on my chest, halting me.

I press against his touch and urge him to let me in, but that just makes him push back harder. When our eyes lock, I'm overcome with the desire to never let him go.

His fingertips travel up my bare torso, dipping into the valleys of my abs before smoothing over my pecs. When I see where his gaze is set, my heart pounds double time.

He traces the thin chain with one finger before cupping both rings in his palm.

"I haven't taken them off since the morning you left," I admit, bowing my head slightly but peering through my eyelashes to maintain our connection.

He yanks on the chain and pulls me closer, then he kisses me with a tenderness that makes my whole body relax. The effect Cory has on me is uncanny.

He's what I crave most. It's not just about the sex or the inexplicable pull we feel toward one another. For the first time ever, I want to let someone in. And I want him to stay. Forever.

"This won't happen again," he murmurs into the narrow space between us.

It would be easy to blow him off or push back and challenge his resolve. But there's a sincerity in his promise that soothes the most vulnerable, insecure parts of me. Letting him in means trusting him, too, so instead of questioning him, I repeat his vow: "This won't happen again."

"I'll take care of your heart," he continues, his eyes darting between mine like he's willing me to understand the gravity of this moment.

He doesn't need to worry. I fucking feel it in every fiber of my being.

"And I'll work tirelessly to trust you with mine."

I shudder at his words, but will myself to stay open and accept his promises.

"I won't give up on us again," he declares, tugging on the chain around my neck for emphasis.

"I love you, Jake Whitely." He gently guides me back to create space between us, then drops down to one knee. "Will you stay married to me?"

A tightness bands around my chest as I gaze down at the man I love. Fuck. His proposal was so much better than mine.

And rightfully so. What started as a practical arrangement with a few extra benefits has transformed into the most beautiful, fulfilling, unexpected gift.

"Yes," I rush to reply, sinking to my knees to match his stance. "But I want a redo."

His gaze narrows in question.

"I want to give you the wedding of your dreams, baby. I want to stay married to you, but I want to have a ceremony and plan a huge party with all our family and friends. And I definitely want to go on another honeymoon." I cock an eyebrow. "I want to make my husband's dreams come true."

I slip the necklace over my head, unhook the ball chain clasp, then slide both our rings off. A dueling sense of calm and smug satisfaction courses through me as I slide Cory's onto his finger, the platinum band slotting back into place. I hand him mine, and he puts it on for me.

Gripping the nape of his neck with both hands, I press our foreheads together as we breathe each other in and commit this moment to memory. But I don't stress about forcing the feelings to linger. We have a lifetime of moments just like this ahead of us now.

"Would now be an inappropriate time to make a joke about you getting down on your knees for me?" I deadpan.

His eyes shoot open and he laughs: the sound of his joy lighting me up and making me tingle all over.

"Some things will never change, will they?" he teases as he tackles me to the ground and climbs on top. I prop up on my elbows before he can kiss me.

"Wait," I interject. "There actually *is* something I want to change. I was thinking I'd change my last name to Vargo." Despite my adamant desire to do this, my words are soft, almost a whisper. I've been considering it for a while, just rolling the idea around in my mind as things grew between us.

Cory's eyes go wide. "Are you serious?"

"Of course I'm serious."

He blows out a long breath, runs his hand through his hair, then smiles down at me. "I love it," he gushes. "It's just hard to imagine a day when the great Jake Whitely won't be, well, Jake Whitely."

I slide my hands over his obliques, then dig into his sides for emphasis.

"You know I haven't been the infamous Jake Whitely since the night you agreed to marry me, baby. I want your last name, if you'll share it with me. I'm proud to be your husband. I want everyone to know I'm totally and completely yours."

His eyes flare with want as I stoke his possessiveness with my words. I'll give this man anything and everything if he promises to look at me like *that* for the rest of our lives.

My body. My mind. My demons. My heart.

Every part of me belongs to him, and I plan to spend the rest of forever making sure he knows it.

Jake

3 Months Later

The Oak is overflowing tonight—people are crammed shoulder to shoulder, screaming over the music and lighting up the dance floor. I'd feel compelled to do a headcount for fire code if this wasn't a private event.

It's not just any private event: it's our wedding reception. Our *real* wedding reception to celebrate our over-the-top dream wedding.

Turns out a wedding can come together fast if you have a lot of money to throw at it. And if your husband already has a dozen Pinterest boards dedicated to every detail of his ideal day.

We chose a destination wedding—something Cory always dreamed about—and timed it during winter break so we could accommodate his school schedule as well as winter breaks for the girls and his siblings.

We flew all our family there—Abuela, Tori and Rhett, both of his parents and their families, Julian, Ashleigh, Fiona and Amelia—and we spent a week at an all-inclusive resort on a combination bachelor party/wedding/second honeymoon extravaganza.

Rhett's still harping on me about spending more time in the room with my husband than living it up at the bachelor party he planned. Sure, I used to have a vision for what one would entail and how much I'd love it. But the rowdy boy in me wasn't feeling the bachelor party vibes. Plus, our honeymoon suite had a private infinity pool and a steam room. Has he *seen* my husband in swim trunks?

Speaking of my husband... I scan the crowd for Cory and find him in the middle of the dance floor with Lia, surrounded by a gaggle of children. He's been taking turns dancing with my nieces and his siblings for the last half hour. It's adorable, but I've made the rounds and accepted a million congratulations by myself. I'm getting anxious to have my turn with him.

I sidle up from behind, gripping his hips as he sways in time to the music. He leans back into me, giving me a subtle hip grind that has me instantly hardening. Lia rolls her eyes at us, but I don't miss her knowing smile. She leaves us alone and heads toward Tori and Rhett, who are not-so-subtly making out in one of the back booths of my bar. The place really is a mad house tonight. I wouldn't want it any other way.

"Co-ry," I purr in his ear, loving the way he melts into me as my hands brush up his sides. "Fuck, baby. I wish this party would just end already."

He spins around and cocks one eyebrow, his gorgeous chocolate brown eyes dancing in delight. He knows I'm messing with him, but he still takes the bait.

"And why do you want our wedding reception to 'just end already'?" he mocks, lowering his voice an octave and doing an impression that sounds nothing like me. "We haven't even cut the cake."

I glance over at the four-tier monstrosity from Della's Bakery. Each layer is a different flavor. The thing could literally feed three hundred people. But it's what he wanted. And all I want is to make him happy.

"I'm tired of sharing you," I whine, pulling him into my body and circling my arms around his neck as he continues to roll his hips to the beat of the music. He's teetering dangerously close to working me up a little too much.

"Baby," I warn, leveling him with a *cool off all your sexy hip swaying* look.

He bites down on his lip and eye fucks me before leaning in close.

"You get me to yourself all weekend," he whispers into my ear. "As soon as we get home tonight, you won't have to share." He rolls the *R* in *share* for so long I feel a drop of precum accumulate on my dick.

Fuck. Me.

I work my hands under his suit jacket and pull his body tight against mine. I press my forehead into his with enough force to get his attention.

"You have to slow dance with me until the raging boner you just gave me goes away," I huff out.

"Oh, do I now?" he teases.

"Yes, you fucking do," I retort as I let him guide us on the dance floor. I roll my hips forward and sway in response to his rhythm. "For better or for worse, baby. This is your lot in life now. You're stuck with me."

He bites down on that juicy bottom lip I just want to suck into my mouth before replying.

"Or maybe we can sneak back to the liquor cage, and I can take care of my husband a different way?"

I'm grinning so big my face hurts.

"Now you're talking." I spin him in my arms, grasp him by the shoulders, and use his body as a shield as we circumvent our friends and family on the dance floor to sneak away for a private party for two.

I *love* being married to this man.

Cory

6 Years Later

"Papi... nigh-nights."

I awkwardly hold my daughter in the narrow waiting room chair and nuzzle her downy soft hair.

"I know, princesa. I know."

"Here. Give her to me." Tori lifts Stella out of my lap and cradles her. My daughter's little hand instantly wraps around Tori's neck. When they lock eyes, Stella's whole body relaxes.

"Thanks," I mutter, rolling out my shoulders and running a hand through my hair. "I hate that we're messing up her bedtime routine. I never expected it would take this long."

"Have they texted you any updates?" Tori asks, her eyes transfixed on my overtired toddler as she softly hums something I don't recognize. Stella is staring right into the emerald green eyes of her godmother. She's completely enamored by everything Tori does. My heartstrings pull as her little hand lifts up to pet Tori's cheek. She does that to Jake all the time, especially when he's gone a few days without shaving. There's no doubt in my mind that my daughter loves her godmother just as much as she loves her dads. Their connection is so strong.

I stop studying them long enough to glance down at my phone to look for an update.

"Nothing."

I stand up and stretch my arms overhead, letting my shoulders pop before rolling them back a few times. We've been here for almost six hours now, and Chloe has been stuck at eight centimeters for the last two.

I'm trying to stay calm, but I'm starting to worry something is wrong.

This whole pregnancy has been different from Stella's in every way. Whereas Stella's birth was textbook and quick, the new baby's been toying with us for two weeks. We've come to the hospital *four times* because of false labor and contractions.

"Why don't you take a walk and check on him," Tori suggests, not bothering to look up at me as she continues to stroke Stella's hair and hum.

I love seeing them together. I never knew my heart could feel this full, that love could feel like this, that I would be lucky enough to have this beautiful, blessed, interconnected family. Never in a million years did I dream that someday I would get to be a father. And that my best friend would be the one to donate her eggs to make it possible.

They say everything happens for a reason. The fact that Tori froze her eggs all those years ago instead of embryos like she had originally planned means that we will forever be indebted and connected to her. Jake was even with her that day. He sat with her after the procedure. He held her hand through it all. Our children came from her sacrifice. It's a gift I'll spend the rest of my life being grateful for.

Jake is back in the delivery room with our surrogate now. He loves to be in the action. He's good under pressure and not at all squeamish like me. I almost passed out when I watched them place Chloe's IV when she was admitted the day Stella was born. I'm not the man for this job. Only Jake will do. Rhett is hanging in the small waiting room down the hall, just in case he needs backup.

Even if I wasn't squeamish, I want today to be about him. The first time around, we both contributed samples and let fate decide for us. We figured we might not know right away, or maybe we'd never know for sure. But it was immediately clear that Stella's jet-black hair and tan complexion came from me.

It didn't matter to either of our hearts. But I couldn't shake the feeling that it mattered to Jake's soul, whether he realized it or not.

When we started talking about trying for another, I insisted we use his sample. He loves our babies no matter what, but I wanted the little boy who grew up feeling like he wasn't worthy of being loved unconditionally to have the chance to break the cycle and to father a child. Tori donated another egg, Jake provided the sample, and miraculously, we had another successful pregnancy on the first round.

What we hadn't counted on? This kid had obviously inherited more than just Jake's looks, because he was already giving us a run for our money.

Every appointment has been something. Weird hcg levels that didn't double in the beginning. Awkward placenta placement that made it hard to see our little guy on the ultrasound. Amniotic fluid levels reading too low at one appointment, then too high at the next. And the one I felt the worst about: gestational diabetes for Chloe over the last three months.

It's a good thing we're done after this. Our poor surrogate probably wouldn't agree to work with us again after having to deal with the rowdy boy antics passed on through my husband's DNA.

Tori's soft humming draws me back into the moment. I'm torn between staying here with her and Stella and going to find Jake. If there was an update, or if he needed me back there, he would have texted.

I don't have time to contemplate my next move, because my husband comes barreling into the family waiting room in a huff that notches up the energy and takes me by surprise.

He frantically scans the space; I'm grateful we're the only ones in here right now. Something is clearly wrong. His expression softens slightly when he spots Tori holding Stella. He blows out a long exhale before finally looking at me.

"Still no progress," he croaks. My body jolts at the desperation in his voice.

I move toward him as Rhett appears by his side. He clasps my husband on the shoulder, then subtly cocks his head and gives me a silent warning.

When I wrap Jake in my arms, he sinks his weight into me and actually lets me hold him. That's how I know something is really wrong.

"Hey," I reassure him with a squeeze. "You're okay. It's all going to work out. They'll be fine."

He nods into the crook of my neck before pulling back and making his way over to the girls.

Rhett gives me a pointed look, then turns to walk out of the waiting room.

I anxiously follow him down the too-bright hall, desperate for more details but not wanting to ask in front of Jake or Stella when emotions are already running so high. Once we're out of earshot, he catches me up to speed.

"Chloe and the baby are both fine," Rhett starts, leveling me with his serious look. I exhale a breath I didn't know I was holding, then nod for him to continue.

"The doctor said labor can stall out around eight centimeters because her body is gearing up for the final push. Since everyone's vitals look great and Chloe delivered Stella naturally, they're going to give it another hour or so. She's bouncing on her yoga ball, walking around, and trying everything she can to get to ten. The next conversation will be about a c-section, but it's not time to talk about that yet."

I've never been more appreciative of Rhett's no-nonsense stoicism than I am at this moment. I blow out another breath and try to muster up a sense of calm. "Okay, that all makes sense. So why is—"

"He got into it with a nurse," he cuts in, raising his eyebrows for emphasis. "They asked him to step out of the room and take a breather, and when he snapped back, they told him he wasn't allowed in the room until he calmed down."

I close my eyes and hold back the laugh threatening to spill out. My poor husband. They say becoming a parent changes a person. I don't think any of us expected Jake to morph into this over-protective helicopter parent when he became a dad.

What the hell did he do or say to get kicked out of the room? Doesn't matter. He's obviously on edge, and it won't help Chloe or the baby if he isn't allowed in the room when it's time to push. Jake has gone through all the birthing classes with

Chloe. It's his job to be her support person. It's *my* job to make sure he gets back in that room.

"I'll talk to him," I assure Rhett as I pivot on my heel and head back to the waiting room. When I turn the corner, Jake and Tori are huddled over Stella, both staring down at our sleeping toddler.

"Hey," I whisper, squatting to meet my husband at eye-level. When he meets my gaze, his eyes are filled with a torrent of emotions. I know he's worried, anxious, and excited. He also has the decency to look embarrassed about his outburst. I fight back another laugh, knowing he needs love and support right now, not a reminder that he screwed up.

"Come talk to me," I urge quietly, offering him my hand as I stand so I can pull him out of the seat. He reluctantly accepts, and Rhett swoops in to his vacated spot, his arm instantly going around Tori and Stella. He kisses his wife's head and whispers something I can't make out, then looks up at me. "We've got her," he assures me.

I pull Jake down the bright hallway and duck into an alcove. He blows out an exasperated breath as he leans back against a soda machine, crosses his arms, and hooks one ankle over the other in his go-to bartender stance.

"Look, I don't know what Rhett told you, but that nurse had it out for me from the moment—"

I cut him off with a kiss, wrapping my arms around his waist and pulling him in to me before he can object. It takes a few seconds, but eventually he goes soft in my embrace, all the tension and defensiveness giving way to the vulnerability he so rarely shows.

"I love you," I murmur against his mouth as I pull back and kiss along his jaw. "I love how you care so deeply about our family. I love how you get so growly and protective of our babies. I love everything about you, Jake Vargo."

He doesn't say anything in return. Even after all these years, he still needs a little time to process it: That he's lovable. That he's worthy of adoration. In all honesty, I don't think he truly believed it in his heart until Stella started saying "love ew, daddy," a few months ago.

"Thank you," he chokes out as he rests his forehead on mine. "And I love you, too," he adds, even though it's not necessary. Everything this man does is for me, for Stella, for our family. I haven't doubted his love for one second of one day since we made things "officially" official and decided to stay married.

"I do need you to get it together now. This baby has your DNA," I remind him, our foreheads still touching as I rub his back through his tight black T-shirt. He was at The Oak when we got the call, so he came straight from work. It's dumb luck that Tori and Rhett are in town this weekend. Dumb luck—or kismet.

"You can't be wasting all your daddy energy fighting with the nurses. We're about to have a mini Jake to contend with, and this kid's already proven he's going to be a handful like his daddy."

He smirks and moves to kiss me. "I'll show you some daddy energy," he teases before crushing his lips into mine. I let myself get lost in him as he shoves me against the opposite row of vending machines and deepens the kiss. It's not until someone clears their throat that I even remember where we are.

"Uh, bro?" Rhett interjects, shaking his head when he finds us making out like horny teenagers in this alcove. Like he can judge. Based on how flushed Tori was when they arrived, I'm almost positive they snuck in a quickie in the parking deck before they met us in the waiting room.

"They sent someone down to tell you it's time. Like, right now."

My husband tenses in my arms before he breaks into the biggest grin. He looks at me, wide-eyed, and I nod at him enthusiastically.

"Go," I urge before I lean forward for one more kiss. "And please don't text me to come back until they take the placenta away this time," I remind him. I wish I was kidding. It's embarrassing as hell to almost pass out multiple times at the birth of your child.

Jake stands up straighter before he strides out of the room, enthusiastically yelling "catch me if you can, Bro!" in Rhett's direction as he takes off jogging down the hall.

Jake

His eyes are identical to Tori's. His hair is barely there, just a few light brown wisps on his slightly misshapen head. I can't stop staring at him: looking at his perfect tiny hands. Admiring the pucker of his adorable little lips. When he suckles, he has a teeny dimple. Just on one side. Just like me.

A love I've only felt twice before overwhelms me as I stand in the middle of the hospital room, cradling my newborn son.

My entire essence somehow leaves my body and is replaced with nothing but warmth as I hold him in my arms.

My son.

Matteo Everhett Vargo.

We have a son.

Cory enters the room; I feel it in my soul, just like I always do when he's near, but I can't tear my eyes away from our boy long enough to look up at my husband. When he's close enough that his frame blocks out the harsh hospital fluorescents, Matteo lets out a tiny whimper, and I finally look up.

Cory's eyes are brimming with tears, but he's got the biggest smile on his face.

"Do you want to meet our son?" I rasp, holding back tears of my own.

He nods, then moves to stand beside me, one arm wrapping around my shoulder while the other cradles the back of Matteo's head.

He's tuned in enough to know not to try to take this baby from me. For as much as he liked to tease me about being a baby hog with Stella, what I'm feeling right now is on a whole new level. It's like this surge of protectiveness and possessiveness blended together to create this fortified shield I want to wrap around my child. He's so tiny and vulnerable and *real*—I don't ever want to let him go.

"He's so beautiful." Cory sighs as he runs one finger gently over our son's hair. "He loves you so much, Jake. Can you feel it? This baby loves you *so much*."

Tears erupt behind my eyes, the weight of it all crashing down around me and trying to swallow me whole. The foundation of unconditional love we've built within our family is this next-level kind of magic I didn't know I even had the capacity to feel. But it's there. And it's real. The way Cory makes sure I feel it every damn day...

"Stella and I love you, too," he adds, tilting his head to kiss me softly. He lingers just an inch from my lips as he whispers, "Thank you for giving us this beautiful life."

My throat clogs with emotion. The tears are already streaming down my face. I'm afraid if I let myself feel anything more, I'll combust. Sensing I need a moment, Cory kisses me again, then makes his way over to Chloe.

She was a fucking champ, especially at the end. It took less than ten minutes from the time I came back into the room until she was on her final push. Letting her squeeze the shit out of my hand as she delivered our son is a memory I'll never forget. And not just because I might have permanent nerve damage.

I scan Matteo's tiny form again. How can someone even be this small? He's no longer than my forearm, and yet he's already taking up so much space in my heart.

"I've got you, little man. I'm so lucky to be your dad. I don't even know you, and yet I love you so much. Whoever you are... whoever you're going to be... there's *nothing* you could ever do to make me not love you."

"And we love you," Rhett says as he wraps me in a side hug. Tori's on his other side, with a half-asleep Stella propped on one hip. Cory joins us, forming a circle in the middle of the hospital room as we gather around the newest addition to our family.

I look at each of them and commit this moment to memory, just soaking it all in. These people, this life—it's more than I ever gave myself permission to dream of.

This is my family.

The two people who have been with me through it all.

The man I have the privilege of calling my husband.

And the tiny people we all created—together.

Want to see Jake, Cory, and the kids in the future? Sign up for my email newsletter and receive a free eBook called Hampton Holiday Collective featuring four holiday-themed novelettes for all your favorite Hampton Hearts couples.

Afterword

Writing Jake's happily ever after has been the highlight of my career. Let's be real: has anyone ever deserved an HEA more than this man?

Whether you're a brand new reader or have been with me, Jake, and the gang since the beginning, I want to thank you from the bottom of my heart for going on this journey and trusting me with your time.

If you're interested in receiving writing updates and shop alerts, you can sign up for my email newsletter.

Be sure to catch more Jake and Cory moments in in Fourth Wheel (Maddie's story) and Full Out Fiend (Fielding's story). And don't forget to download your free Jake + Cory holiday novella, I Saw Daddy Kissing Santa Claus, by signing up for my email newsletter!

By Abby Millsaps

presented in order of publication

When You're Home
While You're There
When You're Home for the Holidays
When You're Gone
Rowdy Boy
Mr. Brightside
Fourth Wheel
Full Out Fiend
Hampton Holiday Collective

Too Safe: Boys of Lake Chapel Book One
Too Fast: Boys of Lake Chapel Book Two
Too Far: Boys of Lake Chapel Book Three

About The Author

Abby Millsaps is an author and storyteller who's been obsessed with writing romance since middle school. In eighth grade, she failed to qualify for the Power of the Pen State Championships because "all her submissions contained the same theme: young people falling in love." #LookAtHerNow

She's best known for writing unapologetically angsty romance that causes emotional damage for her readers. Creative spicy scenes and consent as foreplay are two hallmarks of her books. Abby prides herself in writing authentic characters while weaving mental health, chronic illness, and neurodiverse representation into the fabric of her stories.

Abby met her husband at a house party the summer before her freshman year of college. He had a secret pizza stashed in the trunk of his car that he was saving for a midnight snack—how was she supposed to resist that level of golden retriever energy and preparedness? When Abby isn't writing, she's reading, traveling, and raising her three daughters.

Connect with Abby

Website: www.authorabbymillsaps.com
Instagram: @abbymillsaps
TikTok: @authorabbymillsaps
Email: authorabbymillsaps@gmail.com
Newsletter: https://geni.us/AuthorAbbyNewsletter
Facebook Reader Group: Abby's Full Out Fiends

www.ingramcontent.com/pod-product-compliance
Lightning Source LLC
LaVergne TN
LVHW030315070526
838199LV00069B/6471